TREACHERY AT TORREY PINES

A Shank MacDuff Mystery

By

JOHN VAN VLEAR

Velvet Room Publishing

Newport Beach, California

VelvetRoomPublishing.com

ISBN: 978-0-9857378-0-1

Library of Congress control number: 2012942803

PRINTED IN THE UNITED STATES OF AMERICA

ISBN: 0985737808

Dedication

To Kimberley Ann, my darling bride of treasured years – who inspired me to write this novel, tirelessly applied her training and creativity in editing manuscripts, and prayerfully encouraged me throughout the journey.

Marsha Ford
Editor-in-Chief
(Ford Editorial Services)

Victoria Van Vlear
Publishing Manager; Polishing Editor
(Velvet Room Publishing)

CHAPTER 1

Horrified mourners watched as Buddy Franks's casket began to shudder. No one made a sound. As the rattling intensified, a thundering roar echoed from the chapel's stone floor. Time slowed. My focus narrowed to the pine burial box.

Had the doctors made a mistake? Would my friend's sallow hand suddenly open the lid? Was Buddy trapped in utter darkness, alone and confused? The unimaginable claustrophobia and panic! People around me began gasping and screaming. Was this really happening? My body began to react; butterflies fluttered around in my stomach the way they did during the many earthquakes I had experienced. Finally, I realized what was causing this macabre scene—a temblor was rocking the Southern California funeral.

The shaking stopped. Nervous chatter erupted. Those guests who lived outside quake country were clearly alarmed. And the recently widowed Linda Franks seemed to be in even worse shape than she had been during the many eulogies for her husband. Her flowing red hair looked like molten lava against her ashen face; she sobbed and hugged her children tight. What else could happen to this poor woman?

The funeral director tried to restore some semblance of decorum. As the commotion subsided, the pianist attempted to comfort the mourners with appropriately solemn music.

Buddy's death gnawed at me, the sensation fed by vivid memories of that night in the Midwest. I blame the recklessness on the adrenaline monster that has always prowled my core. It compels me to ride bone-crunching waves, scorch empty highways in fast cars, and ski steep mountaintop chutes. I have always been its willing slave.

That night, as we were finishing dinner in a tavern near our hotel—we were in the same profession, one that required lots of travel—I recounted to Buddy a few stories of my boyhood exploits. That wasn't unusual, but on this occasion, the theme was a new one—climbing. "We'd hunt down these cool structures. Bridges, small buildings, anything with decent features to grab onto. One time we even scaled a gnarly hilltop water tower."

Sitting back and looking totally relaxed in his usual baggy shirt, my fleshy companion asked in his trademark Southern drawl, "How tall?"

"Maybe a hundred feet," I estimated.

"There was a fish *this* big," Buddy mocked while stretching his arms wide.

"You don't believe me?"

"Shank, sometimes you heap it on pretty thick."

"That's it! You've challenged my manhood or at least my boyhood," I complained with playful bravado. "Let's go find a water tower, and I'll prove it."

2

"Now?"

"This very minute."

Buddy was apprehensive. "It's late, it's windy—and where are you gonna find a tower fit for climbin'?"

Excellent points. However, I was undaunted. Working the room, I found a local patron who provided directions to a couple of possibilities.

"Ready?" I asked Buddy upon returning to the table.

"You really want to do this?"

"Absolutely. You can either tower-hunt with me or watch the last few minutes of this lousy basketball game." The Indiana Pacers were whipping our Los Angeles Lakers. Clearly, there was only one choice. We paid our tabs and were off.

After checking out the first tower, I passed. "It won't work because the legs are totally smooth—nothing to grab while climbing." Buddy shrugged and kept fiddling with the radio. The next tower was a big one. Standing over ten stories tall, the tank was held up by six legs. The wind whipped around us as we got out of the rental car for a better look. I pointed at the tower and said, "The leg with the maintenance ladder is the only way to the very top."

"OK," Buddy acknowledged flatly. "But how you fixin' to get past the metal mesh 'round the lower part?"

After considering that obstacle, I solved the problem. "The lattice work on the inside of the other legs forms a series of X's all the way up. I can climb the X's and then access the ladder above the mesh protector, which I'm sure is locked. The only dicey part is that horizontal beam between the legs."

Looking up, Buddy stammered, "You're joshing, right? Walk across? That's a hundred feet up."

"Fun, huh? That'll get my juices flowing!"

"A man climbin' that would be 'bout as comfortable as a Thanksgiving turkey in an ax factory." Buddy's maxims were legendary. After a long silence, my friend added in a determined tone, "I'm goin' with you."

"Yeah, right," I replied. Neither Buddy's temperament nor his body fit the profile of a tower-climber.

"Shank, I've harvested bushels of your wild stories. In a different life, I did reckless stuff too! I'm tired of sittin' on the sidelines. Need to recapture some glory."

He was serious; I was stunned. "Hey, man, it's one thing for unattached me, but what about Linda and the kids?"

"With you leading, what could happen? Reckon I've *got* to do this," he said with rare intensity.

The more I protested, the more agitated he became. "Fine," I ultimately relented. After all, he was his own man. I almost added—ironically, as it turned out—"It's your funeral."

We scaled the chain-link fence and looked up the belly of the beast. The wind was howling. "Let's do it!" I said, encouraging Buddy to join me.

The climbing was easy, since the middle of each metal X provided a natural foothold. Several times I looked down to monitor Buddy's progress. He was not what you'd call an athlete. However, like me he was a professional golf caddy, and his pudgy body was surprisingly fit. When we reached the horizontal beam, my chest pounded beyond what the exertion warranted. This was crazy scary. The steel beam was only about six inches wide. My pulse accelerated wildly.

I yelled above the howling gale, "See the slanting vertical supports on each side, above us and then again across on the other side? The upward angles are so steep that we can only hold on at the beginning and end of walking the beam. Those thirty feet in the middle, where the supports are too high and out of reach, is where we fly solo!"

I waited for a negative reply from Buddy. After all, he had every right to balk. But he merely said, "See you on the other side."

Later, I thought about the multiple meanings of that phrase. However, that night it was merely chatter.

The shaking seemed to increase, both inside me and along the beam. *Calm down, or you are toast.* Focusing intently, I thought about how simple the feat would be on the ground. *Imagine it's a sidewalk curb.* This was a mental exercise, not a physical one, I reminded myself. With that thought, my heart rate slowed a fraction, and my breathing became more regular. Gusts blew randomly. As I crept forward, the structural support above tapered away. Sweat dripped down my back. I held on to the support as long as I could. At last, when the support finally angled up out of reach, my arms let go and smoothly dropped into a horizontal "flying" position for balance. *Do or die.* A healthy dose of adrenaline, nature's thrill drug, surged through my body. *Stay in the moment.* It was not easy to focus or relax, especially since the car looked like a toy down there on the ground. Even so, my concentration never wavered. *One foot in front of the other.* By making decisive but careful movements, I got across in under a minute. Cowabunga!

My attention then turned to Buddy. He looked terrified. He had clearly not challenged fate in years. The noise of the wind made calling to him useless. Buddy waited on the other side for a long time but eventually followed my example. After a few steps, he let go of the upward-slanting support and looked as if he was going to be fine. Unfortunately, near the middle of the beam a violent gust battered him. He lost both his nerve and his balance. My companion started to topple, seemingly in slow motion. He could not recover his balance.

As my stomach twisted, something totally unexpected happened—Buddy sat down. He did not scream, curse, or actually fall. His rotund center of gravity somehow managed to push him onto the beam. He awkwardly twisted sideways, ending up with his back toward the wind. Every fiber within me reacted, and I lunged to help. But Buddy stopped me by raising an open palm in my direction. Like a storefront mannequin, my pal was motionless and mesmerized. Eventually returning to this dimension, he remained seated and started to move. Looking like a clumsy 200-pound inchworm, he slid the remaining distance six inches at a time. When he finally got close enough, I helped him stand. We hugged.

"Do I qualify?" he yelled.

"What?"

"Am I in your fraternity of thrill-seekers?"

"Absolutely, you freak!"

We entered the semi-enclosed maintenance ladder and climbed the rest of the way without incident. In a few minutes, we were sitting on the summit.

"That was intense. What happened?"

"I 'bout fell off," Buddy deadpanned.

"Obviously. I mean afterwards."

"My life flashed before me, real quick-like. Started with stupid stuff—hounds we had as pets, flapjacks, horseshoes, and Friday night football games. Then some dark junk. Finally, Linda and the kids. After that, this weird calmness came over me. I reckoned everything was going to be OK."

We perched on the tower taking in the breathtaking view. Twinkling pockets of lights spread out for miles. Buddy broke the silence. "Can't believe I near-about fell. What if I had?"

"No way—you were cool."

He then looked me in the eyes and asked, "Would you take care of Linda if I die?"

"Oh, be serious."

"No joshing, Shank. If I went to rot in the ground, would you take care of her? Not financially or romantically—more like a brother."

I was touched.

"Sure, man. But hey, this is silly talk. You'll outlive us all!"

How wrong I was.

CHAPTER 2

Death by old age? Of course, that happened to grandparents. Cancer? Yes, I've known some whose lives were cut short by cells mutating out of control. Car accident? Had a classmate killed like that. But murder? Before Buddy, I had never personally known anyone who had been killed on purpose.

"... and because of your friendship, I thought you were the natural one to help."

Snapping back to reality, I muttered, "Uh-huh." My *good* sister taught me to interject sounds like that whenever someone was delivering a monologue, just to make it sound like an actual two-way conversation. On a Tuesday, a few weeks after the funeral, Linda Franks was trying to make a serious request, and I didn't fully comprehend what she was saying.

"Besides, given *how* he was killed, someone in the industry might have an advantage."

I nodded vaguely. The coroner had determined the cause of death to be choking—on a golf ball. Why had someone killed him like that? Rage could have provoked the initial blow to Buddy's head. Those things happen, even at posh digs like the Lodge at Torrey Pines where the murder took place. But once Buddy was down, it was cold-blooded murder to shove a golf ball down his throat. Did the killer have to pry open Buddy's mouth to insert it? How much hatred, or insanity, was behind such a grotesque attack? I flinched, imagining the scene.

"Are you OK?" Linda asked.

"Yeah. A lot of this is hard to fathom," I said, rubbing my temples.

Realizing I was fading in and out of the "conversation," she pleaded—with a tinge of irritation—"So will you help find Buddy's murderer?"

The Franks's living room reminded me of a dangerous surf spot where the ocean appears safe, but toothy carnivores swim below. What lurked where I might have to go to provide this help? Granted, after our tower-climbing escapade, I had promised to look after Linda. But what could I really do? I was a professional caddy who toted a fifty-pound golf bag for a living. I made good money, had chunks of time off, and enjoyed travel, but how did that qualify me to sniff around a homicide?

"Shank? Have I lost you?"

Returning yet again from deep thought, I responded, "Sorry. This is difficult."

"I understand. You and Buddy are good friends. I mean, *were*—" she corrected herself with a voice that trailed off in an unsettling way.

Reengaging, I asked, "Why do the police think you had anything to do with it?"

She held a glass of iced tea in her lap, stirring it slowly with a spoon. I could hear the clock ticking. *Why such a long delay answering?*

At last, she launched in. "Well, I drove to Torrey Pines that Sunday after watching the front nine on TV. I didn't think Tinny's big lead would hold up, or I would have gone earlier."

I nodded. Journeyman golfer Tinny Wilcox, the pro that Buddy caddied for, had never won a PGA Tour event before.

"When it looked like they might finally get that first win, I wanted to be there," Linda continued. "While Tinny would be in the spotlight, Buddy deserved some special attention too. He had been such a loyal caddy. He worked so hard. I asked a neighbor to watch the kids and got ready to go. I couldn't wait to get there."

"From Orange County to La Jolla, that puts you down there in about an hour?"

"That's what I figured. But there were several bad stretches of traffic on the freeway once I hit San Diego County. Then I tried to take the back way into Torrey Pines and got lost. When I finally got there, everyone was leaving. Traffic barricades kept me from getting into the closest parking lots. I ended up walking a couple of miles from one of the remote lots."

She paused for a moment, looked out the window, and sipped her tea. I took a long look at her. Linda was a spunky redhead whose eyes could dance, but the ravages of the last few weeks had tarnished some of that shine. Still in mourning, the new widow wore black pumps and pants, a gold belt, and a black silk blouse with gold-flecked accents. She looked more stylish than I remembered her to be. And for the first time, I noticed how appealing Linda's body was. Had I simply suppressed making that assessment while Buddy was alive? Regardless, if Linda wanted to find another man, she had the bait to hook one. When she turned back toward me, I smiled warmly.

Becoming agitated, Linda said, "By the time I reached the course, their disastrous finish was headline news on sports radio. I was so mad that Tinny tanked again!" I could see her knuckles turning white with rage as she strangled the iced tea glass. Composing herself, she continued.

"I tried calling Buddy, but he hadn't turned his cell phone back on. Since the tournament was over, I headed straight for the Lodge. Buddy had spent Saturday night there, and I figured he was packing up to leave. But the place was swarming with emergency vehicles, and a cop was screening everyone who tried to get in. He didn't care that my husband was a Tour caddy—he would *not* let me in. I insisted on seeing his superior. So this older officer eventually came over, and I told him that I was Buddy Franks's wife. I could literally see his body stiffened. That's when I knew something was wrong."

"They obviously let you in."

"Absolutely. From that point on they treated me with kid gloves—until I became a suspect," she said, shivering as she uttered that last word.

"What changed?"

"They're a bunch of lying—" Linda bit her tongue. "The police say I had a window of opportunity. They calculated I had enough time to get to the Lodge, confront Buddy, leave, and then stage an arrival to cover my tracks. They didn't believe what I told them about traffic and the problems I had finding a place to park."

"Did you stop on the way down or talk with anyone who might back up your story?"

"Not that I recall," she answered without much thought.

"Take your time. This is important."

Linda frowned with the effort. "I didn't stop on the way, and by the time I got to the parking lot, the attendants were gone."

"There must be more to their suspicions than the lack of an alibi."

"You'll have to ask *them*," she said curtly.

We sat in silence. How much did I really know about this woman and her relationship with Buddy? They had invited me to their home several times for family meals, which were pleasant enough. We had also socialized at various events. Apart from Linda's tendency to dominate, they seemed to get along fine. But was there more? An uncomfortable tension was apparent at times. Buddy would take Linda's phone calls, excuse himself, and lower his voice. He would later return looking beaten. Other times when they interacted, Linda made comments under her breath. Buddy would sigh while rolling his eyes. Dark thoughts began to cloud my mind. But what motive could she have to harm her husband, the father of their children? Feeling creeped out, I redirected the conversation. "How did you and Buddy meet? I've never heard the story."

Bingo! Her face relaxed, and a smile blossomed as she started talking. "Buddy had recently arrived in Southern California from Las Vegas. He said he was tired of the sweltering heat there, so he came to the coast. We met at a Super Bowl party. I was definitely *under*whelmed," she added with good-natured emphasis. "He was older, a high school graduate, and a caddy. Whoop-de-do! I'd never played golf or attended a tournament, and I was amazed anyone could make a living by carrying somebody's clubs. He was sweet, though, and of course he spoke with that lovely Tennessee accent.

"We dated for the better part of a year, got married, and moved to Orange County. We settled here in Irvine. I hated the consecutive tournaments when Buddy was gone for weeks. But it was wonderful when he was home for extended periods. We rode bikes with the kids and went to movies. Now—" She couldn't continue.

While this trip down memory lane started out well, it had quickly turned bumpy. Time to change topics again.

I waited until she recovered and asked, "So Linda, what exactly do you envision me doing?"

"Getting me out of this mess," she said with a demanding edge. Realizing how sharply her words had come out, she licked her lips. "Sorry, it's the pressure and stupidity of the situation. The police are all over me, and the district attorney needs a villain. What's going to happen when the police arrest me?"

She looked frightened. The dam finally broke. Sobs and convulsions followed. Typically, guys don't know how to react when women show such open emotion. I was no exception. But I felt compelled to do something. So I moved over to the couch and gathered her close. She melted into me and continued crying.

If she was faking, what an actress! Where did that awful thought come from? Linda was a widow and needed a warrior. But what if she was manipulating me? She seemed to be holding something back. As my thoughts continued to vacillate, her warm tears soaked through my shirt. Sadness and despair permeated the room. I rubbed her shoulder softly. Was Buddy was looking down on this somber scene?

Something clicked, and I was electrified. It felt like that critical moment after I've paused on the edge of a near-vertical ski drop and my body finally screams, *Go, go, go!* I realized that this was more than the fulfillment of the promise I'd made to Buddy—helping Linda was simply the right thing to do.

My parents came to mind. They always said that when someone needs help, they need it right then. Mom was a good seamstress, and people knew it. When my sister's friend had a wedding disaster, Mom came to the rescue. The bride's dress didn't show up until the day before the big event, and it didn't fit right. The bride was distraught. Mom endured sore fingers and little sleep, but she finished the marathon sewing project the morning of the ceremony.

Dad was cut from a similar cloth. We joked that he was California's Statue of Liberty— "Give me your tired, your poor, your orphans, whatever." A neighbor once asked Dad to walk his dog while the man had minor surgery. Days turned to weeks as the poor guy suffered complications. Rebuffing suggestions that he take the dog to a kennel, Dad walked that dog for months until the recovering man could finally claim his pet.

Linda needed help, and I had time. My quiver of skills had several sharp arrows, and I had a thirst to find the murderer. Holding Linda's tortured body tightly to mine, feeling her pain drip into my pores, I was ready to uncover the mystery behind this treachery at Torrey Pines.

CHAPTER 3

My first encounter with Buddy was at a Professional Golf Association tournament at the often breezy TPC Southwind course in Memphis, Tennessee. Before the opening round on a Thursday, Tinsley "Tinny" Wilcox and his caddy were on the practice range. While both were in their early forties, the pair contrasted dramatically. The golfer was tall and thin, the caddy short and stout. The latter's straight black hair, dark eyes, and baggy clothes made him look like Buddy Hackett—stand-up comedian and Herbie's mechanic in the original *Love Bug* movie.

Part of my job as a PGA Tour caddy for pro Cary Cline is predicting how the swirling wind will affect a golf ball's flight. Still a rookie then, I tried exploring the topic with Wilcox's caddy by asking, "Think it's a club more because of the breeze in our face?"

"You reckon I'm a weather vane?" was his terse response, in a thick Tennessee accent.

"Not even close. Your head doesn't spin fast enough," I quipped back.

Both pros made the cut and coincidentally played together in the third round on Saturday. The PGA Tour schedules most tournaments for Thursday through Sunday, with eighteen holes played daily. Only golfers in the top half make the cut and play the weekend—the only way to win *any* prize money. Depending upon the total event purse, winners can earn $1 million or more for the week.

I ignored Herbie's mechanic until he approached me and apologized. "Sorry 'bout the other day. The wife called and chewed my biscuits. I took it out on you. Let's start over. My name is Buddy."

"Seriously?" I laughed.

"My pathetic apology that funny?"

"No," I said gaining control. "It's just that you look like Buddy Hackett—"

"—Got it," he said, cutting me off.

Obviously, I wasn't the first one to see the resemblance. "Better than being Mr. Sunshine like you," he teased with a wry grin.

The good-natured barb was dead on. I was then a 27-year-old quintessential Californian. Standing a few inches over six feet, nature had welded my powerful 195 pounds onto an agile frame. Neat blonde hair and rugged features are Scottish, tracing back through Dad to shivering guys in kilts. My intense blue eyes are a genetic gift from Mom's Viking ancestors— even colder shivering guys! Constant exposure to the sun has tanned my fair skin and deepened the premature crow's feet around my eyes.

While neither of our pros won that tournament, both finished well, and we earned respectable caddy-cuts of their winnings.

At the Memphis International Airport, Buddy sat near our gate reading the sports section of the paper. I approached him and asked, "Do you live in Orange County, too?"

"Yup."

"Say, how about those Lakers?" I asked.

"Soap opera, but entertaining. You a fan?"

"I bleed purple and gold," was my proud response. "Did you patch things up with the wife?"

After searching for a response, Buddy finally said, "You ride bikes as a kid?"

"Sure."

"Remember puncture kits with those rubber patches? Apply glue and hope it holds?"

"Got it," I said, impressed with the analogy. I tried to sound encouraging. "Sometimes the fix is even stronger than the original."

Over time, Buddy and I developed a friendship. We saw each other in Southern California and hung out during tournaments as our schedules permitted. As different as we were in background, talents, and temperament, we were exceedingly compatible. I genuinely enjoyed his company.

CHAPTER 4

After the emotional night at Linda's, I had a hard time getting my typical three hours of sleep. Finally getting out of bed at 2 a.m. Wednesday morning, I felt less fired up about helping. No experience, no leads, no plan. On top of that, a possible headline kept running through my mind: *Caddy Arrested for Interfering with Police Investigation.*

Slipping on a blue Nautica robe and cushy sheepskin slippers from my folks, I headed to the front window. The view always reminds me why I live in such a small apartment. Beyond the parking lot, a mere 7-iron away, is the vast, seemingly limitless Pacific. My address is 2207½ Oceanfront, Newport Beach. The "½" denotes an upstairs unit. The interior motif is early bachelor. Uninspired wood and stucco duplexes on either side mirror mine. The residents access tiny garages through an alley plastered with no-parking signs. My favorite reads, "Hey, you! Don't even think about parking here!" The residences are sandwiched between businesses in both directions. A constant river of human interest flows along the primo boardwalk in front. My humble abode provides a fabulous location without an outrageous Newport Beach price tag. Newport is a magnificent enclave of millionaires and billionaires that anchors Orange County's platinum coast. To the flat north is edgy Huntington Beach, where each July the U.S. Open of Surfing bustles in a circus-like atmosphere around a modern concrete pier. To the hilly south is Laguna Beach, a century-old former artists' colony with quaint streets, dramatic views, and a tourist-filled downtown village.

Newport Beach offers miles of oceanfront real estate and a large pleasure-craft harbor with several chic residential islands. The city's most famous former resident was movie legend John Wayne. The Duke used to host floating poker parties on his conspicuous yacht with pals Bob Hope, Sammy Davis, Jr., and Dean Martin. Newport Beach —which often makes, and sometimes tops, lists of wealthiest cities in the U.S.—is home to famous sports and entertainment personalities, as well as being the locale for fictional TV shows like *The O.C.*

In the early morning darkness, I left the lights off so I could see better. Rod cells in the eye work best in the dark. Cone cells like the light and provide detailed color vision. But once the cones are activated, the rods take time to re-establish sight. This is why people stumble blindly in the dark when they go back to bed after turning on the bathroom lights. With my rods dominating, I could see the promised overhead north swell pounding the beach. Waves before breakfast!

With several hours until dawn, I revived the computer from sleep mode. Needing to organize my efforts for Linda, I created a document with three headings: (1) Facts, (2) Theories, and (3) Thoughts. In naming the file, the words

"Find My Killer, Shank" flew from my fingertips. My intention in typing that was to provide motivation every time I accessed the document. Under the first heading, I tried to detail all the facts Linda told me. Skipping the second section was easy since I had no theories yet. In the third section, I randomly journaled thoughts and feelings. It felt good to unload some of the baggage.

Next I checked the wave prospects on one of the sites that provides forecasts and webcam images of surf spots. One camera showed the Newport Beach Pier. The north camera offered the same basic view as the one out my window. Of course, in the dark, the camera barely showed white foam rolling toward shore. But the site's other features confirmed that big waves were expected most of the day.

Zoning out for a moment, I wondered whether Linda was awake too. Losing a spouse had to cripple normal sleep patterns. It's likely she was a temporary nocturnal loner like me. However, there was a difference. For Linda, time would eventually heal the worst wounds. She would return to full nights of slumber. I had no such hope.

The quickest way for Linda to regain peace was for me to help her. But how? While it would be great to get the police reports, that was going to be way too difficult as my first move. Develop likely suspects? Grand idea, but there were none. Needing more details about the events of that day, I turned to news outlets. The cyber connection soon led me to the *San Diego Union-Tribune*, the largest regional paper covering Torrey Pines. I searched the archives for the Monday after the tournament. Pay dirt:

Caddy Killed at Classic

La Jolla—Professional golf caddy Buddy Franks, who caddied for Tinsley "Tinny" Wilcox, was the apparent victim of foul play after the Torrey Pines Classic on Sunday, according to local police.

San Diego Police Detective Gerald Baker said that shortly after Franks left the course following the tournament, a guest in an adjoining room at the Lodge at Torrey Pines reported a disturbance in Franks's room. When hotel personnel investigated the complaint, they discovered his body.

According to Detective Baker, the assailant struck Franks on the head with a golf putter before forcing a golf ball into the victim's mouth. Wilcox told police that the putter and ball likely belonged to Franks, as he often traveled with such equipment for in-room relaxation.

Buddy also took along a plastic "hole" for putting fun. We would hang out in his hotel room and play a variety of games. How many putts in a row could we make? With eyes closed? Who could make the first one off-handed, through our legs, or on one leg? We would bank them off an armoire or other piece of furniture. We spent hours engaged in those ridiculous competitions. Loved it!

The article continued:

Franks's death followed a dramatic loss by Wilcox in another bid for his first PGA Tour victory. Franks was Wilcox's caddy for the last six years. After the round, Wilcox was on the practice green before authorities escorted the golfer to the Lodge where they told him of Franks's death. The pro turned "white as a ghost" and collapsed, according to witnesses, and emergency personnel were summoned to administer medical attention. Franks, originally from Tennessee, lived in Irvine, California. He is survived by his wife, Linda, and two children.

That's weird. Tinny was on the practice green *after* the tournament? It's common for pros to be seen on the practice green between rounds, but they never go there after the final round. I continued searching for other *Tribune* articles the week after the Torrey Pines Classic. Finding nothing more, I went to the *Los Angeles Times* site. There was a separate column about Buddy next to Monday's tournament coverage. While much of it repeated the *Tribune's* report, the following was new:

> Tournament Director Nick Slate said, "We are all shocked by such a senseless act of violence. Our sympathies go out to Tinny and, of course, to the man's family."

My blood pressure climbed. Slate did not even bother to reference Buddy by name! Realizing the overreaction, I calmed down and let the hottest anger dissipate. I put the computer back into sleep mode, stretched, and moved on. By the time I finished a few chores, it was six o'clock. Time for waves!

After pulling on a full wetsuit, I grabbed my favorite mid-size surfboard, ran across the damp sand, and dove into the breakers. The ocean is my playground. When I was younger, catching waves was my religion. I would cut non-essential classes and even tag along with an older neighbor on the occasional "surfari" to Mexico. Many of my friends were converts to the surfing lifestyle too, even if they did not really surf. But they would go to extreme lengths in their quest to adopt a surfer image. Sometimes, on the rare San Clemente winter day when the temperature stayed in the low 50s, some of them would wear surf shorts with a ski parka on top. I'm not kidding.

I loved being part of the cowabunga crowd. My room at home housed your basic furniture and shelves with a few knick-knacks and trophies—until one day, early on in high school, when the centerfold wave in a *Surfer* magazine caught my attention. It was a huge barrel at Pipeline—the world's most recognized wave, from the North Shore of Oahu in Hawaii. The monster tube, the stuff young surfers dream about, was empty. I taped it to the wall over my bed. Mom was not thrilled, but she figured this was a temporary phase. Wrong. Over the next few months, I neatly taped pictures of other waves from magazines on the wall around the killer Pipeline shot. With each added photograph, a striking collage emerged.

Mom eventually flipped out. "Henry David, you *must* take those down. They will ruin the paint!"

As I vehemently objected, Dad came wandering into the fracas. He thought about the pictures. Mom and I remained silent, each of us hoping for an ally. Finally, he offered a compromise. "Shank, if we let you keep them up, will you agree to repaint the entire room, in any color your Mom chooses, when you go away to college?"

The proposition seemed reasonable. After all, university life was still several years away—an eternity to a teenager.

"Sure, Dad, I'd be glad to paint the room later so I can decorate it with waves now."

Mom's resistance was gone. "I guess the waves are better than other things you could put up."

All through high school, I added more pictures every month. On occasion, a bikini-clad surfer girl would also make the grade. When the wall above my bed was full, the collage turned the corners on either side. By the middle of my junior year, the masterpiece was complete. I had covered every inch of wall space in my bedroom with surfing images. It was relaxing, entertaining, and compelling. A consistent flow of friends, both guys and girls, came to check out the "wave room."

The summer before college, I made good on my promise. After the emotional task of tearing it all down,

I repainted the bedroom in a shockingly bright shade of Tahiti Teal. Mom was thrilled.

On crisp mornings like this one in Newport, nothing says "hello" quite like the icy Pacific in your face. The sun was starting to lighten the horizon, and several other hearty souls joined me. How different surfing would be, especially in predominantly cold-water locales like California, if we didn't have neoprene wetsuits.

Between sets of surf, I alternated between thinking over my last wave and the newspaper articles I'd just read. *Paddle, take-off, slip, oops, thumped. That was lame.* If someone murdered me, I wondered, would my death get more coverage than Buddy's or less? *You dog! That was my wave. You cut me off! Let it go, let it go.* Why a golf ball as the murder weapon? Talk about an unreliable tool. Even if he was unconscious, Buddy could have gagged and spit the ball out, foiling the murder attempt. It made no sense. *Paddle, dig, dig, free fall, I'm up, barreled—out untouched. Super wave!*

After the wonderful surf session, I thawed out in a hot shower. Dressing was standard fare: Levis 501 jeans, golf shirt, Nautica jacket, and a pair of Nikes. No socks. As I looked out over my beach and the solid waves, I prepared a hearty breakfast of bacon, toast, and sliced bananas. My initial game plan came into focus. I needed to talk to people who were closest to the action the night of Buddy's death, including Detective Baker and Slate, the tournament director. Next would be Buddy's pro, Tinny, and the Lodge employee who found Buddy's body. Those four formed my initial interview list. That sounded kind of cool—an "interview list." It may have seemed silly, but this bit of microscopic progress energized me. I jumped up from the table, knocked over the chair, and thrust both arms into the air in mock victory. Look out, Perry Mason and Nero Wolfe; move over, Columbo and Sam Spade—novice detective Shank MacDuff is rolling now!

CHAPTER 5

"Linda, how are you?" I asked when I called her later that morning.

"Better than yesterday. You were very sweet. Thanks for the soft touch."

Was there a double meaning to that? I shook my head and continued, "What do you think about me interviewing Slate, Detective Baker, Tinny, and some of the Lodge employees? We should try for low-hanging fruit first, someone willing and accessible."

"Makes sense. But that leaves Tinny out since he lives in Arizona."

"True. I hadn't thought about the logistics."

"Whatever you could do would be wonderful, Shank."

"What are you up to today?"

"Off for a manicure," she said breezily.

"Really?" I blurted out.

"Just because Buddy's gone, do I have to stop living?" She sounded cold. Linda was obviously under pressure, but nobody likes to be on the receiving end of such a frigid blast.

"You should stay with your normal routine," I offered.

"Oh, I haven't had a manicure in years. Buddy thought my nails would fall off."

So why the sudden urge to primp? Kind of weird.

"Got to go," she said, sounding distracted.

"Sure, Linda. Hang in there."

As the call ended, I hoped she would regain her old stride soon. Then again, maybe this was simply an example of the Linda that left Buddy shaking his head so often.

I called the Torrey Pines pro shop and wandered through various keypad options. Finally getting a live body, I asked, "Can someone provide me the contact information for Nick Slate?"

"Certainly."

After writing down the number, I dialed.

"Slate Sports. How may I help you?" the receptionist bubbled.

"I'd like to make an appointment to see Mr. Slate. My name is Shank MacDuff, and I'm a PGA Tour caddy."

"May I ask the nature of your business with Mr. Slate?"

"It relates to the death of Buddy Franks."

"I see," she said. "One moment, please."

While I was on hold, high-energy music blared in my ear. A moment later, the woman returned and said, "He's free at eleven today. Will that work?"

"Sure, thanks."

After hanging up, it occurred to me how cool it was that caddying provided me freedom to pursue projects like this. My pro, Cary Cline, plays in about twenty-five tournaments per year. Thus, I work about half the time during the year. We had finished the West Coast swing and were in the middle of a week off before heading to a tournament in Florida.

On the brilliant 70-degree March day, the drive down Interstate 5 to San Diego was delightful. My M3, BMW's high-performance sports sedan, settled into the task with style, its custom Caribbean Blue skin color screaming "fun." The last city in Orange County is San Clemente, where I grew up. It's nestled between the coastal range and sandy beaches, and it was a great place to spend my youth.

Next up was the famous Trestles surf spot. The waves were breaking overhead and looked inviting. Trestles is technically part of the mighty Camp Pendleton Marine Base. Pendleton's 250,000 acres make it the largest Marine Corps base in the country, and its massive girth separates Orange County from San Diego. The seventeen-mile stretch of undeveloped shoreline that belongs to Pendleton is by far the largest in Southern California, worth buckets of billions to developers—if they could ever pry the Marines off.

The upstairs office of Slate Sports was in a Del Mar Heights business complex, three miles north of Torrey Pines. Slate's lobby hosted an array of scuba, mountain climbing, and British golf magazines. After I had waited about ten minutes, Slate's secretary fetched me. "Mr. Slate will see you now," she said, as if I had just scored an audience with a king. She led me to the boss's office.

Slate looked up and inspected me. Sauntering over and extending his hand to me, he said oh-so-slickly, "Nick Slate." He was shorter than I am, and his graphite-gray eyes were too deep in their sockets. Styling cream glazed his bushy brown hair, while the man's skin glowed with a tanning-booth sheen. His hip clothes were GQ all the way. He slinked back behind an ultra-modern desk. I sat down on a hard wooden guest chair seemingly designed to keep people from becoming too comfortable. Slate adorned his office with all sorts of sports paraphernalia, from autographed balls and hats to framed photos of himself with famous athletes.

"Are you a sports agent?" I opened.

"Not even close," he smirked, noticing my obvious interest in the high-profile stuff. "I just know the right people."

One prominent item on the wall was a large poster of Magic Johnson, the star of the Los Angeles Lakers dynasty that won five world championships in the 1980s. In his rookie season, with Kareem Abdul-Jabbar injured for game six of the finals, Magic became a 22-year-old legend by playing all five positions, scoring 42 points, and leading his short-handed team to the title. Magic's million-watt smile ultimately helped make him one of the most recognizable athletes in the world.

The poster made me think of Buddy. One night a year earlier, some guy invited him to a Lakers home game. The seats were supposed to be killer. After I watched the game on TV, the phone rang.

"Shank, it's me, Buddy," he yelled into the phone.

"Where are you?"

"Fixin' to leave the game. Sorry 'bout the noise."

"That's OK. Nice victory."

"Yeah, but you know where we sat?"

"Tell me."

"Two rows from the floor, close to the basket!" he said excitedly.

I pictured the location in my mind. "Not *that* end?" I asked, realizing where this was heading.

"Yep, right behind Magic! Can you believe it? Magic Johnson!"

When they retire your number, hang your jersey on the wall, and dedicate a bronze statue of you out front, you get a *really* good seat. TV cameras love to show Magic and high-profile Lakers fans like Dyan Cannon, Billy Crystal, Denzel Washington, and of course, Jack Nicholson.

Buddy continued, "More exciting than a mouse in a cheese festival. Heap of folks talked to Magic; class act every time."

"That's awesome. Did you speak to him?"

"Nah. He nodded in our direction, but I froze. Don't matter. Just thrilled to have lived it from up close." Buddy rode the fumes of this high-octane encounter for weeks.

I returned my focus to Slate's office.

"Our main business is adventure travel," he said, trying to educate me. Seeing the blank look on my face, he added condescendingly, "Arranging exotic sports outings?"

"Got it. Sounds lucrative."

"If you've got serious cash, I'll hook you up on an expedition to Mt. Everest."

"I had no idea an Average Joe could stand at the top of the world so easily."

"You'd be surprised how much people will pay to try the things they see on adventure shows."

One of two cell phones on his desk rang. He nodded in my direction then answered. "Slate. Yeah. OK. Maybe. Uh—Madison. Sure. Later." He hung up and continued as if we hadn't been interrupted. "We offer other trips, like scuba diving on the Great Barrier Reef, alligator hunting in the Everglades, and golfing in Scotland via private helicopter. Like minting money."

"So how did you end up as tournament director for the Classic?"

"Played golf as a teenager, some in college, and I was good. But things happened. I ended up working a few miles down the road at Del Mar Racetrack. Being a San Diego resident entitled me to discount rounds at Torrey Pines. The cheap play brought me back into the sport. There was more long-term opportunity in golf than working the ponies, so I switched."

"Better connections?"

"Different, you know? Over the years, I became more involved in the Classic. Then when the former director moved to Michigan, they asked me to take his place. It's been a good fit." Though he obviously enjoyed talking about himself, he switched gears after glancing at the clock. "I'm sure you didn't come for my life story. What brings you here?"

I tried to settle back in the torture chair, but my effort was in vain. I forced a smile. "As you probably know, I carry the bag for Cary Cline on Tour."

"Hey, let me ask you something," he immediately interrupted. "I read somewhere that Cline is a religious freak. He prays before every round and sometimes every shot. Is that really true?"

"Basically, yeah. Cary says he's a born-again Christian. It seems to work for him."

"What about the golf-tee thing?" he kept pressing.

"You're referring to the press Cary received for printing 'John 3:16' on his golf tees?"

"I guess that's it."

"He once told me it was the same Bible reference that In-N-Out Burger puts on cup bottoms." A bit distracted, I redirected the conversation. "Anyway, Buddy Franks was a friend of mine before—you know. The police are putting pressure on his wife, Linda, and I'm trying to get her off the hook." *Oops.* That made her sound guilty. I would have to watch myself in the future.

"Did she have a reason to want the poor sod dead?"

I shook my head. "Don't think so."

"So, you want to know if *I* killed the caddy?" he asked with a wry smile.

"No. Of course not. I want to hear the story from your perspective."

"Huh," he said under his breath. The other cell phone rang. He put an index finger up to me and answered, "Slate. Oh, hey. That might work. Let me check. Around

lunch is clear that day. Want to book it? Fine. See you then."
He looked back at me. "Where was I? Oh yeah. With Tinny
so far in front going to the back nine, we could hear TV
sets clicking off all over the country. Then he fell apart—
I mean bad. Within a few holes, Tinny is gone. He plum-
meted down the leader board."

"That much was clear from TV," I interjected. Cary
had played poorly on Thursday and Friday of the Classic.
Missing the cut had provided me plenty of relaxation time
on Sunday to watch from home. "What about Buddy's
death? How did that unfold?"

"As you probably know, I'm one busy guy as the tournament wraps up. Once Tinny's group, the final pairing, finished the eighteenth, my only goal was to make sure the
awards ceremony flowed. It did. All the fans remaining in
the grandstands applauded and then headed for their cars.
At that point, there was nothing really different from prior
years."

"What did you do next?"

"Schmoozed; talked with lots of important people. Then
I wandered back to the operations room and saw Tinny on
the practice green by the bar trying to figure out what went
wrong." He paused and then continued. "Once we were
inside, the team worked on wrap-up. We were hashing out
a few issues when a staffer ran in and said that some caddy
got himself killed at the Lodge. What a bummer! I was in
the mood to finish the weekend with a thick steak and a
thin brunette," he leered while winking. "Unfortunately,
given the fact it was a caddy, I had to go check it out."

"Did you go to Buddy's room?"

"No, the manager's office. Found Tinny laid out on the
ground getting medical attention. People said when they
told him what happened to the caddy—"

"Buddy Franks," I reminded Slate, tired of the imper-
sonal and even offensive account.

"OK, Franks. Apparently, when Tinny hears his guy is bound for a body bag, the pro got bleached and hit the floor."

"Excuse me, 'got bleached'?"

"Turned white?" he explaincd with great indulgence. "Whoever grabbed Wilcox from the putting green should have told him right there. It would have saved his face." Slate smirked.

"I don't understand."

"Had they told him there, instead of waiting until he was in the manager's office, he would have landed on soft grass instead of hard floor. Get it?"

"Got it," I said, disgusted. This callous jerk was getting to me.

"Just kidding. Lighten up. Anyway, someone on the Lodge staff told me what happened, about the golf ball and all that. Somebody was really steamed and took care of business with flair." He glanced at his watch again. "Got a lunch meeting in a few. Are you getting what you want?"

"Sort of."

"Have you talked to the cops yet?"

"That's on my list."

"So you haven't had the pleasure of dealing with Detective Baker," he said sarcastically. "Good luck. The giant redneck is a real pain."

I needed more than he had given me, but I didn't know what to ask next. This was like trying to climb a mountain of peanut butter. "Was there anything out of the ordinary?" I asked lamely.

"Like throat-seeking golf balls?" he joked.

My patience wore even thinner. "Like something during the tournament?"

Again, he was flippant. "You mean apart from Tinny choking and then his caddy doing the same?" This time he laughed out loud at his own morbid humor.

Just as I was about ready to jump over the desk and throttle his neck, the second cell phone rang again. He answered and shrugged his shoulders helplessly at me. Into the phone he said, "My man, it's been a while. What's happening?" Slate settled back to talk, this time showing no indication that our conversation would resume anytime soon. Standing up, I bailed. He gave me a two-finger salute goodbye.

Would all my interviews be so dissatisfying?

CHAPTER 6

While I was still in Slate's parking lot, I called the police department that covered La Jolla. A monotone voice answered with, "Northern Division." While waiting to be connected, I wondered if the police would belittle my efforts. Real cops did not have to indulge a gumshoe masquerade. I asked for the officer mentioned in the news articles. After I had been on hold for at least two minutes, a booming baritone answered, "Baker."

"Detective, my name is Shank—"

"MacDuff, right?"

"Correct," I answered, surprised.

"What can we do for you?"

"I'd like to discuss the Buddy Franks case, in person if possible. I'm in Del Mar Heights. Could we meet this afternoon?"

Without hesitation, he asked in a friendly tone, "Two hours?"

"Great!" I agreed. The detective provided directions, and we hung up.

My next move was clear. I ignited the M3, and we headed for the scene of the crime, taking the coastal highway so I could get my fill of the crashing surf. Soon we approached the Torrey Pines State Reserve. It's located within San Diego city limits, but the reserve is a wild stretch of land. Chaparral, rare and elegant Torrey Pine trees, and an unspoiled lagoon grace the 2,000-acre beachfront oasis. Anyone wandering the reserve's trails can easily imagine what California must have looked like to the early settlers or Spanish explorers.

Once it gets beyond the waves and next to the reserve, the road seduces drivers as it climbs inland to a stretch without cross-streets. The M3 viciously accelerated as its horses stampeded, shoving me back in the seat. The Caribbean Blue streak was quickly going over a hundred miles per hour. Even before mechanics enhanced some of the critical components, the car had nearly track-ready performance. At the top of the hill, with the golf course in view on the right, the eager BMW reluctantly relaxed. Gravity brought us back down to freeway speed. To me, driving fast in this urban environment is like surfing—you take a calculated risk, hit it hard while trying to come out cleanly, and patiently wait for the next opportunity.

Turning into the parking lot, the M3 glided into a cherished end spot away from potential door-dingers. Stepping out, I noticed a truly overweight man sitting on his car's bumper, trying to shove swollen feet into worn-out golf shoes. The car was dipping toward the back, the poor shocks straining under the weight. As the man gave one mighty push of his foot, he lost balance and rolled on the ground.

"Whoa!" I said, rushing over to help him up. "Are you OK?"

"Yeah," the round man muttered, wiping himself off. "Happens more than I'd like to admit. I'm top heavy."

I tried not to laugh at the understatement of the year. Seeing his predicament, I tentatively offered, "Can I help you with the shoes?"

Without a hint of embarrassment, he said, "Sure."

He perched again on the bumper, and I shoved the shoe on like an unlucky prince in a Kafkaesque *Cinderella*. After I tied the laces, we repeated the process with the other foot.

"Thanks. You probably think I'm a real clown, but my game is actually coming around. I work nights and play here all the time. Lots of bang for the buck."

"Good for you. Well, hit 'em close."

So here's what I know about Torrey Pines, or at least some of what I know. It opened in 1957, on an expansive ocean bluff across from the University of California, San Diego. In 2001, the city upgraded the South Course in an effort to snag a U.S. Open Golf Championship. Changes included placing greens on the edge of seaside canyons and cliffs. Seven years later Torrey Pines was selected for the U.S. Open—a particularly sweet victory since the other main contender was world-famous Pebble Beach Golf Links just north of Carmel, California.

Just past the parking lot, I passed the two large practice putting greens that are wedged between the Lodge at Torrey Pines and the functional, older clubhouse, which budget-conscious city administrators built. I headed for the Golfer's Grill at the corner of the Lodge and saw that the bartender that day was a hip kid with spiky hair who looked as if he really could make any drink you dreamed up. Since he was busy with an Asian tourist, I looked back outside. The bartender's view was onto the practice greens, with the closest one starting fifteen feet from the entrance. A Tolleson's Weeping evergreen blocked part of the view of the green.

The juniper tree brought back memories of one we had at my childhood home in San Clemente.

"You really must water that poor thing," people would plead with Dad.

He would sigh and reply, "This tree is in great shape. It's *supposed* to look that way—you know, *weeping*." Dad liked gardening and took pride in nurturing special plants like that one.

Noticing that the tourist had left, I stepped back inside the Golfer's Grill. The bartender eagerly asked, "What can I get you?"

"A little information?"

"I'll try," he beamed.

"Did you work on the Sunday of the Classic last month?"

"Sure did—best money I've ever made. This place was packed. Big tippers!"

"Did you see Tinny Wilcox after the event?"

"Are you kidding? That poor sucker was right out there," he said, pointing to the practice green. "I'd be bumming too if I blew that much dough. Did he ever choke! Everyone was watching on the TV," he said, nodding toward a wall-mounted flat screen. "The moans got louder and louder as he missed all those putts. After it was over, there he is on the practice green. People were pointing and whispering. He was one sad cat, all droopy and deflated. Putt, putt, putt, for a long time."

"Did you see him leave?"

"When security came, he split with a staffer and never came back."

"Was he alone the whole time?"

"Far as I can remember."

Just then, a couple who looked to be in their 60s arrived and wanted a cocktail. The hipster had satisfied my curiosity, so I thanked him and walked back outside. Turning right into the Lodge and up the stairs, I followed the route the players use during the Classic. I emerged in a hallway next to the Charles Reiffel Room, named after and early 20th century impressionist painter from California. During the Classic, the pros used the converted conference room as a temporary locker.

I walked out to the terrace above the pool and recalled the days not so long ago when the old lodge limped along as a mid-priced golfer's hotel. By the 1980s, all its former pizzazz was gone. But then as part of the U.S. Open bid, the place was demolished, though designers spared several huge pines that they incorporated into the new hotel, to stunning effect.

The Lodge is ubiquitously fashioned in a "California Craftsman" theme. The lobby is particularly impressive with its stained glass Tiffany lamps, Jatoba woodwork, and Gustav Stickley-style furnishings. The centerpiece is a roaring fireplace beneath an original Maurice Braun painting. Such attention to detail helped the Lodge at Torrey Pines vault near the top of luxury coastal resorts in Southern California.

I approached the front desk and asked to see the manager.

"May I ask why?"

"If it's OK, I'd rather just speak with the manager."

Unruffled, the desk clerk made a call, and we waited. Eventually, a professional-looking middle-aged woman headed in my direction. If you could describe a woman as "burly," this former swimmer—or current weight lifter—fit the bill. We shook hands.

"I'm Shank MacDuff, caddy to Tour pro Cary Cline."

While I could not tell if she recognized Cary's name, the manager nodded courteously.

"Buddy Franks was a close friend, and I'm doing follow-up for his wife, Linda."

She nodded again without committing or yielding her position.

"I'd like to see the room where he was killed."

With a very discerning eye, she finally spoke. "Would you mind if we called Mrs. Franks to confirm that you are indeed her representative?"

This lady was good.

"No problem," I responded nonchalantly. Pulling out my cell, I found Buddy's home number and hit "call." The manager extended her hand for the phone. I complied and gave it to her.

"Mrs. Franks? This is the manager of the Lodge at Torrey Pines. I have a Mr. MacDuff here who says he is acting on your behalf." She nodded, as Linda apparently spoke. "Yes, yes, I see. Given the circumstances, we cannot be too careful. On a personal note, I am so very sorry for your loss. If we can be of any further assistance, please let us know. All right then. Yes. Thank you."

She handed the phone back to me with a polite smile. I was golden—the widow had anointed me.

"Let's see if that room is occupied," the manager commented while walking behind the counter. She looked up the information on the computer. After a moment she said, "I'm sorry, there are guests in occupancy until Friday morning. Would you like to see a similar room? The police immediately scoured that room, and in the several weeks since we made the room look like new."

"I understand. But I really want to look at *that* room."

"You may come back Friday and look at it then, anytime between noon check-out and four o'clock check-in."

"OK, that might work. Were you working on the Sunday of the tournament?"

"No, that would be one of the other managers." She went back to the computer. "As luck would have it, that gentleman is working on Friday. You can look at the room and speak with him on the same visit. I will leave a note confirming your representation for Mrs. Franks and your desire to inspect the room."

I smiled. "Sounds like a deal. Thanks."

Wandering past the roaring fireplace once again, I looked out the large picture window toward the ocean. The sparkling pool and beautiful wood deck were in the foreground and behind that a work of art that some people might call merely a hot tub. It had an infinity edge, so the bubbling water appeared to drop onto the eighteenth green beyond. Past a cluster of century-old pines was the rest of the picturesque South Course. Finally, there were several hang gliders hovering above the shimmering blue Pacific. About as good as it gets—sublime, striking, spectacular.

CHAPTER 7

enry David is my given name. But everyone calls me
Shank. The nickname is unbecoming at first blush,
since a "shank" describes a golfer's mistake that sends
the ball sideways, often frightening other players or local
wildlife. I did not choose it by design.

One day when I was 14, I was golfing with some friends at
San Clemente Municipal. We reached the 12th hole, which
is so close to a street on the right side that at the tee box, a
sign reads: "Please aim to the left side of the fairway to help
reduce the impact of errant golf balls on people, cars, and
property along the course."

As a typical teenager, I ignored the warning and
aimed advantageously to the right. "Watch me draw this
ball out over the edge of the street and back into the fairway," I announced with panache. I swung hard. The ball

started to the right but never drew back. Instead, it flew wildly across the street. To my complete horror, the ball went through an upper bedroom window of a street-front home.

"Run!" suggested one of my helpful mates.

The irresponsible suggestion was tempting, but a gust of responsibility blew it away. As I approached the driveway of the damaged home, I could hear screams. My blood ran cold. Was someone injured? The front door opened, and an angry man rushed out holding the innocent-looking golf ball. He yelled, "Is this yours?"

I was boy enough to admit it.

"You killed our cat!" he roared.

My reaction to this feline tragedy was to throw my head back with a relieved sigh. After all, it was only a cat. The red-faced man did not see it the way I did. Storming back inside, he reappeared with the lifeless animal.

When something bizarre happens with a golf shot, people invariably say, "It was a million-in-one-shot." On this occasion, it really was! The ball traveled the length of two football fields and into a house, and nailed a cat that was looking out the window. What must the cat have thought as the strange "white bird" crushed its skull? Thanks to several months of extra chores, I finally paid my parents back for the damage and an upscale burial at a local pet cemetery.

Understandably, the story spread, and my friends started to call me Shank. Lots of kids thought the nickname was even more hilarious since it was followed by my last name, MacDuff. A "duff" in golf lingo is a misplayed shot—topping the ball so it goes only a few feet or missing the ball entirely, for example. Similarly embarrassing, "duffer" refers to a *very* unskilled golfer.

I good-naturedly endured the well-deserved jokes. I expected the abuse to taper off, but the reverse happened. Soon, others at school—in fact, the whole school including teachers and administrators—started using the nickname. Then it spread to neighbors and relatives. Ultimately, everyone who knew me even remotely or who had simply heard the story called me Shank. I planned to start over at college as the sophisticated Henry David, but I discovered I couldn't do it. The nickname had become part of my identity.

At times, even Cary must deal with my name. Around the edges of tournament golf, there are always groupies and even hecklers. More than once, we've been walking down a fairway or between the crowd-control ropes, and someone will say, "Hey, Cline, you 'shanked' one back there. Better have your caddy change his name!" The insults are uncomfortable when Cary is involved. I'm thick-skinned about it by now, but the collateral damage to my boss is a different story. Yet, true to form, it slides off Cary as if he's Teflon. He even encouraged me once by saying, "You realize the amount of free publicity we get because of that great nickname of yours? I must be underpaying you!" Cary always seems to say the right thing. As we laughed, my Shankness grew ever deeper.

CHAPTER 8

Lunch seemed appropriate that Wednesday before meeting Detective Baker, so the M3 motored down Torrey Pines Road to nearby La Jolla. Aptly named "The Jewel" in Spanish, the seaside resort town oozes affluence and charm. The downtown village is home to designer stores, art galleries, restaurants, and hotels. After wandering into a tree-lined arcade above La Jolla Cove, I tried a sandwich from a café name "Deli-icious." It was! The pastrami, Swiss cheese, and green chilies on pita bread perfectly offset the chilled Mountain Dew.

As the well-heeled shoppers strolled by, I contemplated my upcoming meeting. Would the police ignore my efforts to help Linda? Grill me? Or actually help? Catching the wavy image of myself in a nearby shop window, I realized I was not exactly dressed like a sleuth. Oh well, no sense trying to be someone I wasn't. Flexibility was going to be crucial, given my lack of experience. Stay alert and be willing to accept whatever the cops will give.

After the five-minute drive from La Jolla, the M3 found an opening next to a handicapped spot in front of the Northern Division. I've found that parking really close to the blue line typically provides ample protection from door-dingers and still allows room should a handicapped person need it.

As I entered the law enforcement area of the joint fire/police facilities, a live recruiting poster greeted me. "May I help you?" the uniformed male receptionist asked.

"Hope so. I've got an appointment with Detective Baker." He took my name. Looking around the Spartan lobby, I saw portrait photos of the San Diego police chief, assistant chiefs, and the person the staff had affectionately labeled "Our Captain." A voice like a tuba shattered the silence. "MacDuff?"

I spun around. My eyes climbed a mountain of a man who had to be 6'8" tall. He reminded me of Shaquille O'Neal during his prime—proportionately huge with arms the size of my thighs. In contrast to the flabby fat man I had helped in the Torrey Pines parking lot, this detective seemed almost fit. He had cropped brown hair that was graying at the temples, granite features, and steely dark eyes. Wrinkled suit pants clung to his legs. Since he wasn't wearing a jacket, I could see large sweat marks drenching each armpit of his light-blue dress shirt. Thrift shops would probably reject his wide paisley tie. I shook his overwhelming paw.

"Come on back," Baker said as he led me to a conference room. On the table were a file, yellow pad, and pencil. "Water? Soda?" he asked.

"No thanks. I'm fine." The detective struggled to fit his massive frame into one of the cheap conference room chairs. The giants of this world have my sympathy. Everything must feel child-sized. Professional basketball players can afford custom-made everything, but civil servants and other mortals don't have that luxury.

"You knew Buddy Franks?" he asked.

"Yes, sir. We were both pro caddies and friends."

"Who killed him?"

"No clue," I responded to the refreshingly direct question.

"Any guesses?"

"A burglar?" I stabbed in the dark.

"Unlikely. There were no signs of forced entry. Also, apart from the putter and golf ball, not a single item in the hotel room appeared to have been touched. Mr. Franks showered after the tournament, so it doesn't appear he surprised anyone already in the room. Neighboring guests heard arguing. No, it wasn't a burglar."

Down in flames with a thoughtless guess! I decided to let him speculate this time. "So you think Buddy knew him?"

"Or her," Baker said with an emotionless face. It was not hard to figure out that he was including, or singling out, Linda.

"You think his wife is involved?" I said with an edge.

"Maybe."

"I know that the police think Linda had a window of opportunity to kill him. That's why I'm here. She's asked me to help."

At this, Baker's stony expression washed away, and he cracked up. Not a small chuckle but a side-splitting laugh. "Being a caddy qualifies you?"

His condescending attack made me defensive. "I have a college education and free time."

"So?"

"I also attended the FBI Academy for a while."

That got him. After a framework-adjusting pause, he asked, "What do you mean for 'a while'?"

"I was within days of graduating when…there was an accident." Bam! The topic hammered me again. I think about the accident every day, but sometimes the memory floods over me far too vividly. This was such an occasion.

Baker realized I was struggling. "And?"

"I ended up, well—broken. Except for my left eardrum, all the physical injuries eventually healed. But the incident ended my desire to keep going in that direction."

Baker sat back in contemplation. "Maybe we can help each other. To tell you the truth, I don't think Mrs. Franks did it. But some cops here at the department have her at the top of their list." With a shrug of his massive shoulders, Baker added, "Motive and opportunity will do that."

"What motive?"

"The millions in insurance money," he said coldly.

"Insurance?" I stammered.

"Apparently your new 'client' hasn't told you everything. It's a chunk of change," Baker said, raising eyebrows so bushy that they looked like a unibrow.

Backing up mentally, I recalled the Sherlock Holmes books from my childhood. London's master detective once told Dr. Watson, "Deduce a motive, and the criminal shan't be far behind!"

Baker continued. "Some things don't add up that you may be able to shed light on. For example, Franks simply appears out of nowhere in Las Vegas, as if aliens dropped the guy on The Strip."

"He was born and raised in Tennessee," I said, stating the obvious.

"Then it was an invisible youth. No birth certificate, Social Security number, driver's license, or public school information. No records indicating that a Buddy Franks ever lived in Tennessee."

Surprises seeped out of every coffin crack. *Stay flexible, keep engaged.*

"Did you try other first names? Buddy was probably a nickname."

"Sure did. All sorts of angles. No Franks from Tennessee matching his gender, age, or description. You've been to his house, right?"

"Yeah."

"Did you ever see pictures of his parents? A childhood home? Friends? How about memorabilia like a school yearbook or ring? Was he a big Tennessee Volunteers football fan like virtually everyone else in the state? Did he ever say exactly *where* in Tennessee he was from? Near Nashville?"

"No, no, no, no, no, no, and no," I said, whimsically counting on my fingers to make sure every question received a response.

Baker seemed amused. "You're sharp—that's good. I could have predicted your answers, though, because that period in his life doesn't appear to exist or at least not in Tennessee or under that name. While it gets better in Las Vegas, it's still not much. Apart from a few utility bills that required a name, address, and deposit, there are no other Nevada records referencing him. No driver's license or credit cards. He caddied for cash at a ritzy private club, and that enabled him to pay cash for everything."

"Did he drive? If so, without a license? Or did he hoof it everywhere?"

"No, no, and apparently so," he said mocking me and counting on the giant digits protruding from his palm.

My turn to look amused.

"He lived in the Greystone Park Apartments, east of The Strip. From there, he could have 'hoofed it,' as you said, to most places. We've still got ground to cover in Vegas, but our resources are limited for an intensive effort like that," Baker said. He was less than thrilled.

"Can't the local police help?"

"Out-of-state requests get fairly treated in larger departments, but they must be focused and of limited scope. No agency is keen on fieldwork for a distant investigation. We did find out, however, that Franks had one public friend—a male, maybe 60 now. They used to hang out at bars watching sports. No name yet."

One time in Vegas, when Buddy and I were both working a tournament, he introduced me to a guy that might fit that description. However, I could not fill in the details and thus hesitated discussing it with Baker.

"Did that jog a memory?"

"Not really."

The detective looked at me cautiously but smiled anyway. "That's OK, keep trying. By the way, exactly why did you come to see me?"

"I need to understand who the suspects are to help get Linda out of the cross-hairs."

With hesitation and pursed lips, he asked, "Well, *Mr.* Nancy Drew, list a few possibilities yourself."

The Nancy Drew comment stung. My sister used to read those mysteries. He was turning the tables. I would play. "Tinny might have had a motive if he thought Buddy screwed up his best chance at that precious first victory. But how? A caddy might be wrong on yardages or the break of a putt, but the player always has the final say."

"Agreed. We've looked at Wilcox, or I guess 'Tinny,' but it does not look promising. After the tournament on Sunday, a bunch of witnesses saw him on the practice putting green trying to figure out what went wrong. That behavior is apparently abnormal; he looked pathetic. The scene made an impression. We also secured all the camera footage, not just the broadcast cuts the TV audience saw. A golf fanatic here reviewed every minute showing the final foursome. Mr. Franks's actions revealed nothing suspicious. We also talked with some of the other players and caddies, including those in his group that day. They didn't see anything Franks did, or could have done, that would have made a difference.

I'm not a golfer, but our guy said Tinny's problem wasn't club selection or anything a caddy might interfere with. His misery was a lost putting stroke. Can't that happen to the best of them?"

"Sure, but not usually in such a dramatic fashion. Putting is the most fickle part of the game. It's a mix of proper green reading, stroke, nerves, confidence, conditions, and a dozen other factors that all get jumbled together."

"And millions of ordinary folks pay to play and endure that frustration?"

"The endless challenge is addicting. But it is odd that he practiced after losing. Who remembers seeing him?"

"Several people who were in a position to see, like the bartender."

"True. I talked with him on my way over here."

Baker took notice and then proceeded. "Even Slate, the tournament director, saw him," he said with a sharp edge.

"Again confirmed. I talked with him earlier also. Not too fond of the man?"

"No."

"He was similarly warm and fuzzy about you."

"Next topic," was Baker's curt reply.

I went back to his suspect-listing game. "What about a business partner or even another woman?"

"That would be marvelous. Got any?"

"No," I said, feeling silly. "Nothing indicated that he had other business ventures beyond caddying and, while Buddy would flirt with the occasional waitress or groupie behind the ropes, I never sensed he was unfaithful."

"You are now about as far along as San Diego's finest. That's why his wife keeps surfacing."

"Understood."

"Franks was a gambler, right?"

"Some football, March Madness, and the like."

"Do you know how much he was losing?"

Good way of putting it, since if you bet for long, you eventually lose. "No idea how much," I answered.

There was a knock on the conference room door. A stunning, uniformed blonde entered who looked like movie star Meg Ryan. Both the actress and this square-shouldered beauty reminded me of someone I once deeply loved. Officer Valentine, or so her badge read, looked at me and then addressed Baker. "Sorry to interrupt, detective, but your next appointment is here. He's early and extremely anxious. Poor man looks like he might get ill. The sergeant told me to alert you."

"That's fine," Baker said. "Anything else, MacDuff?"

"I'm good for now."

The detective pushed away from the table and went vertical. Once again, he towered over everything. I felt sorry for the criminals.

"Thanks for stopping by. Here is my card. If you think of anything else, call. Do you have a card?"

"I'm a caddy, remember?"

Both officers grinned. His was an amused grin; hers was something else. Since Baker hadn't taken any notes on the yellow pad, I wrote my contact information on the top page. As he reviewed it, I found Ms. Valentine staring at me. We locked eyes, and my pulse quickened. Most people turn away when they're caught gawking. Not this soldier of sex appeal.

After the detective ripped off the sheet and shoved it in his shirt pocket, the young lady and I both headed for the door. Botching the maneuver, we collided and awkwardly bounced apart. She blushed. I stifled a gasp of delight. Waving my hand toward the hallway like a butler, I let her power out first. Baker smirked and winked, looking like a good-natured Cyclops.

CHAPTER 9

Back in my apartment later that same Wednesday, I kicked back in the recliner with another Mountain Dew. Had the detective disclosed Buddy's mysterious past figuring I would snoop on Linda? Not a bad move. I was in a better position to get information than Baker was from behind his badge. What if I refused? He had lost little in trying.

I grabbed the phone and punched in the number from memory. "Hey Linda, it's Shank," I said when she answered.

"Hey stud, how goes the hunt?"

Ignoring the strange greeting, I summarized my day and then zeroed in on the reason I called. "Linda, we need to talk about a couple of tough topics. You ready?"

Silence.

"Baker unveiled a financial motive for you." I let that fact hang there like a half-broken piñata.

"It's the stupid insurance, isn't it? Well, it was bound to come out. I saw this depressing TV ad where a man dies and leaves his wife and children broke. A real sobering 60 seconds. I could not stop thinking about where we'd be if Buddy died. Things would be OK for a while, but soon everything would start to unravel. So we bought life insurance."

Had she rehearsed this explanation?

After clearing her throat, Linda continued. "The problem is we got carried away. It's a rather large policy."

A long pause ensued. Since she was not going to offer any more information, I asked. "How much?"

"Several seven figures."

What a weird way to describe millions of dollars. I waited again. This was like trying to coax the last drop of honey from an exhausted Sue Bee Honey bear. "And?"

She was more emotional this time. "I know, that ridiculous sum sounds terrible, doesn't it? With his charts and smooth talking, the agent convinced us the amount was our 'peace of mind' level."

"Why didn't you tell me?" I asked, trying to keep the irritation out of my voice.

"Forgot," she responded with no hint of being sorry.

Even considering the stress Linda was under, was such a glaring oversight possible? *Be open-minded; keep going.* "Baker also told me that his men couldn't find any information about Buddy's past. During his Las Vegas years, there were a few more records, but still, any evidence of his past is thin. He finally became paper-traceable in California. Is any of this making sense?"

"Somewhat. Buddy was always reluctant to discuss details of his childhood. There appeared to be some very unpleasant memories. For a long time, I thought his father might have been an alcoholic or beat him or did something even worse. But over the last few years, I began to think it was something else."

"Did you ever meet his parents or talk to them?"

"No, they're both dead."

"Really? I had the impression that they were still around but estranged from Buddy."

"Doesn't surprise me," Linda said with an edge to her voice. "He was frequently inconsistent about things like that. I never questioned him, because one thing was clear—that chapter of his life was none of my business."

"Did he ever mention exactly where he was born or grew up?"

"Never. He was simply from Tennessee, as if the entire state was his home." She paused, and her tone changed. "How does this tie in to his death?"

"Good question. If something he did in the past was enough to provoke someone to kill him, why did the murderer wait so long?"

"I don't know, Shank. It's all so sinister and depressing."

"Sorry, but we've got to go through this. Tell me about his Las Vegas years."

"Buddy liked life in Nevada, except for the desert heat. That's where he learned about golf and how to caddy. He was living in an apartment near The Strip at the time. He never talked much about friends, except for some guy named Milton."

That was the guy's name! "Milton Reily, right?"

"Yeah. I think there were also some caddy pals, but their names escape me."

"Spare time fun?"

"He watched a lot of TV. We'd watch a show in reruns, and he would say, 'I used to watch this in Vegas.' That's also where the gambling started," she added with a mixture of anger and disgust.

"Baker talked about that too. How much money are we talking about?"

"It wasn't so much the amount but the frequency. He was constantly hooking up with Milton. Between football, basketball, horse racing, and who knows what else, he would place bets daily."

"I was with him a lot and had no idea. That frequency surprises me. How much would he bet?"

"It was always hard to tell. He kept the gambling money separate. The losses were his version of a country club membership."

"So in your mind it was significant but not crippling?"

"That's fair. At times, especially when Tinny went cold, we could have used the cash. Do you know how he and Milton did their thing?" she asked.

"By phone?"

"By *Milton's* phone. For frequent clients, the bloodsucker provided a free cell with only one number on speed dial."

"Wow, I had seen Buddy with different phones but never asked about that. Are you sure Buddy wasn't into Milton for a sizable amount? Not rocket science to deduce a possible motive there."

Linda sighed. "Believe me, that was one of the first things that crossed my mind. I went back and double-checked our regular finances. Nothing abnormal. Then I tracked down Buddy's gambling account. I'm still hassling with the bank to gain access. It was in Buddy's name alone." She sounded defeated.

"Was there anything strange before the Classic? Like confidential letters, odd voicemails, hang-up phone calls, that sort of thing?"

"Not really. Although that call after the funeral might qualify. You'd have to ask my ...." Her voice trailed off.

"What was that?"

"My brother, you'd have to ask him. I was pretty out of it. Thankfully, my family was here. The phone rang, and my brother answered. He got into a heated exchange with the caller. That call sticks out because everything else that day was so subdued."

I could sympathize. During a trying time in my life, certain incidents stood out like a burst of color on a charcoal sketch.

Linda continued, "I have no idea what they said. My brother never mentioned it again. Do you want his number?"

"Sure." I jotted it down.

"Shank, I can't tell you how much it means to have you fighting for me. It's—"

I could sense her rocking through the tears.

"Hang in there, Linda. We'll figure it out."

Then, she was gone.

CHAPTER 10

I t was a little early, but dinner sounded good. I went to my bedroom and looked into the mirror on the sliding closet. The jeans were fine, but everything else needed an upgrade. I took off my shirt, tossed a three-pointer into the hamper, and slipped on a new yellow polo. As I looked out the window onto the back alley, my mind wandered. A frequent question echoed again: *What are you doing with your life?*

Though my parents had never asked me that question directly, I had heard it in their hints. Mom would ask, "So Henry dear, remember so-and-so from high school? I saw his mother the other day, and she says he just entered his medical residency or whatever. Isn't that wonderful?"

"Great," I would respond without taking the bait.

Dad would try another tactic. "I read an article recently about how this-or-that is going to be a huge growth area.

I bet there are going to be many opportunities there for years to come. What do you think?"

We would have a nice conversation, exploring the dynamics of this-or-that. At times, it seemed he was on to something. After all, where did Tour caddying lead? Leather skin. A bad back. Alone and unfulfilled—maybe.

How different my life would have been had it not been for that accident. I sang softly, "Pain, pain, go away, come again another day." Hadn't it been long enough? Was I damaged goods? What about a bigger purpose—did I have one?

Shaking my head, I returned from oblivion. One Topsider peeked out of the closet, so I dropped down to look for its mate. After I did some scrounging, the couple was reunited, and I slipped on the comfortable leather deck shoes, without socks, of course. For now, helping Linda was a positive move. It felt satisfying in a new and meaningful way. Yet, I was increasingly aware of a hole inside of me. Could good deeds fill the void?

There was a knock on my door. As I left the bedroom, I could hear Sage singing to herself. I opened the door and she planted a wet one on my cheek. Sage is a neighbor surfer chick. Dark brown hair with blonde highlights breaks in waves over her tanned shoulders. She was wearing tight jeans and a top with a plunging neckline. Sage has a dynamite body—and she knows it. She may not be the sharpest coral in the ocean, but she's been wonderful to me.

"Shankee, how are you?"

"Small and choppy."

"Such a bad emotional report! I came to borrow an egg, but first tell me what's the matter."

She turned a kitchen chair backwards and straddled it causally. The move was raw and seductive. She has used that type of natural maneuver to build quite a reputation.

Sage and I have an unusual relationship. Soon after moving to Newport, I saw her on the beach posing for a modest-budget swimsuit calendar. Later it came to light that she lived nearby. I found her to be an entertaining lightning bolt who was fun company. She wields her curves like a sexual sledgehammer, but she simply does not do it for me in that way. She could sense my lack of interest, and soon our interactions became more comfortable. One day she announced, "I enjoy hanging with you and want it to continue. So I'm going to keep the voltage turned down low. Work for you?" I assured her the arrangement suited me fine. We have been chums ever since.

Grabbing a chair, I sat down and answered her. "Self-reflection over my caddying."

"Having trouble with Cary?"

"No, just the opposite. Everything's going great, but where do I go from here? There's no advancement. I've already achieved the top rung on the caddying ladder."

"What else are you cut out to do?"

"Probably lots. Have I ever told you about my schooling?"

"Don't think so." Twisting a strand of hair, she encouraged me to continue. "I'm all ears."

"Well, you know, I grew up in San Clemente, and like every other guy there, I tried hard to sell myself as a carefree surfer. In reality, I was compensating for being an academic powerhouse. From early on, my parents challenged me intellectually. We always had puzzles and books lying around, and worked on home science projects."

"How sweet," she commented. "Not my old man—he was too busy chasing skirts."

Frowning in sympathy, I kept going. "As every year passed, I observed the growing gap with classmates. While there was the occasional math wizard, reading buff, or science nerd, nobody was close overall. By high school, even rigorous classes like physics were a breeze."

"Is that where you try and read people's palms?"

"Nah, that would be a psychic. *Physics* is the science of matter and its motion, as well as space and time."

"Oh," she said, still clueless. I never talk down to Sage and she is never embarrassed.

"Near the end of my sophomore year, I took the first of a handful of advanced placement classes at a local junior college. The initial symposium was entitled *Democracy in America—How Did Alexis de Tocqueville See Our Future?* The pompous professor used the Socratic Method. He would ask questions openly in class and guide students through their efforts to answer."

"Sounds horrible," Sage said wrinkling her cute nose.

"On the first day, the professor asked a big hairy guy near me, 'Why do we care about de Tocqueville today?' This was a knee-high wave anyone could ride. But, the caveman froze."

Sage giggled.

"The professor turned up the heat with cynicism. 'Oh come now, are you unable to offer a single reason—even if it is likely incorrect?'

"As the guy stammered, I foolishly smirked. The professor saw me. After looking at the seating chart, he raised his voice and attacked. 'Mr. MacDuff! You must have *the* answer. Please, enlighten us.' The other students sat quietly waiting for the slaughter.

"I licked my lips and went for it. 'Strangers can often observe things with great clarity. Take de Tocqueville. He came to America from France in the 1830s and immediately recognized how important the common person was to democracy and how dangerous majority rule could turn out to be.'

"The room was silent. Everyone stopped looking at me and, like at a tennis match, every head turned to gauge the professor's reaction. 'How long did it take you to read this?' he finally asked, struggling to raise de Tocqueville's 500-page masterpiece with one hand.

"'A week, but I still had my regular school work to contend with.'

"'How old are you?'

"'Sixteen.'

"'So you're the one,' he said while rubbing his pointy beard.

"After class, the hairy professor cornered me outside. 'Watch your back, brainiac. If you make me look bad again, I'll cut your tongue out!' To emphasize the point, he flicked his thick middle finger painfully against my forehead."

Of course, Sage had to try it. "Ouch!" she yelped, rubbing the spot.

"Told you it hurt. So the rest of the semester, I walked a tightrope between pleasing the professor and protecting my mouth's pink appendage."

Sage's cell rang. She stood and looked to see who was calling. "I've got to grab this. Friend in distress over a breakup that won't stick. I'll catch the rest later." She answered the call and started to leave.

I stopped her and pointed at the fridge.

Sage waited as I grabbed an egg for her. "Thanks," she mouthed with lip-glossed emphasis before heading down the stairs deep in girly counsel.

CHAPTER 11

The sun was melting over Catalina Island as I walked up the boardwalk sixty paces to Mutt Lynch's, a favorite hangout of mine. When the weather is warm, Mutt's opens sliding front windows. The interaction between people on the boardwalk and patrons inside creates an inviting street scene.

Cristanos was sitting at the bar sucking on a schooner of dark beer. The crazy Brazilian began embracing a bohemian surfer lifestyle once he arrived in Newport several years ago. He waits tables to eat, pay rent, and buy surfboard wax. His 5' 5" lean body seems too small for a rather large head. Permanently tousled black hair creates a halo around his elfin face and dark eyes. As usual, he wore baggy shorts, surf shirt, and comfortable leather sandals.

"What's up, Cristanos?" I once tried shortening his name to Cris, but he straightened me out.

"Shanks, how goes it?" He gets my name slightly wrong on purpose.

"Pretty good. I didn't see you surfing this morning. Lazy?"

"No. I work late. Surf before lunch. Waves good, huh?"

"Juicy, for sure."

Just then, a middle-aged patron in a business suit entered and said loudly to his wife, "It's unbelievable. Mutt's has barely changed in twenty years! I logged many hours here in college. Honey, you should have seen it when ...."

"Do you work tonight?" I asked Cristanos.

"No, I'm a footloose. Where caddying for Cary next?"

"Florida. I fly out Monday."

"Any fun today?"

"Went to San Diego. I'm trying to help figure out what happened to Buddy. The police think his wife, Linda, is involved. Can you believe that?"

"Muito mau," he said shaking his head. I knew that meant "very bad" in Portuguese, the predominant language in Brazil. "I like Mrs. Buddy." Being uncharacteristically serious, he added, "If you need help, Cristanos ready."

I ordered a schooner of Sam Adams lager, a smoked albacore platter as an appetizer, then a build-your-own-burger with grilled onions, bacon, and bleu cheese.

"Who you think kill Buddy?"

"Don't know. I'm going back down to Torrey Pines on Friday and hopefully see the room where it happened."

"Why? Maids no clean good?"

"They did," I assured him. "There won't be bloodstains or anything. I want to see the place for myself. Maybe a clue will jump out."

"Like Rockford?"

"Sort of."

Cristanos watched more old TV reruns than anyone I knew. We ate and then played two quick games of eight ball on the front pool table. While some nights I can give him a game, I didn't on this night. Smooth-sticking Cristanos won handily.

After returning from Mutt Lynch's, I called Linda's brother. His wife answered and passed the phone to him without asking who I was.

"Hello?" Linda's brother asked.

"My name is Shank MacDuff. I was Buddy's friend."

"You caddy for Cary Cline, right?"

"I do indeed."

"Good player, and seems like a nice guy too. Buddy talked about you both. What can I do for you?"

"Linda mentioned that after the funeral, she was in a daze but remembered hearing you argue with someone on the phone. What happened?"

"I sure do remember that encounter. When I answered, a real sarcastic Southern voice demanded to talk to Buddy Franks, 'or whatever he calls himself nowadays.'

"It was a heavy day for all of us, and I couldn't believe what I just heard. I said, 'Excuse me?'

"He got feisty and said, 'Just put the dirtbag on.'

"I lost it and told him that Buddy was dead.

"He asked me, 'Since when?'

"I told him that the shirt on my back was still damp with sweat from carrying his casket. Instead of changing his tone, he got rougher and started cussing. He insisted I put the 'yeller traitor' on. Now I was really getting hostile. He swore again and hung up. My blood was boiling, so I hit star-69 to dial him back. The front desk at some L.A. motel answered. I tried to make the clerk track the guy down, but he said he had no way of telling which room made the call. I cooled off a bit and thanked him. And that was that."

"Recall the motel?"

"I don't. All I wanted was to find the sucker. When that became a hassle, I dropped it."

"Did the caller identify himself?"

"Not that I recall."

"Did you recognize the voice?"

"No. It was uncomfortably raspy, like he was sick or smoked a lot. With his accent, the jerk sounded like a less refined version of Buddy."

"Could you tell about how old he was?"

"Middle-aged, maybe?"

We chatted a bit longer about his sister, then Buddy. He concluded by saying, "Catch the murderer, Shank. Get him. OK?"

"I'll give it my all."

After hanging up, I called Linda. After summarizing the call with her brother, I asked, "Is your most recent phone bill handy?"

"It came this week. Hold on." After about thirty seconds, she was back. "Got it."

"Look at the afternoon of the funeral."

Papers shuffled. "There are about ten calls. It looks like three are long distance. One is for the 212 area code."

"That would be New York. Next one?"

"It's the 916 area code—that's in Sacramento where my brother lives. But it's not his number. He must have been checking on his kids—they were staying with friends while he was at the funeral. Wait. There's a 310 number."

"Bingo. That area code is near L.A. That has to be it."

After a few minutes of small talk, I hung up with Linda and dialed the number she had just given me.

"Ocean Verandas," a man answered.

Having no plan, I said "sorry" and hung up. I did an online search, which yielded a generic home page for the Ocean Verandas Motel in Inglewood. It was described as a business retreat center in coastal-breeze Inglewood. With nine "custom" rooms, the motel awaits the cost-conscious business traveler. I had to chuckle at *that* description.

Inglewood is inland of Los Angeles International Airport, or LAX, in a perpetual ghetto. Its only claim to fame was the Forum, where the Lakers won six world championships. But in 1999, Lakers owner Jerry Buss moved the team to Staples Center in downtown Los Angeles. A coastal breeze was probably the best thing the Ocean Verandas now had going for it. I thought briefly, very briefly, about driving up there right then. However, Inglewood is not even remotely safe at night.

Staying on the computer, I retrieved the "Find My Killer, Shank" file. Recalling recent events and organizing my notes took a few hours of diligent work. I detailed many of the conversations word for word. No patterns or revelations surfaced.

After slipping into volleyball shorts and a T-shirt for bed, I first watched the end of a Lakers victory over the San Antonio Spurs. My evening ended with the final hour of *I, Robot* starring Will Smith. Good movie, but I never seem to catch the beginning.

CHAPTER 12

The next morning, Thursday, the nice swell was fading, so I opted for a run. First onto my naked legs were black performance tights that fit like another skin. Next, the watch-like receiver of a heart rate monitor went on my left wrist, while the thin radio transmitter fit around my chest. The brilliant little device shows how hard I am working by measuring my heart rate against a target level calculated on age, weight, and fitness level. An old Pinehurst golf course sweatshirt and Nike running shoes, this time with socks, finished off my running garb.

It was still dark, and the morning was cold by Southern California standards. The thermal tights felt good. Along the boardwalk, I ran past the Newport Pier to the south where the ocean view homes are a hodgepodge of plain rentals, gorgeous multimillion dollar customs, and eighty-year-old classics. The first mile of a run is always painful. Then I break into a sweat, and the effort becomes more comfortable. The boardwalk route took me past the Balboa Pier, then a block inland at E Street, and finally to residential roads paralleling the beach to the end of the Peninsula.

The rising sun finally forced black from the sky as I ran across ice plant-covered sand dunes. Arriving at the Wedge, I circled the lifeguard stand with its dire sign: "Warning, diving in the ocean surf or bay is dangerous. Remember! Hazardous and changing conditions may exist." The alert is particularly appropriate here at the world's most famous bodysurfing and bodyboarding theater. Long ago locals gave the name the Wedge to the place where the beach intersects with the western jetty entrance to Newport Harbor. Southern swells "wedge" against the large riprap rocks, rebound sideways, and combine with the next wave to create liquid behemoths. As they break, the freakish waves thunder onto the sand in the ultimate shore break.

I can remember driving up from San Clemente during high school as a New Zealand swell hammered away. There must have been two hundred Wedge spectators but less than a dozen brave souls in harm's way. Some waves were actually breaking over the jetty into the harbor entrance. Those were the largest waves I have ever personally seen. Nobody died *that* day. But over the years, other adventurers were not so lucky at the deadly boneyard.

On the run back, I again pondered my new endeavor. As is apt to happen when I'm exercising, a patchwork of questions floated in and out of my mind. Was tracking down Buddy's past worth the effort? Where were Buddy's parents or siblings? Was the mystery caller relevant? Was he indicating that Buddy had changed names? Why a golf ball as the murder weapon? The killer had apparently already hit him over the head with a putter; why not keep smashing him with it? Was there really a gambling undercurrent?

Clearly, Buddy and Milton Reily had a betting link. Did Nick Slate, with his horse racing history, also play a part? Could I believe Detective Baker, or did he simply need my help? Was Linda being honest? Would she kill her husband for millions of dollars?

Then my concentration vanished, and I wondered, "How much wood could a woodchuck chuck if a woodchuck could chuck wood?" That tongue twister has always been easy for me. I have a much tougher time with saying, "You know New York, you need New York, you know you need unique New York." However, the toughest for me to repeat five times really fast are "stupid superstition" and "toy boat." Mindless fun.

The six-mile workout felt solid. My heart rate exceeded the target level 70 percent of the time, a decent ratio for a flat run. Back inside my apartment, I drank a quick protein supplement, a usual post-workout habit that helps repair and build up muscle. After a shower, I put on jeans and a clean white T-shirt emblazoned with the logo of the golf ball Cary plays. His sponsors are always giving us promotional stuff like that. On my feet went fresh Nikes, no socks.

Minutes later, I was driving north on the 405 freeway to Inglewood and the Ocean Verandas. My destination turned out to be a motel that was at least forty years old. Someone had attempted to spruce it up with ultra-blue paint. A true parking dilemma developed, at least for me. There were no end spots in the small motel lot. Rarely does the M3 park in between other cars where door-dingers abound. Unfortunately, the street was no bargain either. The hot BMW with personalized "SHANK" license plate stuck out like a sore thumb in this part of town. Would it be there upon my return? Weighing the two options, I opted for the lot and hoped it was a slow day at the inn.

As I entered the small lobby, the counter appeared to be empty. But as I drew closer, I saw a middle-aged black woman in a wheelchair. She looked up from her needle-point and lifted her soft, dark eyes over the top of bifocals. With a broad smile she asked, "May I help you?"

"Please. I need some information, and I'm willing to pay for it." *Swift move!* I had planned to use money as a last resort, but I spilled my guts like a schoolboy. What an amateur.

The woman put her project down. "Honey, let's first see what you need and why, and then we'll see if you need to pay for it."

"OK," I said, exhaling an unconsciously held breath. "My name is Shank MacDuff, and I'm helping the widow of Buddy Franks, who was a friend and a fellow professional caddy. He was killed a couple of weeks ago in La Jolla. After the funeral, the widow's brother took a strange call from someone who was staying here, but we don't know who. The clerk on duty that night wasn't able to help. We want to find the man."

"That wasn't so hard, was it? Young man, while you're all sugar and spice, how do I know you're telling the truth? You could be another debt collector or worse."

Seeing a rather sorry-looking computer on the desk, I took a shot. "Does that hook up to the Internet?"

"Mostly. Why?"

"I want to show you a web page where there's an article with my name and picture."

She looked at me skeptically but then smiled again in her warm way. "All right. To tell the truth, I was bored sitting here with my needlepoint anyway." She turned her chair with enthusiasm and wheeled to the desk. After a journey onto the Internet that was best timed with a calendar, I led her to a web site focusing on professional caddies and had her click on "Featured Caddy Stories." Next to a piece entitled "Shank MacDuff Gets All Wet," there I was, smiling and holding a surfboard.

The article detailed how the previous generation of professional caddies used to fish, hunt, or play the ponies as hobbies. It portrayed me as part of the new breed who embraced adventure sports like surfing, mountain biking, and skiing. The clerk read the whole thing while keeping up a constant flow of "mmm-mmm-mmm's" and looking back in my direction.

Finally, she wheeled around and came back to the counter. "How did the other caddy die?"

I explained in summary fashion, and she shook her head. Her penetrating eyes searched me. Finally, she smiled. She'd made her decision.

"Exactly what do you want?"

I wasted no time. "On the Thursday of the third week in February, how many men were registered?"

She flipped the pages in a large red notebook. "That would be three."

"Do you recall if any of them had a Southern accent?"

With no hesitation she said, "Surely do. Mr. Lenny Hayes of Dallas, Texas, or at least that's what the book says. The man sticks in my memory because he was mean clear through. Usually some good comes out of people after I get 'em talking. Not that one. Nasty as an old toilet plunger."

"Is there an address?"

"Uh huh." She took a pen, scribbled it on the back of an Ocean Verandas card and handed it to me.

"What did he look like?"

She thought back. "White. Older and shorter than you, pretty much bald. Mean eyes. Bad scar on his face, kind of like this." She made a motion with her hand from an area near her left ear down to her chin. "Three or four inches long. Walked with a limp, had a twitch, and a raspy smoker's voice."

"Nice," I commented, rolling my eyes.

Figuring we were done, I started to reach for my money.

She looked insulted. "Just put that away. I helped because you seemed on the level. Hope this information helps."

"Fair enough. Thanks."

"Mind if I ask *you* a question?"

"Certainly."

"On a bike, you really jump off rocks, over logs, and such, like the article says?"

"Yes, ma'am. Mountain bikes are made for that kind of abuse. They have full suspension, knobby tires, and other such features. Lots of fun."

With furrowed brows, she cautioned, "Be careful, you hear? Would be tragic if a healthy young man like you ended up in one of these." She struck the sides of her well-worn wheelchair.

"Agreed," I said. "By the same token, life is meant to be lived and adventure is a big part of who I am. Reasonable caution and calculated risks, yes; afraid to embrace the challenge, no way."

She smiled again. "Enjoy yourself then, and, Lord willing, you'll only bleed a little now and then."

My turn to smile.

CHAPTER 13

On the way back down to Orange County late that Thursday morning, I tried to get hold of Buddy's bookie in Las Vegas. I was pleasantly surprised when I discovered that his phone number was listed. The phone rang, and an elderly woman answered, "Hello."

"I'm looking for Milton Reily. Is he in?"

"There's no such man here. Don't call again." She hung up.

Next, I called Linda. After updating her on my Ocean Verandas victory, I asked, "Have you ever heard of a Lenny Hayes before?"

"Never."

"Might not even be his real name. By the way, I tried getting hold of Milton through 411 but no luck. They had him listed, but I think the number was old or incorrect. Do you still have Buddy's special betting phone?"

"Right here. You can have it; I have no use for the thing."

"I can swing by and pick it up later since I've got a doctor's appointment in your direction this afternoon."

"That's OK. I'll be up in Newport, so I can drop it off."

"Deal."

I was getting hungry, and In-N-Out Burger was calling to me like the sirens of Greek mythology. The M3 pulled off at the Wilmington exit and into the drive-thru behind at least ten cars. Always busy, this chain is astounding for its simplicity and popularity. The menu offers several versions of the same basic hamburger and fries. Getting food takes longer than at other fast food places since they cook everything fresh. I ordered my customary cheeseburger combo with a chocolate shake. A second straw is necessary, given the dreamy thickness of the pure ice-cream concoction. I also purchased a gift certificate from the white-uniformed Barbie impersonator. The helpful clerk at the Ocean Verandas deserved a surprise "thank you" in the mail. I drove off nibbling the piping hot fries. Regardless of price, In-N-Out is a top-five meal for me anytime!

After I'd been home about an hour, Linda arrived. She gave me a prolonged hug. The embrace was not one of those polite shoulders-only jobs, but a full-body hug that lasted a bit too long for a respectable social greeting. Was she desperate for physical contact after losing her husband— or seeking something more? I couldn't tell. On occasion, Buddy suggested that Linda was not all she appeared to be.

"Shank, assume you're married. One day, your purdy wife shows up with an expensive ring on her finger that you didn't give her."

Sensing the strain in his typically relaxed voice, I cut through the smokescreen by asking, "Linda?"

"Yup," he acknowledged, sounding disheartened. "I got home from the last trip, and she's wearing a new ring that's peppered with diamonds and green stones. When I asked her 'bout it, she said a great aunt died back East. But she'd never mentioned any such lady before."

"Distant relatives don't always warrant discussion."

"Possible. The ring looks new," he mumbled.

"Is it gold?"

"Yup. Why?"

"Gold doesn't tarnish. Heat, moisture, and most corrosive agents have very little chemical effect on it. Objects from King Tut's tomb still looked new after 3,244 years."

"Those the exact years?"

"Close. Tutankhamen ruled until he died in 1,323 B.C. Howard Carter discovered the tomb in 1922. Subtract one for the missing zero year in the A.D. calendar, and that's 3,244."

"You're too much, Shank, you truly are," he said with a slight shake of his head.

I shrugged and continued. "I've got another thought. Gold is the most malleable metal—in other words, it's soft. If the great aunt had worn the ring regularly, it would inevitably pick up nicks and other signs of use. Take a close look and see if it's been worn a lot."

Buddy never mentioned the ring again.

Linda finally let go of me and stepped back. She looked better than she did earlier in the week, but she still looked battered. I wondered if she would ever truly regain the luster she had before Buddy's death. I remembered how Bill Clinton had aged so quickly during his impeachment, and I knew that sleep deprivation and the constant trauma of war had a similar effect on soldiers during combat. Did the loss of her spouse—or involvement in the killing of him—cause the stress lines on Linda's face?

Not wanting to say she looked haggard, I simply asked, "How are you holding up?"

"Fair. I feel better now that you're involved." She then reached into her purse. "Here's Buddy's betting phone. Anything to be gained from it besides Milton's number?"

"Maybe nothing, but I'm trying to be thorough. Did you see Milton much?"

"Not really. We exchanged pleasantries several times. He was here every summer for the horse racing at Del Mar, but most years he just saw Buddy."

We chatted for a while, and then Linda started to leave. She paused and said, "I would never have guessed how lonely it would be without Buddy. The house is so quiet, the bedroom so desolate. When he'd travel, it was different. I knew he was coming back. Now—"

Feeling a bit uncomfortable, I managed to say, "I'm so sorry. Time should make it easier. Just keep plugging along."

"That's what others have told me too."

Linda kissed me tenderly on the check and left, her red locks fluttering behind her as she descended the stairs from my second-floor apartment.

I closed the door and turned my attention to Buddy's phone. I hit the power button, and it fired right up. The battery indicator showed precious little charge remaining. Linda didn't bring the charger, so I would have to hurry. Fiddling with the onscreen menu, I found the phone number list. There was only one. I hit "send," and the phone rang several times before someone answered cautiously, "Yeah?"

"Milton Reily? This is Shank MacDuff, Buddy Franks's friend."

He was not happy. "How did you get his phone?"

Caller ID had betrayed me. No wonder he answered with caution; it must have been like a call from the grave.

"Linda gave me Buddy's special phone."

There was a long silence. "Why?"

"Because I asked her to. I'm sure you know about Buddy's death. The police think she had something to do with it, and I'm trying to help her. When was the last time you talked to Buddy?"

No response.

"Look, Milton, Linda filled me in on Buddy placing bets through you. That's irrelevant except as it might help find his killer."

Still nothing. *Keep digging.*

"Did the pattern of Buddy's bets change over the last few months? Did he have a particularly bad streak? Since you were friends for a long time, I thought maybe he told you something he wasn't sharing with Linda."

Silence no longer. "Listen carefully, MacDoff, Diff, whatever your name is. I'm sorry about Buddy, but you're sticking your nose where it does not belong! You need to forget you know me and move on. Understand?" His voice had turned menacing.

Being threatened definitely rubbed me the wrong way. "Well, Milton," I said with more emphasis than I intended, "your attitude gives me extra motivation to go deeper, and—" There was a click, and the call was over. That didn't go so well. While I displayed a little bravado, to what end? Shutting off Buddy's phone, I picked up mine and punched in the detective's number.

"Baker," the deep voice resonated.

"Detective, this is Shank MacDuff."

"Inspector, how goes the snooping?"

"Slow. I had a very unproductive call with Buddy's Las Vegas bookie, Milton Reily."

"So you remembered his name?"

"With Linda's help." I summarized the details of Buddy's gambling. "She also gave me Buddy's betting phone, and I used it to call Reily."

"What phone?"

Score one for Shank! "Reily provided frequent customers with a call-only-me phone. The service was still active. I dialed the only number in the memory—his."

"Impressive."

"I said I knew he was Buddy's bookie and asked if he could remember anything different or unusual in their dealings before his death."

I could sense his huge head shaking from side to side. "Nice frontal assault. Do you think you could've been any more direct?"

"A lot of good it did me. He made a veiled threat and hung up."

"Got it."

"Say, are bookies in this country common? With all the casinos and Internet gambling, are they a dying breed?"

"Maybe the herd is thinning, but they're still in business. What else did you learn?"

Time to share the Lenny Hayes story? Not yet. Deciding it was green fruit that needed to ripen, I responded, "Nothing really."

"Can we have a look at the phone?"

"Sure, but the only number in the directory was Reily's."

"Just the same, we'd like to try."

"OK. I'm coming to San Diego tomorrow; want me to drop it by the station?"

"If it's not too much trouble, that would be appreciated."

After disconnecting, I debated my next move. The Ocean Verandas effort had produced a rewarding feeling that at least I was taking action. I wanted another crack at Milton Reily. I could drive to Las Vegas and try to meet him face-to-face. The trip would also allow me to look into Buddy's cash-only existence. Given my minimal sleep needs, I could complete the road trip overnight. Detective Baker had complained about his thin resources for that kind of work, so I would be helping where the police needed help the most.

Regarding the massive San Diego detective, was I being a fool? Even with my FBI Academy experience, I was not in the same league as an experienced cop. Was he playing me like a chessboard pawn?

CHAPTER 14

Mid-afternoon, I arrived for my appointment at a sleep disorders clinic. A month ago, I had undergone the first of a series of bizarre tests. I arrived at my normal bedtime as I was told to do, and a sleep technician pasted electrodes on my temples, chest, arms, and knees. She told me they were also going to make audiovisual recordings. It was painless but creepy. With the technician stationed outside my testing bedroom, they encouraged me to sleep. Yeah, right. After a tortuous night, I finally got up at 4 a.m., having managed only forty minutes of "agitated" sleep. I would have to try again. The following week, I suffered through another night and slept a lousy fifty-five minutes.

On this day, the doctor entered with a thick file. We shook hands and briefly made small talk about the Lakers.

He then said, "I've got detailed notes from your prior visits, but tell me the background story one more time. Tricky case. We don't want to miss anything."

With a small sigh, I launched in again. "Can't recall when I first recognized my abnormal sleep patterns. On occasions like Christmas Eve or when there were other important events the next day, I would wake at two or three o'clock in the morning but attributed that to excitement. It wouldn't happen all the time, only sporadically. The problem got worse during puberty.

"The issue really surfaced during my freshman year at Caltech. I was never a night owl in the traditional sense. I would get tired around midnight and go to bed. By 2 or 3 a.m., I was awake and rested. At first, I tried studying in my room, but turning on the lamp during the wee hours every night was unfair to my roommate. So I'd go to one of the communal study areas. The pattern continued when I was home for holidays and the summer.

"In my junior year, I dated a classmate. She tried to hang with me by getting up early to study. But she became zombie-like and eventually fell behind in her studies. After blaming yours truly for her poor grades, she dumped me."

The doctor looked at his notes, nodding his head slowly. "I have most of that. How about the effect of stress? Let's cover that again."

"Doesn't seem to matter, at least in terms of sleep hours. But since my mind is always active, the pressure is relentless. Most people find relief while they sleep, maybe six, seven hours a night. I only get a break of two or three hours."

"How much stress are you under?"

"It comes and goes."

The doctor wrote diligently. "What about your mother's history? Can you go over that again?"

"Sure. As children, we would play games with Mom while she talked in her sleep. After she dozed off on the couch, she would start talking. Not babble, but clear sentences like, 'Why don't we get off this plane?' My sisters and I would fight to sleep-talk with her. One of us would respond, 'You'll have to stay on board.' Then she might reply, 'But my dog, what about my dog?' We'd roll with laughter. As the years progressed, Mom started *doing* things in her sleep. She was a scary somnambulist."

He looked up with raised eyebrows. "Most people don't know the clinical name for a sleepwalker. Very good. Sorry, go on."

"No worries. The first incident I recall was finding a trash can dumped in the middle of the living room. Had to be Mom, but she had no recollection of the incident. Another time, she awoke screaming. We all ran into my parents' bedroom and found Mom near a potted plant spitting out dirt. She was fine, but everyone freaked. Then the final straw was one morning before dawn when I rolled into the kitchen to grab breakfast before heading off to surf. I turned on the light, and there on a breadboard was a French roll, split in two. Mom had covered it with lye-based Drano.

"It could have killed her, or nearly so. When she realized what she had done, Mom was terrified. She had no memory of making the lethal sandwich. That afternoon, Dad took her to see the first of several doctors. Ultimately, she was diagnosed with a REM sleep disorder."

"This is important," the doctor emphasized. "You do understand what rapid eye movement or REM sleep is, correct?"

"Sure. REM sleep is associated with dreaming."

"That's the basics, good." Like a professor, he continued with a detailed explanation of REM sleep and the disorders associated with it—including physically acting out dreams, as my mother had apparently done that night.

When he finished his mini lecture, he added that one of the standard treatments was a drug called clonazepam, an anticonvulsant.

My turn to nod in agreement. "That's what they gave Mom. But I don't have a REM sleep disorder–or at least not yet, right?"

"True. My purpose in giving you all those details about sleepwalking is so you can be on the alert in the future." Then the doctor paused, clearly searching for a good way to say something difficult.

A knot developed in my stomach. "Spit it out, doc. What's my deal?"

Awkwardly, he resumed. "Our best diagnosis is that you are—how to put this—a freak of nature."

"Is that a technical term?" I laughed.

He appeared to relax. "Let's try that again. We believe you inherited a problematic REM sleep gene. Your mother's disorder manifests itself in a lack of paralysis during REM, allowing her to act out dreams. You, on the other hand, are usually unable to *enter* REM sleep."

"Makes sense," I acknowledged. "That explains why, on those exceedingly rare nights when I sleep five or six hours, I remember dreaming and wake up feeling euphoric. My body actually enters REM sleep."

"Exactly."

"So where does that leave me?"

"People who have trouble getting into REM mode typically become sleep deprived and show related symptoms. For example, constant yawning, the tendency to doze off, exhaustion, poor concentration, or irritability. But you're symptom-free, right?"

As objectively as possible, I evaluated the symptoms he mentioned. "I'm typically high energy, both in the mornings and throughout the day. I do get tired around bedtime, but once I'm awake again I'm sharp. My ability to concentrate remains strong. Admittedly, I get frustrated, but no more so than other people. Using your list—no symptoms."

"We've run the full battery of tests, and your physiological data concurs. Vital signs are excellent, including an athlete's low blood pressure and heart rate. Your cholesterol levels, anemic indicators, and so forth are all fine."

Then I asked the big question. "Is there a cure or anything you can do for me?"

The doctor hesitated. He glanced down at his papers and then lifted his eyes to meet mine. "There is no treatment. We are hesitant to medicate, because there are no symptoms of illness. Every senior doctor has looked at your file. We simply think you are on the extreme edge of the bell curve for sleep. You seem uniquely adapted to being awake about twenty-one hours a day. Even your core temperature rhythms support this conclusion. Most people have the strongest urge to sleep between 3 and 5 a.m. when their body temperature dips. But your temperature *rises* at about 2 a.m."

Sensing my disappointment, he tried to be encouraging. "Look at it this way. Be glad you're not on the other end of the curve. There are people who require fourteen hours of sleep a day."

"Absolutely! That would be inconceivable. But that's better than being a brown bat."

The doctor looked confused.

"Discovery Channel—they require twenty hours a day!"

"Yes, that would definitely cramp your lifestyle."

"So, am I hearing 'full steam ahead'?"

"You got it. Continue to monitor your sleep patterns and look for changes or symptoms. I know that isn't very satisfying, but that's the best we can do."

After years of increasing concern about my vampire-like tendencies, at least now I knew that being awake most of the night was not a cause for concern or medical intervention. Perhaps that knowledge would make it easier to accept my sleep pattern.

As we stood, we shook hands.

"Appreciate the effort, doc. I'll call you with any questions—at a normal wake-up time, of course!"

CHAPTER 15

Even though the sleep disorder clinic was en route, my drive to Vegas was still going to take five hours. Traffic getting out of the greater Los Angeles basin is always a grind, so I settled in for the journey. Before I got too far, I called the FBI's Las Vegas field office and asked the receptionist for Special Agent Timothy Fisher.

"Agent Fisher," answered the business-like voice.

"Tim, it's Shank."

"Mr. MacDuff, how are you?" he asked. I could practically see his ramrod posture relax a fraction. It had been a year since I last saw Tim, one of a handful of guys from the academy that I kept contact with at least by email. After graduation, the agency first posted him in the Midwest. Tim later transferred to the bureau's growing Las Vegas office.

FBI life suited him; it was a natural follow-up to being an Army Special Forces Green Beret.

"I'm OK. Enjoying caddying."

"You must be making some serious dough. I saw that your man Cline finished up there on the money list last year."

"Can't complain. How about you?"

"Let's say Nevada's unique. It is the seventh largest state, but the federal government owns 90 percent of the land. And even more bizarre, the 1.5 million people here in Clark County represent 80 percent of the state's population." I always got along well with Tim, in part because he was into facts and figures like I am. We shot the breeze a little longer, and then he turned to business. "So, why the on-duty call?"

I filled him in on Buddy's murder, Linda's situation, Detective Baker, and the Reily thread I was following into the Nevada desert. Then I asked, "Could you run Milton R-e-i-l-y through the bureau's databases and let me know what I'm up against? If you're uncomfortable with that, no hard feelings."

I could hear the wheels turning on his end. Tim was a by-the-book type, and the FBI would definitely not approve of using its security resources for a civilian request. "I'm off work soon. Let me get back to you on that."

"Great."

We hung up, and I continued the slow drive away from traffic and the metropolitan world. There would be vast stretches of nothingness ahead of me on the way to Las Vegas.

About two hours later, my cell rang. "Shank, it's Fisher. I'm on my way home and can talk now. Here's where I came down on this deal. First, bookies are dangerous, and I would never forgive myself if you got whacked after I declined to help. Second, you are doing law enforcement work, even if it's unauthorized. Third, you're seeking basic background information. It's not as if you're asking me to wiretap someone. So, we're good, but don't reveal me as the source, or I'll have to whack *you*."

"Worst case of amnesia ever," I readily agreed.

"Printed this out before I left the office. Milton Carlisle Reily, born 1953 in Linwood, New Jersey. He was one of the original dealers hired at Resorts when legalized gambling came to Atlantic City. The company bought a grand old seaside hotel, converted it to a casino, and made its money back in its first three weeks of operation. In the early 1980s, Reily moved to Las Vegas and established himself as a bookie.

"He's spent some time in federal lock-up as part of a money-laundering bust, so we have a detailed profile. It indicates a reputation for both benevolence and brutality. If someone gets into debt and has any decent record of paying him back, the man gives extra time, plus interest, of course. But if you get on his bad side, things can get ugly. You better watch yourself, MacDuff—*really* watch yourself." The way he said it made me shiver slightly. "We don't have an address—no surprise for a bookie, but we understand he's well-known on The Strip. That's about it."

"You're awesome, Tim. I appreciate it."

"Let me know how everything turns out—in one of your famous 3 a.m. e-mails."

"I will." We talked for the balance of his commute home, catching up on people from our academy days. Despite some painful memories, it was nice to reminisce.

I arrived in Las Vegas about 9 p.m. and drove The Strip to view the spectacle. Neon, noise, people, and taxis everywhere. Total mayhem on a Thursday night in March. I turned right at Sahara Avenue, where The Strip basically dies out, then two blocks over turned right again on Joe W. Brown Street. At the corner of Karen Avenue was the Greystone Park Apartments where Buddy once lived.

Turning into the complex, the M3 parked in an acceptable end spot near the office. The older, plain buildings were showing their age. This was a part of The Strip's support network, unseen by most visitors, where workers live in the dusty shadows of the bright lights.

As I entered the building, *déjà vu* hit me. Was it really only that morning that I had tried in the same way to get information from the manager at the Ocean Verandas? Experience made all the difference this time. I confidently strode up to the counter and waited for the ancient night manager to inch toward me. This guy's wrinkles had wrinkles!

"Greetings," he said in a surprisingly spry voice.

"Hey. Can I ask how long you've been working here?"

"Since six o'clock."

I chuckled. "Bad question. I meant at the Greystone Apartments."

He mentally counted. "Thirty-three years. Why?"

"A friend of mine, Buddy Franks, used to live here. Black hair with—"

"I remember Buddy. Nice man. He would bring me golf balls. I've seen him on TV caddying for that Tinny Wilcox fellow. How is he?"

Sighing unconsciously, I related the bad news. "Unfortunately, he's dead. Someone killed him at Torrey Pines." I briefly summarized the facts about the murder that had been made public and told him about my relationship with Buddy.

"Sorry to hear that," the great-grandpa said with resignation but without much emotion. After years of hearing hard-luck stories in a place like this, he was understandably hardened.

"Tell me about the golf balls Buddy used to give you."

"I liked to play the game—that is, until my hip finally went out. Buddy was a caddy down the street and knew I didn't have a lot of money. So he'd bring me all the extra balls he found. Hundreds over the years. I'll tell you, he saved me plenty."

"When did you two first meet?"

"When he came rolling in here with nothing. Told me he had trouble back home, somewhere in the South, and was flat broke. I took pity on him."

"Did he have a car?"

"Said he sold it somewhere near town for a few bucks, but he had already used that money on a motel and food. We had some vacancies, so I set him up. Looked like he needed a break. Across 450th, I mean Karen Avenue, as they've renamed it, is the Las Vegas Country Club. Going back before my time, it was a thoroughbred racetrack. When it went under, Joe W. Brown—you know, the street name—bought the land and built the golf course. Guys who caddy there have always liked these apartments because they didn't need a car to get to work. I introduced Buddy to one such fellow who got him a job. Buddy eventually caught up on the back rent and became a good tenant. Paid on time, in cash. Lived here maybe ten years."

"Did he ever say what the old trouble was?"

"Nope. It must have been bad, though. In the early days, he'd hang his head. You know, not look you in the eyes. Like he was ashamed. Later he perked up all right."

"Did you ever see him with a guy named Milton Reily?"

"The bookie? Yeah, sure. Although I don't know what he saw in that vermin."

"Any other friends?"

"Oh, on occasion he'd make company with other caddies, but mostly he was a loner."

That description did not fit the later version of Buddy. At tournaments, he would always be hanging with other caddies. We'd go out at night when we were on the road. Sometimes it was just the two of us, but more often we were a cohort of caddies invading some poor bar or restaurant. He had turned from a loner to a social creature. Interesting.

"How about women?"

"Only a few over the years; never anything serious. Didn't seem too important to him. You mind if I sit down while we talk?"

"Not at all, please."

The old man painfully lowered himself onto a bar stool next to the counter.

"You OK?"

"Fine. Seems like every night it gets a little tougher to get around. Can't give in and stopped fighting, or I'll be pushing up daises."

"Did family ever visit Buddy?"

"Might have. Don't know."

"Anything else you can think of?"

"He didn't want to be found by whoever was looking for him."

"What do you mean?"

"I agreed to warn him if anyone nosed around. It never happened, until you showed up. Buddy would remind me now and again about the promise to warn him. He was afraid."

If he was scared of being found, his real name would have been a dead giveaway. Linda's brother said that after the funeral Lenny Hayes asked for "Buddy Franks or whatever he calls himself now." I followed up with the old man.

"Did he ever use another name?"

"I see where you're headed. But no, he was always Buddy Franks."

"Did he get a different car?"

"Nope, he was a walking man. Took the bus if he needed to go more than a few miles. The stop is across the street."

"Do you know how to get hold of Reily?"

"That's easy. People like him always want to be accessible so they can bleed people dry. Slip the valet at Circus-Circus a twenty, and I'll wager—no pun intended—Reily will appear." Then leaning forward, with vigor in his old eyes, he said, "You find who killed him, OK?"

He knew my mission, and I hadn't even told him what it was. Was I that transparent? Denying it was useless. "Give it my very best," I assured him.

Driving straight to Circus-Circus, the M3 proudly pulled up in front. A young valet appeared. Emerging from the car, I asked to see his boss. The kid took the request in stride and went away. Shortly, a senior valet who looked to be in his 40s came strolling up. This was more like it. Figuring inflation had at least doubled the old man's suggested service fee, I leaned close and passed him a fifty as we shook hands. "I'm looking for Milton Reily. My name is Shank, S-h-a-n-k, and I'll be in The Venetian's main casino, near the central highest-limit slot machine, at 2:30 a.m. tonight. He's *going* to want to see me, so please make sure he gets the message." Stepping back, the valet openly examined the cash. Satisfied, he nodded and went back to work without uttering a word.

CHAPTER 16

Before thinking about where I would sleep, I needed to eat dinner and scope out the site of my upcoming rendezvous with Reily. At the Venetian's busy parking structure, the M3 happily slid into a prime corner spot that provided ample door-ding margin.

I headed to the Grand Canal, where a cobblestone indoor mall wraps around a meandering waterway. The entire structure is designed to replicate the atmosphere of Venice. Patrons were riding in gondolas, shoppers were wandering in and out of trendy boutiques, and visitors were seeking to be entertained by costumed performers and Italian opera singers. The painted blue "sky" with clouds imitates a pleasant sunny afternoon.

I got a table at Canaletto's, ordered homemade saffron fettuccine with smoked salmon, capers, and brandy cream sauce. Buddy would have *hated* the meal. He had simple tastes, did not like his food groups to "touch," and put ketchup on everything. Buddy's lack of culinary exploration caused him to regress to fast food. Only the countless miles he walked as a caddy saved him from an early heart attack. He seemed to eat better when he was at home, with Linda in charge.

After my late dinner, I scoped out the centralized high-dollar slot machine in the casino. The place buzzed with activity under the watchful eye of security personnel and cameras. The meeting place was exceedingly public, great for anti-whack protection.

My original intention was to get a cheap Las Vegas hotel room and sleep before meeting with Reily. But after the filling dinner I'd just had, getting a room seemed too much of a hassle; my car would do fine. I needed to park somewhere safe and relatively quiet, so a residential area seemed to be the best option. Driving west on Sahara away from The Strip, I soon entered the city's suburban sprawl.

Passing Fort Apache Road, the M3 made a few turns deep into a forest of modest tract homes. After retrieving a blanket from the trunk, I slid into the passenger seat so the steering wheel and pedals wouldn't be in my way. As I reclined to near horizontal, the clock read 11:04 p.m.

Two hours later, I awoke and drove the short distance back to the Venetian. The M3 easily found a ding-free parking spot in the now mostly empty parking structure. After using the bathroom, in part to throw some water on my face to try and erase the telltale signs of sleep, I walked back into the cavernous main casino at 2:28 a.m. The crowd had thinned out, but the owners were still minting money.

The smoke-filled casino stood in stark contrast to the Disney-like atmosphere of the Grand Canal. No matter how high-class the hotel is or upscale the shops are, gambling reduces humankind to its lowest common denominator. The saddest people in any casino seem to be the slot machine addicts. In one area, a large woman sat mindlessly punching the repeat button on several slot machines that were adjacent to each other. Nearby, an elderly man wearing a hat that had seen better days was still working the quarter slot machine where I had noticed him sitting hours earlier. What a tragic way to burn through your retirement savings. Finally, there were the newlyweds. At first blush, they seemed thrilled to be living large on their honeymoon. But a closer look revealed that the spinning fruit had mesmerized only the groom. The bride definitely looked concerned as she got a glimpse of her new husband's darker side.

Even though most end up losing in the long run, a few patrons appeared to be in control. At one roulette table, an Asian woman who looked to be in her 50s quietly sat with her purse in her lap, betting only pink chips. Not your typical high roller. Yet, as the young guns, drunks, and know-it-alls lost huge quantities of other colored chips, she methodically placed multiple bets on each spin and consistently added to the neat pink empire growing in front of her. While the house would eventually beat her also, for now she was more than holding her own.

"You wanted to see me?" The gruff voice shook me back into action. Turning, I looked into the face of Milton Reily. He was a wiry man, probably in his 60s, with dark eyes peering out from beneath tufts of matted gray hair. His snowy beard added a touch of Rumpelstiltskin to his appearance.

"Hey, Milton," I said while extending my hand.

Disarmed by my ultra-friendly demeanor, he reluctantly shook my hand. His hand was cold and reptilian.

"Can I buy you a drink?" I offered.

"Sure" was his measured response.

We moved to the Oculus Lounge, located in the middle of the casino, and sat at a small table. The bar was sparsely populated. He ordered a Scotch, and I went for a Sam Adams Boston Lager. My monologue about the hotel, dinner, and

Vegas in general continued until the cocktail server returned with our drinks. The bookie responded with a series of nods and "uh-huhs" without ever taking his eyes off me. When we were alone again, he turned to business.

"So now what?" he asked with a distinct New Jersey accident.

"Our brief phone call ended poorly," I said. "Sorry about that. I'm trying to help a nice lady who's in trouble."

No response. Even the nods had stopped.

"The details of your business don't matter. What I need is insight into Buddy's last few weeks alive. You two must have talked during that time."

"Maybe," was the non-committal reply.

Plugging away to try and break down the barrier he had put up, I kept going. "Buddy was frequently on your special phone. After Linda explained its purpose, I recalled him talking to you often when I was with him. There had to be a lot more calls that I wasn't aware of."

"You guess I did Buddy with a golf ball?" Reily hissed.

"Nah. Buddy had been a solid customer of yours for what, twenty years? He might not have been extravagant gambler, but he was consistent. Why would you kill a golden goose, or at least a silver swan?"

As he stared at me, the bookie's tongue constantly darted in and out between his teeth. The perceptive ancient manager at the Greystone Park Apartments was right; even Reily's mannerisms resembled those of a snake. Making up his mind about something, he finally opened up.

"You're right about several things. I liked Buddy; we used to hang together. As a client, he was a steady ride, one of the rare breed that has a betting budget and sticks to it. Finally, I didn't kill him. Haven't been to California since the ponies at Del Mar last summer."

He downed the rest of his drink in one long shot. Then, in a vicious tone, he bore down on me.

"That's all you get. I warned you once to stay out of something that isn't your business. Too bad you didn't listen." Standing abruptly, he headed toward the street without ever looking back.

I twisted my upper body from side to side to relieve the stress that had crept into my back over the last few tense minutes. Reily had at least confirmed that there was *something* going on. Did it relate to Buddy's death or merely to gambling? No clue.

After paying for the drinks, I approached security. "I'm not thrilled about walking alone to my car this late. Is there someone who can escort me?"

"Certainly, sir," the guard responded politely. He radioed for another guard. I was man enough, and smart enough, to ask for protection in case some of Reily's enforcers were waiting near my not-so-subtle ride, the one with the California plates that read "SHANK."

Shortly after 3 a.m., I headed home deep in thought. It was time to tell Detective Baker about Milton Reily and the information I learned about Buddy's Las Vegas days. Maybe the disclosures, whatever the value, would earn me a few credibility points in our perceived give-and-take relationship.

Cruising on Interstate 15 about 90 miles from Vegas, half an hour after crossing into California, I entered the town of Baker. You can't miss this rural outpost—its 134-foot-high thermometer commemorates the day when it hit 134 degrees in nearby Death Valley. It was the hottest temperature ever recorded on Earth.

The M3 was thirsty, and the first gas station I saw was vacant. After the credit card routine, I started pumping the premium gas. A van stopped on the other side of the service island.

Popping my trunk, I intended to grab the yellow-shafted Momentus golf swing trainer that hangs out next to my golf bag. Like any serious golfer, I always keep the clubs in my trunk. When getting fuel, I often make use of the three or four minutes to swing the weighted club behind my car. People often stare, but sometimes men give me a "that's a good idea" smile as they stand around idly waiting. The heavy club's weight generates momentum and causes the club to follow a proper swing plane.

As my right hand pulled the club out, I saw a man about to attack me from the back. He was a menacing-looking thug raising a metal pipe to strike. I swung the heavy Momentus as hard as possible at his lowered left arm. The swing generated a lot of club head speed, and there was a violent impact above the man's elbow. The sound of smashing bones was nasty. Without skin to contain the pieces and keep his arm together, his arm might have detached.

My FBI training took over. *Assess all threats.* Turning away from the first attacker as he crumpled to the ground screaming, I saw another thug pouncing from the pump island. Adrenaline continued to surge; it was like water gushing from an open fire hydrant. Things slowed as my senses absorbed the scene. The effect was like that of a basketball point guard who can see the whole floor. The man moved toward me and reached into his jacket pocket. *Everything is a potential weapon.* While the bureau intended this training maxim to be a defensive warning, on this occasion it was an offensive insight. Removing the pump nozzle from the side of my car, I fired it like a gun into the face of the horrified target.

The strict Air Quality Management District requires all hose assemblies in the Los Angeles basin to have vapor recovery systems that turn off the flow of fuel when the customer separates the unit from the car. Thankfully, the town of Baker is outside of the AQMD's jurisdiction. This nozzle was simple metal tubing. As the shower of raw gasoline hit the assailant's eyes and open mouth, he stopped in his tracks. I kept blasting the gasoline at him as he cried in terror and agony. Falling backwards, he blindly clawed his way back through the pump island.

Hearing a third attacker getting out of the van, I dropped the nozzle. The driver had at first stayed in the car, probably figuring the other two could handle me. Sprinting to the door of my car, I jumped in, fired up the ignition, and hammered the accelerator. The M3 executed a controlled slide through the pool of gasoline. The whole incident had lasted maybe thirty seconds.

Once on the street, I could see the three men. Destroyed-Left-Arm was still writhing on the ground. Gasoline-Shower-Guy was desperately rubbing his face with a soaked jacket in a useless gesture. Too-Late-Thug appeared frozen between his two fallen comrades.

Every fiber of my being was in flight mode. I flipped on the high beams, and a tunnel of daylight lit the road. We ran a stop sign and hit the lengthy interstate access road at full throttle. The trunk, which had been down but not latched, banged shut. The road was empty, and the M3 on steroids kept accelerating. As we blazed into the darkness, the speedometer nudged past 170 miles per hour. The van had no chance of catching us at near racetrack speed.

As my heart rate finally slowed, so did we. Once the car had slowed to a comfortable 110 mph, my brain began returning from animal instinct to analytical human mode. What had happened? Robbery? No, it was more than that. I knew the attackers had to be Milton Reily's men. Security cameras and the guard likely deterred an assault at the Venetian. They probably followed me, waiting for an opportunity. I had obliged, ending up alone in a deserted gas station.

Reily was trying to send a painful mind-your-own-business message. Don't bookies use tactics like that all the time when people don't pay up? Or more ominously, was he trying to remove me from the picture—permanently? Should I call the police? No. Even if I could force the M3 to turn around, I did not want to spend hours fielding questions that had no answers. Anyway, through Detective Baker I'd be giving information to the authorities. I had no evidence linking the thugs to Reily, but he *had* to be involved. After all, he had threatened me twice. Despite his denial, did he kill Buddy?

I'd have to be more careful. The snake had tried to eat the mouse but found a mongoose instead. But tonight's victory was not all that significant, because the cobra was still coiled to strike.

CHAPTER 17

Arriving back home Friday morning around sunrise, I could tell that waves were definitely in my immediate future. Even though there was not much of a swell, I seriously needed to unwind. The ocean felt invigorating. After riding one breaker but wiping out awkwardly, I emerged from the whitewater to hear someone yelling, "No pictures in a surf magazine for Shanks!" Cristanos laughed as he paddled past me on his board. We talked briefly about my night, but mostly we surfed. It was a welcome two-hour therapy session after the Las Vegas lunacy.

Cristanos and I met again later for breakfast at Mutt Lynch's. I gave him more details as we ate, and his eyes got saucer-big when I recounted the gas station melee. "Why you not blaze them, like Rambo? Toss a match on petrol and boom!" He illustrated his suggestion with his arms exploding upward.

"I wanted to stop their attack, not kill everyone and blow up half the town."

After breakfast, we had our choice of empty pool tables and played for our maximum high stakes—loser pays. Of course, Cristanos won, but at least I took two of five games. Most women seem to bond by talking, but guys bond best by *doing*. My morning with the Brazilian jester was a prime example of male bonding.

I wasn't in my apartment for more than five minutes when Sage arrived. She wore shorts that would make a modern Marilyn Monroe blush and a shirt at least a size too small.

"I felt bad bailing on our talk about your education. Had to help that poor girl with her lousy boyfriend. But I'm back and all ears."

"You really want to hear this?"

"Yes brainiac, I do."

"So you *were* listening."

We sat on either end of the couch facing each other. Sage wrapped her firm arms around her bronzed legs.

"I'm not quite sure where we finished, but let's move to my college years."

"Okey dokey."

"Remember SATs? Used to be called Scholastic Aptitude Tests? I don't know if you took them, but I did, and I got one of the highest possible scores, a combined score of 1590 out of 1600. I scored a perfect 800 on the verbal portion and 790 on math."

"Seriously? Sage interjected. "I never took the SAT. I was lucky to finish high school."

"Never too late for college."

She rolled her eyes.

"Anyway, I had to decide on a school. Oxford—that's in England—sounded interesting, but a European education wasn't for me. Harvard and Columbia are both in the Northeast where the weather is too cold for my SoCal blood. Stanford was a close second, but in the end I chose Caltech."

"Where?"

"The California Institute of Technology in Pasadena. I decided to go there because of its academic reputation. Albert Einstein was even a visiting professor once."

"Is he the guy who looks like the crazy professor in *Back to the Future*?"

"That's him. Caltech is exceptional. Lots of its graduates and professors have won Nobel Prizes. Being an extrovert, I wasn't interested in doing pure research in isolation—I'm too social to spend the rest of my life in a laboratory."

"That's for sure!" Sage said flirtatiously. She stretched out a leg and ran her rose-painted toenails around my ankle.

"Yeah, yeah. So in my second year, I entered a law and technology program that brought together scientists, engineers, and attorneys. I've been fascinated by DNA testing and other technology used to solve crimes ever since the O.J. Simpson trial. So, before my senior year, I ditched my plans to go for a Ph.D. and instead decided to apply what I'd learned to the real world. What really cinched it, though, was a lecture by an FBI agent who gave us an overview of the agency's high-tech equipment. I was hooked. The stuff was awesome. After, I asked the speaker what the most direct route was to becoming an agent. He smiled and answered, 'So my dog and pony show worked, huh?'"

"Dog and who?" Sage questioned.

"Means a fancy presentation. Anyway, the FBI agent told me that in addition to passing various examinations, I'd need a bachelor's degree and two to three years of full-time work related to my target emphasis. He said my Caltech degree would help if I wanted to focus on technology, but he encouraged me to gain experience in civilian technical support."

"What kind of work is that?" Sage asked. I was gratified to know she wasn't getting bored.

"Jobs with supply contractors for law enforcement or the military."

"Oh," she said. I wasn't sure she understood, but she was being a good sport.

"Finally he said that if the bureau accepted me, I'd go to the FBI Academy in Quantico, Virginia, for eighteen weeks of training—truly one of the coolest experiences imaginable for law-and-order types."

Sage said, "Was he cute?"

"Who?"

"The FBI agent?"

I laughed. "Burly guy with a crew cut."

"Yuck!" She sounded like a teenager.

Shaking my head, with a smile I continued. "The seed was firmly planted. How great would it be to become an FBI expert on things like surveillance tools, forensic machines, and high-tech weapons? If what the agent had shown was for public viewing, imagine what the top-secret stuff was like. I got tingles thinking about it!

"Ultimately, I accepted a position with a company that had developed a method for making metal behave like plastic." Thankfully, Sage didn't ask for details. "Great job. I was involved in hands-on testing and manufacturing. It was a perfect stepping stone for my dream job with the bureau and allowed me to move back to Orange County with its endless supply of sun, tanned girls, and waves."

"Now you're talking," Sage perked up.

"After my rigorous four-year tour of duty at Caltech, that was the ticket."

"So did you go to that Qualcomm place?"

Qualcomm? Then it dawned on me what she meant. "That's actually where the San Diego Chargers play football." I stifled a laugh. "But I did go to Quantico, at least for a while." I looked at the clock. "Unfortunately, kiddo, that part of the story is for another day." Actually, that's a story for *never*, I thought. "I've got an appointment near La Jolla and need to get going."

"Aw," she pouted, like a child being asked to wait.

CHAPTER 18

Racking up the miles, early Friday afternoon I headed south to Torrey Pines. For kicks, the M3 wanted to valet park at the Lodge. The doorman was dressed in full Scottish regalia, kilt and all, emphasizing the origins of golf.

Inside, I asked for the manager. Moments later a tailored man who looked to be in his 40s greeted me with a slight British, New Zealander, Australian, or South African accent—I can never tell which. "Mr. MacDuff? So good of you to come again." If his female counterpart from midweek was professional, this guy was downright scary. He escorted me past the gift shop to a solid wood security door boasting a peephole and an electronic keypad. The manager shielded the pad with his body and plucked in a few numbers. We gained access and moved into his modest office. "How may we assist you?"

"I'm working for Linda Franks, the caddy's widow. I understand you were working on the Sunday of the Classic."

"Quite right. Nasty affair. I'm sorry for your loss."

"Thanks." It was nice to have someone realize that I had lost a special friend. "Tell me about the events as you remember them."

"Things were crazy, as expected on the final day of the Classic, but in a predictable hotel way. People everywhere, extra staff, lots of commotion. The guests next door reported a disturbance in Mr. Franks's room. They were getting ready for dinner when several indistinguishable voices erupted, and then they heard a loud thud on the wall. After that, it went silent. And then they heard the door close and footsteps. The wife was concerned, but the husband wanted to stay out of it. She persisted so fiercely that he gave in and called the front desk. Given the quality of our clientele, especially on that weekend, we felt it appropriate to have someone check on it."

"How long after the disturbance did you get the call?"

"By the couple's estimation, perhaps five minutes. When security went to Mr. Franks's room, they could hear the TV, but nobody responded to their knocking. No bath water was running, and we knew that Mr. Franks had registered alone. They overstepped their authority—one of the men used the master key and entered. Within seconds, they had radioed the office. Of course, we called the police straight away."

"Was he dead at that point?"

"Quite so. Security checked for signs of life and removed the obstruction from his throat."

"The golf ball?"

"Exactly. Sadly, it was too late. They restricted access to the room until the emergency personnel arrived and took over."

"Did you personally go see?"

He visibly flinched. "Unfortunately, yes. I will never be able to erase those images from my mind. I've actually had trouble sleeping since then."

I empathized. While most images dim with time, I was beginning to believe that only death could vanquish others.

"The poor man—what a horrid way to go," the manager continued.

"There aren't many good ones."

"Quite so," he said, rubbing his temples. "Mr. Franks was sitting crumpled against the nightstand, his head tilted backward. There was a nasty gash across the left side of his head." As he spoke, the manager verified the description by moving his hand to the same spot on his own skull.

The location of the blow had not been in the newspaper accounts. At first, this new fact seemed important in narrowing the suspects. A right-hander facing Buddy would have struck him on the left side. But on second thought, Buddy could have been facing the other way or bending down, so right-handedness was not necessarily a requirement for guilt.

"Security said they hadn't touched a thing except to remove the ball and check for a pulse on Mr. Franks. The bloody putter was properly resting across his legs."

"Let me stop you for a second. Do you mean actually 'bloody,' or is that just colorful British speech?"

"Sorry, the latter. I don't recall any blood stains on the putter."

"OK, thanks. Also, why did you say 'properly'?"

"Because it was. The killer had taken care to place the putter very neatly before leaving."

"It wasn't security?"

"No, we confirmed that."

"What happened to the ball?"

"That's a tad embarrassing. After it was removed from Mr. Franks's throat, the ball was understandably grotesque, and one of the security men wiped it off. The police later scolded us for that."

I didn't know what else to ask, but I kept trying. "If you had to put together a murder scenario, what would it be?"

He became excited and said, "I feel like I'm on a crime show! Let's see. Mr. Franks probably knew the person and let them in. They argued. The killer struck him across the head with the putter, knocking him into the nightstand, which banged the wall. That's what the neighbors heard. Then the man shoved the ball down Mr. Franks's throat, placed the putter across his legs, and made a getaway."

"Did it look like there had been a struggle?"

"No, definitely not."

How weird was that? I knew Buddy, and he would not have gone down without a fight. If he had been arguing with someone who started wielding a putter in his direction, the man I knew would have gone into full defense mode. No struggle? Impossible, unless… There had to be a deeper explanation.

"Did the police say if they found any fingerprints?"

"Security said they later heard through the grapevine that Mr. Franks's prints were the only good ones on the putter and door handle leading out, the two most obvious places. Our lads spoiled the ball."

"Anyone see someone suspicious leaving the room or in the hallway?"

"No, sir."

Wanting to see how the manager's descriptions matched the physical scene, I asked to see the room.

"Certainly, if our guests have checked out." He buzzed the desk and confirmed that the room was empty.

We exited security and made a quick left through the door to an outdoor center courtyard. The area was unique. The rooms here, which didn't have an ocean view, opened onto a living replica of the Torrey Pines State Reserve. We walked through another set of doors and into a long interior hallway with green paisley carpet, yellow walls, and dark brown wood accents. Every so often, there were paintings of various California beach scenes. The hotel is large and rambling, with many angles; someone could easily have wandered the halls unnoticed.

Buddy's former room was spacious. On the right, there was a mini-bar and a closet with a small safe, terry cloth robes, matching slippers, and a "Do Not Disturb" pinecone for hanging on the entry door. Past the typical TV armoire, there was a desk. I walked to the end of the room and opened the large sliding-glass door that looked out onto the state reserve replica courtyard. The balcony was peaceful and secluded. Back inside there was a comfortable wooden chair and an amazing standing Tiffany lamp with hand-cut scenes of the Torrey Pines State Reserve. Very custom, very theme. A large bed dominated the middle of the room. On each side were wooden nightstands holding more Tiffany lamps. The stand on the right also held a Bose audio unit.

"Where were the radio and lamp when you first entered?"

"The Bose survived on top, but the lamp was knocked down. I'm sorry if I failed to mention that before. So many details, you know."

"No problem," I assured him.

An Asian picture near the bathroom seemed out of place. The decorator probably selected the painting to make frequent Japanese and Korean golfing guests feel more at home. In the bathroom, there was a magnificent marble floor and a huge mirror. Walking back into the room where the manager lingered, I asked, "What had to be done to clean up?"

"Plenty," he responded. "After the police finished their work, we got a crew in here directly. While they tried to clean the carpet, a hint of the bloodstains remained. Thus, in went new carpet. Of course, we replaced all the washable or edible items like bedding, towels, and mini-bar food. Staff scrubbed fresh every remaining inch. There could be absolutely no remnant of that terrible evening."

"Where was the plastic practice putting hole?"

"Over there," he said, pointing to an area in front of the balcony slider.

"Were there any balls left sitting in the hole?"

"I think two. Why?"

"Just checking. Most golf balls come in sleeves of three. Therefore, the killer took precisely one out and shoved it down Buddy's throat, leaving the other two in the hole. Seems like a calm maneuver under the circumstances."

The manager's eyes were glazing over. I continued, "What was the state of his personal belongings? Were his bags packed?"

He cocked his head slightly and thought back. "There was some stuff lying about, and the place looked lived in. Beyond that, I don't know."

"What was he wearing?"

"Slacks, a T-shirt, no shoes. Although he was in dreadful shape given the attack, it was clear that he had showered after the tournament."

I poked around for a minute or two more, but since the room looked new, there was not much more to see. My mind wandered, recalling Buddy's description of his life flashing before his eyes during our water tower-climbing adventure. I wondered if there was a picture show this time. Did he know he was going to die? Did he even see the blow coming? If not, maybe that would explain the lack of a struggle.

As we walked back to the office, I said, "Tell me about Tinny Wilcox, Buddy's pro."

"All right. After viewing the scene, I returned to the management offices and got sick in the lavatory. After I recovered, staff reported that Mr. Franks was the caddy of Mr. Wilcox. As the golfer was also a guest, I told them to go find the fellow, but not to tell him what had happened. They located him on the practice putting green."

"How long did the search take?"

"Maybe ten minutes at most. I'm glad the disclosure occurred in private. When we explained what had happened, all the blood drained from poor man's face, and he collapsed. I rushed to his aid and asked staff to get medical assistance. We tried to make him comfortable. He finally came around after one of the emergency lads administered smelling salts. I later saw the police talking to Mr. Wilcox but don't know what they were discussing beyond the obvious."

When we got back to the area outside the security door, he turned to me. "Is there anything else I can help you with, Mr. MacDuff?" While most people say that kind of thing as a courtesy, he appeared to mean it.

"Not right now, but may I call you if something comes up?"

He shook my hand vigorously. "By all means."

I made my way back to the Lodge entrance and rescued the M3 from the kilted valet, tipping him accordingly.

"Do you need directions, sir?" he asked politely.

"Only if you can tell me where to go for answers!"

The Scottish wannabe had no clue.

CHAPTER 19

Five minutes after leaving Torrey Pines, the M3 glided into a parking spot at the Northern Division station. I tried to drop off Buddy's phone up front, but the desk officer informed me that Detective Baker should handle it personally. Acquiescing, I stepped back and waited. The officer spoke to someone on the phone, hung up, spoke to a second person, and then hung up again.

While I was expecting the giant detective to appear, my heart leaped when the dynamic blonde cop came to fetch me. Although she was wearing a uniform, there was no way to hide her figure. Moreover, because of some slight change in her hairstyle, she looked even more like Meg Ryan—and my Jill. This woman was like a ghost from my past—exciting, yet torturous.

"Mr. MacDuff, I'm Officer Claire Valentine," she said while offering her hand.

"Of course," was all I could muster. Realizing I couldn't refuse to shake her hand, I submitted. My arm tingled when we touched. Locking eyes, I could see her pupils dilate. This was good for her too. We let go a fraction of a second after politeness would dictate.

"Please follow me," she finally instructed. We walked down the hallway to the same conference room as the other day. "Would you like coffee or something else to drink?" she asked.

"That would be great. Do you have any sodas?"

"Coke, Sprite, Orange, or Mountain Dew?"

Ah, the magic words. "A Dew would be great. Thanks."

As she left, Baker entered. "Shank, how are you?" he asked as we shook hands. His hand was huge, and it engulfed mine. Baker looked just like he had the first time we met. Same wrinkled pants and a dress shirt drowning in armpit sweat. His wide striped tie looked as if it had not seen the light of day since the 1970s. He smiled and said teasingly, "I wasn't really that busy, but wanted our secret weapon to escort you."

"Excellent," I replied, reliving the experience fondly.

As Baker settled himself, the young lady reappeared with my drink. She put my Dew on the table and gave me a genuine smile that lingered. "Anything else, detective?" she asked.

"No thanks. We're good for now."

With one final inviting look, Officer Valentine turned and left the room knowing that our eyes followed her. For beautiful women, was the constant staring irritating, arousing, boring, or creepy? Probably depends on the circumstances. I shook visibly, and Baker snickered. I wondered if she really *was* one of Baker's weapons against me.

Placing Buddy's phone on the table, I told Baker, "Tried it on the way down here, but Reily turned off the service."

He briefly examined it with a pencil and then said, "The lab boys will check it out anyway. As far as you know, the fingerprints should be yours, Mrs. Franks, and Mr. Franks?"

I hadn't thought about fingerprints. "As far as I know. Sorry if I messed up the evidence."

"No problem. Real long shot, but we want to cover everything."

I sighed and said, "I've got a few things to unload on you, including a wild adventure during my dark hours this morning. I became your unofficial gumshoe in Las Vegas." His eyebrows raised in surprise. "I tracked down the manager at the Greystone Park Apartments, and we chatted about Buddy." I recounted every word the old man said. This time Baker took notes. Next, I provided a blow-by-blow account of my encounter with Reily and the thugs. The detective asked a lot of questions and continued taking notes.

When I finally finished, a furrow crept into his brow. "You're correct; it may be difficult to connect Reily with your attackers. For all we know, they really could have been robbers, maybe car thieves, or felons out for evil kicks. Could you tell if they were high on something?"

"No way. It happened too fast."

"OK. For our part, we don't have much on Reily."

That comment presented a decisive fork in the road. Do I tell him about Tim's research? Can I trust him? What the heck. "Detective, some of Reily's background has come to me from a confidential source. If I tell you, do you promise never to reveal that it came from me?"

His giant fingers put down the tiny pencil, and he looked me straight in the eyes. "I promise."

I then relayed everything, obviously leaving out my source. Baker tapped his fingers like pistons on the table while he was thinking. Suddenly, I had an idea.

"If Reily really did send those bruisers after me, because they crossed state lines could the FBI become involved?"

"Sure."

"If that's the case, you might put a call into the FBI's Las Vegas field office. Ask for Special Agent Timothy Fisher. We went to the academy together, and the personal connection might help. Tell him everything *you've* uncovered."

He stared at me, not getting it at first. Then the light bulb went on, and he smiled. "That's a fine idea. Maybe Agent Fisher can do some research on Reily and get back to me." This cop was no fool. He understood where I got the information and the implications for Tim if his unauthorized help to a civilian became known. However, if Baker relayed the profile *his* investigation had uncovered, then Tim could simply confirm it. The official FBI files would catch up with Tim's prior work, and everything would be kosher.

I changed the subject. "Is it true that you didn't find any helpful fingerprints on the putter or door handle of Buddy's room? That's what the Lodge manager told me."

"The grapevine is accurate again. The only good prints on the putter were from Franks and security. The ball was useless, both because of the inherent difficulties in getting prints from the dimple pattern and the fact that security wiped the thing. As with any hotel room, we found prints all over the place, including on the door. It's been a royal pain trying to track down the strays. Most were either hotel employees or recent guests."

Grabbing for logic, I said, "Since there were *some* prints found on the putter and door handle, does that indicate the killer wore gloves? If he had wiped the surfaces to cover his trail, you wouldn't have found *any*, right?"

"Again with the correct analysis," Baker complimented. He then paused as if debating which way to go with me. Finally, he asked, "Has Mrs. Franks been any help with more history on her husband?"

So I was right! He did want to use me as a mole to get information from Linda. While I was satisfied at figuring out that angle, I felt used. But it was probably fair since he was providing information to me. I would play along.

"No help, really. Buddy kept her out of that chapter of his life. She knows it was something dark but never learned what *it* was. Early on, she thought he would share more about his past once they became more comfortable together. But that never happened. She respected his privacy and moved on."

"That's too bad. If Franks was from Tennessee, he was a ghost. We've tried everything."

Despite feeling guilty about withholding the Lenny Hayes lead, pride kept me silent. After all, my work uncovered his name. If there was a buried nugget, I wanted to be the prospector. Baker might have suspected I was holding out, but he did not press me.

Claire Valentine came charging into the room with an all-business look. "Detective, you're needed *now*." She was not kidding.

Baker rose immediately. Grabbing my shoulder as if I was a toy, he warned me, "Be careful, MacDuff."

After the big man left, I found my voice and spoke to my companion. "Sounded serious, but don't disclose it or you'll have to shoot me."

She laughed. "What you're doing for Mrs. Franks is sweet. You must have enjoyed her husband's friendship very much." Wow, she was even saying the right things. Yet, the cynic in me wondered if Baker staged the emergency to leave us alone. Was this my way of rationalizing the need for distance? What is wrong with me! I am still haunted. This beauty in uniform brings it all rushing back.

"Buddy was a good man, and his widow needs help. What else could I do?"

"Nothing; most people would do nothing. You're doing *something*. I respect that." She stood casually now, letting a tantalizing right index finger play with her luscious hair.

"Hopefully, justice will be served," I said. "How do you like working with Detective Baker?"

"It's good but challenging. You never quite know what he hides up those huge sleeves. I've only been here four months. Maybe he's easier to read with more experience." She paused. "Say, I understand you live in Newport Beach."

"Guilty as charged."

"I haven't yet been up to Orange County. I hear there are some nice spots there. I'd love to see for myself sometime," she said, luring me in.

"It's a wonderful place," I responded, without taking the bait. Desire pushed me toward asking her out. But deep-seated emotions held me back. How could I not be ready yet? Light interaction with women was no problem. I had even dated a little for fun since Jill's death. However, anyone who might become special still caused me to freeze. Officer Valentine's resemblance to Jill made my hesitancy even worse. Will this torment never end?

As I started to leave, she touched my arm gently, but I could feel the electricity she generated. "If you want to chat, or *whatever*, give me a call." Her hazel eyes were delightful. She slowly moved her other hand up and reached into the pocket of her tight shirt. *Breathe, Shank, breathe!* In a delicate maneuver, she removed a folded slip of paper. She took my hand and placed the note in my palm. She then folded my fingers into a fist over the paper. "It's my cell number," she finished.

Amazing. With nothing but green lights ahead on a gorgeous road, all I could do was turn into the same dead end. I nodded, tried to smile, and walked out.

CHAPTER 20

The next day was Saturday. I halted full-time sleuthing to get ready for a business trip to Florida. Cary Cline, my pro, had played in the two Southern California tournaments immediately after the Classic. He enjoyed this stretch in the schedule because he could compete yet stay at home with his family. After the week off, Cary was playing the tournament in Palm Beach Gardens, Florida. He had played well there last year and finished third, earning us both sizable checks. We would be back shortly, however, since Cary was not playing the following week; it was his daughter Rebecca's eighth birthday.

While we sometimes fly out of Orange County, on this occasion we were leaving from LAX. Monday morning, Cary and I drove separately to the airport in Los Angeles since I was going to be making a detour through Dallas on the way home. I had made up my mind to see Lenny Hayes personally.

Leaving a car at the airport is always a hassle, and for a protective parker like me, risky. The solution is Wally Park, a six-story structure north of Century Boulevard. While the business sounds goofy, it is *the* place to park at LAX. Once the car pulled inside, a maroon-vested valet eagerly greeted the purring M3. With restaurant valets, it often seems like the fox is guarding the hen house. I imagine the sneaky kid picking up his girlfriend and going for a joy ride. Not at Wally Park! Here, the valet army appears ready to defend your car from bumper to bumper. I arranged for the BMW to get a bath during the week and then boarded the complimentary shuttle to the terminal.

Cary was waiting at our flight gate. "Cutting it close, Shank. Good waves?" He knew me well. While his 5' 11" frame is stout, Cary looks good wearing logo-emblazoned golf shirts and tailored slacks for tournament play. He dresses just as nicely when traveling. Straight brown hair and matching brown eyes complement his clean-shaven boyish look.

Although he is a bit serious, Cary is good-natured and a joy to work for. He takes responsibility for his own actions and relishes the hunt as much as the catch. Most Tour players and caddies do not have much of a relationship off the course. We do. It developed gradually over the last few years. We both live in Orange County, and our differing personalities mesh wonderfully. His family includes me in some of their activities. Since my folks moved to Palm Springs, two hours away, I appreciate the gesture.

We first met several years ago at a charity golf event played that December at his home course, Dove Canyon. I had mostly recovered from the accident at the academy when a friend asked me to join his father's group. Cary, whom my friend's dad knew from church, rounded out the foursome. We hit it off right away. After a few holes, the conversation inevitably turned to my name. I relayed the whole story.

"Quite the tale. Thanks for sharing," Cary said, smiling. "So, if you wear jewelry above your foot, is it called a 'Shank-let?'" He laughed heartily.

"That one's new, although I've heard a few hundred others."

"Like?"

"'Is the ugly thing on your lip a Shanker-sore?'"

"At least you have a healthy attitude about it."

"Shank-you," I said wryly.

With Cary as our ringer, and the rest of us solid golfers, we won the team event. Near the end of the round, Cary said to me, "You know, I've been without a caddy since letting my guy go recently."

"Why?"

"I'd rather not go into it," he said with a frown. "Anyway, while the PGA Tour season doesn't start until January, I've got the Challenge next weekend and need a good man on the bag." Following the end of the regular PGA Tour, there are various invitation-only made-for-TV events. Cary had agreed to play in a Southern California version.

"Is that an offer?"

"Indeed it is. I'm sure you can manage the task, and I thought it might be a good fit given your post-academy situation." I peppered him with questions over the last few holes and then agreed. Taking the assignment seriously, I read everything on caddying I could find. Cary played great, and we both earned some serious cash. A week later, he called. "Shank, it's Cary Cline. How are you?"

"Good. Hey, I really enjoyed the caddying gig; thanks for the opportunity."

"Any interest in continuing?"

"Seriously?"

"I'm still without a caddy for next season. You understand the game, and with the Caltech training, you're uniquely *over*qualified to handle the distance, wind, and elevation calculations. It would be cool to have the smartest caddy on Tour. The physical demands are no problem, and you have excellent eyes to help track balls. Most importantly, I like you. We'd continue to make a good team." I talked to my folks and decided to go for it. We have been together ever since.

Settling into our adjoining seats on the plane, Cary asked, "How was your week?"

"Bizarre. Linda Franks asked me to help with Buddy's murder. The project took most of my energy and almost more." I filled him in on everything, even the Las Vegas fiasco and the Lenny Hayes lead.

He listened attentively and then said, "While I'm not keen on being attacked by thugs, what you're doing is a blessing for Linda. You're solid, Shank. Crystal and I will be praying for you."

I never quite know how to respond when he says stuff like that. He does it all the time, but it still makes me uncomfortable. My parents were barely "C and E" folks; they struggled to go with my grandmother to church on Christmas and Easter. We never prayed for anything. Cary's family seems to pray for everything. It's beyond me.

But since he raised the religious stuff, I said, "Slate asked me about what you have printed on your golf tees. I couldn't really explain the significance. What is it?"

As if waiting years for me to ask, his eyes twinkled. "John 3:16 is the Bible reference to the Gospel of John, chapter 3, verse 16. Most Christians have this 'golden text' of Scripture memorized: 'For God so loved the world that he gave his one and only Son, that whoever believes in him shall not perish but have eternal life.' It means that God sent his one and only son, Jesus Christ, to earth to show people what God was really like. He was then willingly crucified on the cross, taking the sins of all people on himself. Three days later Jesus rose from the dead, conquering both sin and death. Anyone who believes in Jesus and his saving work on the cross, admitting that they are sinners and asking for his forgiveness, can live with Him in eternity."

Wow! This is what In-N-Out Burger and the clothing chain Forever 21 print on millions of cups and shopping bags a year? Rarely am I at a loss for words.

Realizing my bewilderment, Cary came to the rescue. "Do you want to keep talking about this?"

"No, thanks. You answered my question, but I'm not ready for a serious religious conversation. Merely curious."

"OK. Whenever you want to satisfy that curiosity further, just ask." Ever the diplomat, Cary did not miss a beat. "Is Linda Franks compensating you?"

"Not really. She offered, but I'll probably only ask for significant expenditures. I can cover the little stuff."

Cary and I have a very open relationship when it comes to money. We have to. Like other teams on Tour, we base our verbal arrangements upon trust. Players generally want to reserve the option of firing a caddy if things go sour. Similarly, caddies want to be free to move on, since staying with a player who consistently misses the cut would be financial suicide. Players typically pay caddies a guaranteed weekly salary throughout the season. We pay for our own expenses, such as hotels, food, and travel. The only other compensation we get is when the pro makes the cut and earns winnings on the weekend. Cary has always given me a base 5 percent, rising to 7 percent for a top-ten finish. If we win, it's 10 percent.

Last year, Cary played in 21 tournaments, had seven top-ten finishes, and earned several million in winnings. That total was good enough for 28th on the Tour's official money list. Add Cary's endorsements for clubs, balls, and non-golf products, and his earnings double. The trickle-down effect means that I make real money in the form of salary, percentage of winnings, and a very generous Christmas bonus that seems to grow yearly.

Buddy and I talked about my situation frequently. He would argue that I should be challenging myself more. "You got a college degree, big-time *Caltech* degree. You could do anything, Shank."

"True. But caddying has become 'golden handcuffs' for me." His hands turned palms up; he didn't understand the reference. I explained. "Typically it refers to attractive financial benefits that a corporate employee will lose by quitting."

"So in your case, the money from caddying is so good you feel locked into the job?"

"Right."

"But what if Cary gets hurt? Or worse, simply loses his game?"

"It can happen," I agreed. "It was sure hard to watch the public meltdown of Duval and Baker-Finch. Their caddies were brutalized financially." Former world number one David Duval, and before him British Open champion Ian Baker-Finch, both simply lost their games. The press chronicled their plummets to unimaginable depths. Try as they might, neither returned from oblivion. I continued, "But really, how many professions allow a young guy to pocket so much dough? It's the rare doctor or lawyer at my age that makes as much. I'll guarantee you, none of them have as much free time or probably enjoy work as much as I do. There's also the travel and outdoor lifestyle. Golden handcuffs indeed!" Buddy could only nod in appreciation of my dilemma.

Back in the plane, Cary asked, "What are you going to say to Hayes?"

"I'm going to see why he made that strange call to Linda's house the day of Buddy's funeral."

"What if he pulls out a gun and starts shooting?"

"Never thought of *that* possibility. I figured the worst he could do was slam the door in my face. So, I'd run fast?"

Cary rolled his eyes. "Well thought out."

A nice-looking brunette walked down the aisle and looked my way. I smiled as she walked past.

Cary shook his head. "No dice, pal. She was with a swarthy fellow in a tank top who had his hands all over her in the security line."

"'Swarthy fellow?' Nice description!"

"I read a book now and then. So what's your working theory of Hayes's connection to Buddy?"

"The Texan must be part of the past mystery life. He asked Linda's brother for 'Buddy Franks or whatever he calls himself now.' With any luck, he can outline Buddy's life before the Las Vegas years."

"Have you talked to Tinny?"

"Not yet."

"You know he's playing this week for the first time since Torrey Pines."

"Yeah, I saw his name on the players list. I'll make a point of speaking with him early in the week so as not to disrupt his concentration once the tournament starts. Do you know who's carrying for him now?"

"No idea, but those are big shoes to fill. Buddy was a good caddy." Cary looked out the window for a minute then changed topics. "By the way, would you like to come to an appetizer party in honor of Rebecca's birthday? Crystal thought it would be fun to have a party at the house next week. Neighbors, people from church, Rebecca's friends and their parents. The birthday girl asked if 'Mr. Shank' was coming."

Rebecca was a cute waif of a girl whose hair seemed to fly as she scampered. She liked to show me her new treasures, like stuffed animals, games, or accessories for her prized American Girl dolls.

"Sure, I'd love to. Thanks. Appetizer party—does that mean I should bring something?"

"Nah. Crystal's friends have it covered. Your smiling mug is enough."

CHAPTER 21

During Tuesday's practice round in Florida, Tinny was a few groups behind us. It was sad and strange to see someone other than Buddy carrying his bag. While the replacement caddy looked familiar, I could not place him. After the round, I hung out waiting for Tinny to finish. When he did, I approached him and offered, "I'm so sorry about Buddy."

"I know, Shank," he said in his typically squeaky voice. Tinny wore traditional golf attire, but he looked shabby. With Buddy's generally frumpy look, they had always looked like unkempt bookends.

"Can we talk for a few minutes?"

He frowned. "I guess. Over lunch?"

"Fine."

"Let me wash up. I'll see you there."

After a few minutes, we met in the restaurant. We each ordered a burger. He had an orange drink while I scored a Mountain Dew. After shoptalk, I started in earnest. "As hard as it may be, I'd really like to hear about that Sunday at Torrey Pines. Perhaps you noticed something, even something small, that might be useful."

"Aren't the police supposed to handle that sort of thing?"

"Of course, and they are. But Linda asked me to help."

"All right," he said reluctantly as darkness enveloped him. He wore the trauma like a death mask. "Worst day of my life, and that's saying something. I've had more than my fair share. Not only did a golden opportunity for my first Tour win slip away, but my caddy died."

"Understood."

"As I'm sure you saw, everyone saw, I couldn't make a putt to save my life on the back nine. Mild shock set in. Kept expecting my weeklong touch to return. It never did. Down in flames. The 'choker' again," he said sullenly.

I knew the basics of Tinny's history. At first, he kept failing Qualifying School, the grueling tournament that non-exempt players endure to get PGA Tour playing privileges. He eventually qualified, but he failed to earn a top-125 money list exemption his rookie season. Back to Q-School. This scenario repeated itself several times. Many years, however, Tinny did play well enough to stay on Tour. It was during those later good years that Buddy was on the bag. Tinny simply could not win. Half a dozen times, he was in contention on Sunday and blew it. Receiving increasingly harsh press, the horrible label "choker" seemed to haunt him. While making a decent living, he plodded in mediocrity like a *Star Wars* Imperial Walker. As younger players hit the ball farther past him, Tinny could hear the clock ticking on his career.

He continued. "When we finished the round, I was stunned. Must have signed my scorecard, but don't recall it. I walked through the crowd toward the lockers in the

Lodge. There were a few rude comments but mostly just pity. I stopped at the practice green. Admittedly it was lame, but I had to figure out what happened."

"Did you? Figure it out, I mean?"

He hesitated. "Nope. Putted for I don't know how long until a staffer from the Lodge found me. He said that the manager wanted to talk. In the office, this English guy told me what happened to Buddy. Must have passed out. My nerves were shot."

"You don't remember?"

"Not really. Mostly bits and pieces. I recall paramedics; a cold towel on my forehead; orange juice; commotion; cops asking questions. Finally, they let me go."

"Why was Buddy staying at the Lodge?" After asking the question, I realized this was unknown background. I never asked Linda, Baker, or the resort manager. *Be more thorough!* Caddies usually stay cheap, even sharing rooms to save money. Moreover, Buddy was only an hour from home. Thus, it was odd indeed that he was staying at the lush Lodge at Torrey Pines.

Tinny continued, "He started out at home as usual for the Classic. But since we had the lead Friday, I told Buddy if we were still there Saturday, I'd put him up at the Lodge as a treat." Our food came; the burgers were huge. Tinny tried cutting his, but the knife slipped and stabbed the back of his hand. "That was bright," he groused. The wound wasn't too serious but did start to bleed. He got up and found the waitress. They were gone a few minutes, and he returned with a bandage near his right knuckles. "Were you asking something?" he asked, picking at his coleslaw.

"Did you notice anything about Buddy during the round, that week, or even before, indicating something was wrong?"

"Like what?"

"Anything. Was he quieter than usual? On his cell more often? Distracted?"

"Not that I noticed."

Tinny had aged since I last looked at him closely. His hair was definitely turning gray throughout. His eyes looked dull, with deep circles around them. For an athlete of his age, his posture was not good. Undoubtedly, many of these traits were current manifestations of long-term trends. Yet their pace had accelerated. How many years had the stress of the last few weeks had taken off his life? Sad situation.

"Did Buddy ever talk about his past?" I asked.

"His past?" Tinny awakened, as if from a daydream.

"Yeah, Buddy's childhood and later. He's got no background before Las Vegas. Did he ever talk about growing up, his parents, friends, things like that?"

"Nope. It was all a big secret. He mentioned Tennessee, but precious little else."

"Same here. Buddy was consistent on that score, even with Linda." Not really knowing where else to go, I asked the ultimate question: "Do you know who could have done this?"

Tinny stared past me. "No idea. Who would want to kill an honest, loyal guy like Buddy?" he said without emotion. The combination of tragic events that Sunday had affected him. He was messed up. It would be a heavy load for anyone. While they had different temperaments, Buddy's mellowness seemed to smooth some of Tinny's sharp edges. The conversation lagged. We soon split the bill and left the restaurant.

"Good luck this week."

"OK," he muttered.

Unfortunately, Tinny needed more than luck. After miserable outings both Thursday and Friday, he was three *over* par and tied for 130th on an easy course where five *under* par was necessary to make the cut and play the weekend. We fared significantly better. Cary played well again, this year finishing tied for eighth. Nevertheless, it had been worth the trip. Since he finished in the top ten, my 401K got an extra slug of dough.

CHAPTER 22

On Monday morning, Cary and I parted ways at the Palm Beach Airport. While we normally would have flown out on Sunday night after the tournament, on this occasion Cary invited me to join a business dinner with one of his corporate sponsors. From Florida, my boss took the non-stop flight back to L.A while I went to Texas. As I walked through Dallas/Fort Worth, the excitement slowly rose within me like mercury on a warm afternoon. What if Lenny Hayes held the key to Buddy's death? Even the possibility gave me goose bumps.

As I drove east on Highway 183, sparkling downtown Dallas soon appeared. After a development boom into the 1980s, most of the oil industry relocated to Houston. Urban renewal ground to a halt. For twenty years, nobody added a single high-rise. As the new millennium dawned, money once again flowed into the downtown loop.

Fifteen minutes down the I-30, I exited on Dolphin Road. The area had once been a desirable neighborhood, but the years had not been kind. After a few turns, I found Hayes's address. It was a small one-story home with faint reminders of grass in the yard. A thrashed blue Chevy Impala sat dejectedly in the driveway. I parked across the street. The earlier excitement became a knot in my stomach. What was I thinking? The neighborhood's pallor added to the feeling of dread. I took a deep breath and tried to look casual walking up to the house.

After I rang the bell, a woman yelled through the door, "What do you want?"

I stood squarely in front of the peephole, smiling in an effort to appear friendly. "Is Mr. Hayes around?"

"Who wants to know?"

"My name is Shank MacDuff, and I want to speak to him about Buddy Franks."

"Who?"

"A mutual acquaintance."

"He'll be here after work, 'bout sunset. Come back then!"

Given the nasty tone of her voice, it was clear the brief conversation was over. Walking back to my car, I could feel the woman's gaze burning a hole in the back of my shirt. Resisting the temptation to turn around and check, I got in the car and drove away.

Having six hours to kill, I decided to play golf. While scoping out directions online from home, I noticed a nearby golf course—Tenison Park. Built in 1914 and once hosting a Texas Open, the track supposedly "wove through pecan, sycamore and oak trees, presenting an assortment of challenging holes and shots for an enjoyable day of golf at affordable prices." Sounded perfect.

Buddy and I frequently chased the white ball around similar low-budget layouts during lulls on the road. While some were in poor condition, an equal number were local gems. Buddy was not a particularly good golfer, although his solid putting helped. During one such round, Buddy confided, "I reckon golf saved me in a way."

"What do you mean?"

"I was adrift, out of kilter. Toting golf bags and learning to play in Vegas provided me direction. A rudder. You understand?"

"Absolutely," I sympathized. "Caddying has done the same thing for me over the last couple of years."

"Guess golf got 'er done, straightened two bent nails," he observed with his thickest Southern drawl. I never could figure out if his ancestors had passed those maxims down through the generations or if they were pure Buddy. Either way, I enjoyed the resulting mental pictures.

As it was midday on a Monday, the starter had no problem getting me out. Although I prefer golf shoes for traction, sneakers worked fine. I rented clubs and bought two sleeves of balls. Tenison Park had a cool layout that lived up to its billing. Large trees lined the fairways, and a hazardous creek meandered through the course. Walkers and joggers, several with dogs, enjoyed the park atmosphere. A few pro caddies are excellent golfers, but most can't break 80. I hold my own, playing to a consistent four or five handicap. While it always feels awkward to use rented clubs, on this day I shot a respectable 78 by making birdie on the uphill par five finishing hole.

After returning the rental equipment and washing up, I headed back to the Hayes house. The blue Impala was gone. There were no other cars parked nearby. A predictable silence followed my ringing of the doorbell. Seeing no signs of life, I departed once again.

It was time for dinner. I drove toward White Rock Lake and found a rib joint that was busy—always a good sign. My restaurant radar proved accurate; the place cooked a tasty rack of baby-backs. I had to settle for a Coke, however, as they did not "do the Dew" in that part of Texas.

At dusk, Hayes's gloomy street appeared in my headlights for the final time. A tough looking man about 50 years old was getting out of a dented pickup truck in the driveway. He wore a tired tan suit and dusty brown loafers. This had to be my quarry.

"Mr. Hayes," I said enthusiastically as he turned to watch me approach. Even in the fading light, I could tell this was a man sculpted by the harsh winds of life. The street light illuminated the ugly scar on his face. As the Ocean Verandas clerk had noted, it was about three inches long and ran from his left ear to his chin. He had deep-set eyes and skin so tough you could grate cheese on his forehead. His mud-brown hair had receded to the point where it would take an expert to determine baldness.

"Who 'er you?" he snarled with the raspy voice of a heavy smoker.

"My name is Shank MacDuff. I was around earlier in the day and your wife—"

He interrupted by barking, "Ain't my wife, just my woman."

"Okay," I replied slowly. Trying to connect better, I tried, "Your *woman* said you'd be home after work."

He swore and added, "She don't know when to shut her flap. What do you want?"

"I live in California and was a friend of Buddy Franks."

That got him. While it seemed impossible, his scowl deepened. With gritted teeth, he advanced toward me. "Any friend of that dog ain't no friend of mine." The vicious look in his eyes was beyond description. What in the world had transpired between them?

"You know he's dead, murdered?"

"So? That news is only sad 'cause somebody beat me to it." A real poker player, this one. His neck and right shoulder twitched.

"Be that as it may, I'd still like to talk."

"Ain't fixin' to tell you nothing. Why should I?"

Good point. If he hated Buddy as much as professed, pleading Linda's cause would fall on deaf ears. A heavy hand was worth a shot. "Look here!" I said raising my voice and pointing a finger. While I may have puppy-dog tendencies, the right motivation produces a ferocious streak in me. He pulled back a fraction as I continued to press the advantage. "If you can explain a few things, *perhaps* you won't be arrested for murder. I know all about you checking into the Inglewood hotel the day before Buddy's death. So you can deal with me now and maybe it goes away, or the police get involved!" My heart was racing after the speech. I put my finger down, hoping he hadn't seen it shaking. This was stupid. What if the ornery cuss had a gun, as Cary suggested? Were these the last few seconds of my life?

As Hayes stood there, his tongue searched for moisture to ease the sudden cottonmouth. Then like a pit bull, he struck. His right fist came at me fast. All I could do was move my head several inches. It was just enough to cause him to miss. As the man's momentum carried him forward, my forearm landed a restrained blow on his back. He toppled clumsily to the ground. Getting up with his eyes blazing, he began to cough terribly.

My hands went up, palms toward him. "Whoa, Lenny, take it easy. This is *not* smart." I had the advantage in youth, weight, and muscle mass.

Hayes finally stopped coughing. His shoulders slumped, and our brief physical encounter was over. "Inside," he growled. He walked with the limp the wheelchaired clerk had described. Admittedly, it was foolish for me to go into the house and lose what little protection the public front yard offered. But something about his demeanor had changed. Lenny resigned himself to the task at hand.

The home's interior was a dump, literally and figuratively. As Lenny turned on the lights, I could see trash everywhere. The distinct smell of pet urine filled my nostrils. Throwing his keys on the kitchen table, and sitting down in one of the plain wooden chairs around it, he asked, "The man's for sure dead?"

"Yes, sir. Went to the funeral myself."

He took a cigarette pack out of his shirt pocket and lit the cancer stick. "Sit," he ordered after sliding back a chair with his foot.

"No thanks. Given your performance outside, I'll stand."

"Suit yourself." Wasting no time, he launched right in. "I growed up with who you called Franks, but his real name was Benjamin Hazletine Fulner. I was three years older than Ben. We was born and raised in Horse Cave, Kentucky, a piddlin' town split in two by the South Dixie Highway."

"Kentucky?" I mumbled.

"What?" he said, irritated.

"I'm sorry, but Buddy—uh, Ben—told everyone he was from Tennessee."

"That were the neighbor state, not ours. Ben and me had lots of kicks. Small towns is kind of boring, though, so we drunk a bunch and made mischief. We got to serious drinking one night. Real JD, not cheap stuff. We went—"

"I'm sorry—JD?"

"Jack Daniel's whiskey," he said in a condescending tone.

"Uh, thanks," I said sheepishly.

"We drove my piece-of-junk car, drinkin' all the way. Ended up in Bowling Green, 'bout an hour away. Pulled into a gas hole for Ben to use the toilet. I was always hurtin' for money and got stupid. While Ben was doing his business, I went to robbin' the place with a hunting rifle. In walks Ben. He gets all high and mighty and starts grabbin' my gun. The fool! We fought, and the worker pulls out a shotgun.

"Ben took my gun just as the station man starts swearin' and shootin' at us. Ben shoots too. The sound was bad, results worse. Ben's bullet finds a home in the man's head. He flew straight back, a goner before hittin' the floor. But the corpse's buckshot nails me. Tore me up bad. Still got the limp and twitch to prove it."

I couldn't believe it. Buddy, a killer?

As I mulled over the shocking story, Hayes started babbling. "There was these cigs behind the counter. Death knockin', and all I could sees was cigarettes. Strangest thing." He stopped, as if instant replay was running in his head.

I was spellbound. "And Ben?"

Hayes erupted and slammed his fists on the table. I jumped. "The dirty mongrel, he run out on me! Saved his own hide and left me to die. After Ben drove off, a woman came for somethin' like candy. She got a treat all right, two men lyin' in pools of blood. I was near-about dead. What saved me was her being a nurse. She slowed my bleedin' and got help."

"Obviously, you survived?" I added, speaking before my brain engaged.

"Why of course, you moron! The docs operated 'til morning. Took me months to even partial recover. Lot of good it did; my life was ruined. Lawyer done a lousy job. Jury convicted me of all sorts of things leadin' to a killing. Served eleven long years in the Kentucky State Penitentiary at Eddyville. That's where I got this," he said, pointing to the nasty facial scar.

"And Buddy—or Ben?"

"Long gone. Probably kept driving 'til he was broke. Far as I know, never set foot in Kentucky again."

"Makes sense," I joined in. "He appeared in Las Vegas with no prior history."

Hayes didn't hear me and kept talking. "Sittin' there in prison, I did in ol' Ben over and over. Shot him, strangled him, and strung him up. If he had just let me be while rob-bin' that gas hole, we'd made out fine." He was way off somewhere now, staring into space.

"What happened after you got out of prison?" I asked, trying to bring him back.

"Left Kentucky and drifted, movin' town to town. Stole to eat. Sometimes worked. Slept under bridges, trucks, any-where dry. Had a hankerin' to settle down so stopped here in Dallas. Got me a real job with a garage door maker, you know, the kind that rolls up in sections."

"So why were you in L.A.?"

"I travel for work ever so often, and that time it was California. Flew in on Sunday and went to that lousy hotel. Flippin' TV channels and started watching Torrey Pines golf. They kept showing Tinnery or Tinnsy, whatever his name is, and all his misery. I was only part payin' atten-tion, but then I sees him. Was that Ben caddyin' for the feller who was givin' the tournament away? I later did some checkin' and found out he changed names. Now called himself Buddy Franks. That clinched it!"

"I don't understand."

"Ben Fulner. Buddy Franks. BF! Get it, you idgit?"

I've been called many names before. "Idgit" was a new one. I nodded in understanding. "Let's back up. What did you do right after you saw Ben on TV?"

"I went out for supper then back to the hotel."

"Can anyone corroborate that?"

"Don't believe me?" he seethed.

"Just asking what the cops would. Remember, I'm trying to eliminate their involvement."

Calming a tad, he muttered, "Nobody. Ain't so easy to make friends." I didn't know whether he meant on such a business trip, or for him in *any* setting.

"OK, I had to ask. So why did you call Buddy's home?"

"If you'd shut your trap, I'd tell the story!"

"Sorry. Please continue."

"Found out he lived in Orange County. But that flower had a thorn when the man tells me he's dead." Linda's brother was right; Hayes did talk like Buddy, even peppering his speech with Southern sayings. Lenny kept rolling. "I didn't believe him, or didn't want to. We both got ornery, and I hung up. Later I found out about Ben's killin' at the fancy hotel. Reckoned that was that. Did he live happy out West?"

"Seemed to."

"I 'bout bleed to death, rot in prison, limp for life, and he lives high and mighty. Ain't fair," he smoldered.

The incident must have tortured Buddy, gnawed at him like a tapeworm even though he put himself in a position to start over. His view that golf and caddying were a rudder during the tempest now made more sense.

Suddenly the vicious look returned to Hayes's face. "You got what you want, now git!" He didn't have to ask twice. After thanking him, I was out the door and in my car in less than a minute.

Sitting by the window on the flight home from Dallas, I saw the puzzle pieces floating in my mind. While there was no complete image, I could start placing some of the outside edges and grouping certain colors together.

Did Lenny Hayes give it to me straight? Perhaps my threat about the police worked. He must have told the truth about the basic facts, since they would be easy to check. Assuming the "gas hole" incident was based in reality, was that all of it? The part about Buddy grabbing the gun and shooting the station attendant was hard to believe. Yet, it would explain why he beamed down into a Vegas existence—escape, change his name, and bury the past.

Hayes certainly had a motive to kill Buddy. Hatred like that has driven lots of people to violence. He also had the opportunity. Was his travel schedule mere coincidence? He had arrived in Southern California the day of Buddy's murder and left shortly after the funeral. He had no apparent alibi. While the police could check with the employees at the Ocean Verandas, it would be unlikely anyone noticed the movements of a low-rent guest like Hayes. Was his call to Linda's home some sort of sick game after he killed Buddy? The flight attendant interrupted my musings by offering a mini bag of nuts. I'm never one to turn down the salty morsels. Settling back and munching, my thoughts turned to Linda and the kids. How brutal to find out that your husband or father had such a dark past. Perhaps the kids didn't need to know. Yet someone had to tell Linda. Guess who? Leaning back and closing my eyes, I worked the puzzle all the way back to the Golden State.

CHAPTER 23

On Tuesday morning, the clock read 1:06 a.m. as I tumbled out of bed. It was early, even for me, but my body was still on East Coast time. Having maximum dark hours, I replaced my volleyball shorts with gray sweat pants, pulled on a Bandon Dunes sweatshirt, and settled in front of the computer for a long session. Before the trip to Florida, I had put the unit in sleep mode instead of turning it off completely. Now trying to wake it up, something was wrong. It was frozen.

Wasting time staring at the screen while the computer restarted, I realized how these electronic devices are still in their teenage years. They have hard drive crashes, incompatible programs, and other technical glitches. I figure that computers will reach maturity when they are as quick and reliable as the light switch. When you enter a dark room and hit the switch, you *know* that electricity will flow and the lights will go on. Apart from the occasional blown bulb, it always works. Will computers ever match the lowly light switch in this wonderfully reliable way?

When the machine was up and humming, I opened the "Find My Killer, Shank" file. I typed in my conversations with Tinny Wilcox and Lenny Hayes verbatim, and then added sections with various headings, including one recounting the conversation with Cary.

Themes started to emerge. Through *Golf*, Buddy connected with his pro Tinny, tangentially with tournament director Slate, and Linda from a financial provider perspective. His *Past* involved childhood friend Hayes, Reily from Vegas, and Linda. It seemed too much of a stretch to include the ancient manager from the Greystone Park Apartments in that group. Via *Gambling* Buddy linked to Reily as bookie, Linda as wife, and perhaps Slate with his racetrack experience. Since everyone except Buddy was a theoretical *suspect*, Detective Baker touched everyone.

Creating a simple spreadsheet, I listed topics on the horizontal axis and names on the vertical axis. Even though the answer may be absurd, I endeavored to put something in every box. The result was this:

	History w/Buddy	Golf	Gambling	Motive	Opportunity	Distrust
Buddy Franks	---	Yes	Yes	---	---	---
Linda Franks	Yes	Yes ($)	Yes ($)	Yes ($)	Yes	?
Lenny Hayes	Yes	No	No	Yes (hate)	Yes (in L.A.)	?
Milton Reily	Yes	No	Yes (bookie)	?	?	Yes
Nick Slate	No	Yes	Yes (Del Mar)	?	No (*Classic*)	Yes
Tinny Wilcox	Yes	Yes	?	?	No (putting)	No
Det. Baker	No	No	?	?	?	Maybe

While the chart looked scientific, it wasn't. Some of the responses were very subjective, like "distrust." In addition, there were huge data gaps. Was the murderer even on it yet? One thing for certain, Linda was up to her neck in it!

Moving on, I decided to research Lenny Hayes's story. My first Internet efforts focused on Horse Cave, Kentucky. There it was, about an hour northeast of Bowling Green in Hart County. I discovered that Horse Cave dated back to the 1840s and got its name from folk tales involving Indians and horse thieves. Developers ruined the main attraction in town when they flooded the biggest cave with waste. The odor was terrible, and the cave's famous "eyeless" fish population began to decline. By 1943, the cave was closed, and the town has suffered with the stench ever since.

So Buddy grew up in Horse Cave, a poor rural backwater of Kentucky, where they still probably bemoan the loss of the eyeless fish. And I grew up in San Clemente, an affluent city nestled on a gorgeous coast, where I chased tanned girls in bikinis. Thanks to a country where people have freedom of movement without class restrictions, we were able to become friends and live as we pleased. Awesome!

I tried a bunch of different Web searches, but nothing came up about the alleged gas station shooting. This could be because the town's older newspaper stories hadn't been converted to digital format yet, or Lenny was lying. Completing my research, I checked emails and answered several with lengthy replies. After working on a few other items, I noticed that it was getting light outside. Wandering over to the front window, I saw nothing but shapeless, mushy, wind waves. No decent swell. Time for a run. After getting ready and emerging onto the boardwalk, I headed up the coast this time. It was early, and there wasn't a lot of activity outside. The occasional person going to work or exercising was about it.

At 36th Street, the boardwalk ends. I went inland half a block then continued up the coast on Seashore Drive where there is a painted bike lane behind the oceanfront homes. Continuing past 62nd Street, I reached the River Jetties at the mouth of the storm channel separating Newport from Huntington Beach. The River Jetties frequently offers excellent surf due to silt accumulation on the ocean floor. At the same time, it can be nasty, given the high bacteria count from urban runoff.

On the way back, my rhythm was good. At 43rd Street, a danger signal flashed in that mysterious area of my brain that no research will ever isolate. The same thing happens when I drive through an increasingly dicey neighborhood and *know* it's time to lock the doors. People often refer to the sensation as raising hairs on the back of your neck. Whatever the mechanism, the phenomenon is real.

At first, the nature of the threat was not clear. However, as the milliseconds raced, the menace became a sound. My dead left ear eliminates the possibility of me hearing anything in stereo. Thus, at first I have trouble determining the direction a sound is coming from. To compensate, my head now automatically turns until the good right ear finds the source of the sound. On this occasion, the maneuver probably saved my life.

Rotating my head to pinpoint the sound behind me, I caught a glimpse of something black bearing down on me. The information rocketed to my brain. My muscles fired. My left leg pushed hard. The reaction combined with my running momentum, and I dove to the right. Pumping adrenaline masked the pain as my body crashed into several metal trash cans. I tumbled over and slammed upside down into a wooden gate between two beachfront homes. There was a deafening crash. I could hear metal on stucco, a deep engine at full throttle, and the cans flying. Never saw the black truck that almost killed me.

Crumpled like a rag doll, I was dazed. How badly was I hurt? Ever since I was a child, right after an accident or impact, be it on a bike, football field, or skiing, I would start an inventory to make sure all my body parts were still there and functioning. This time was no exception. Both arms moved; so did the hands and fingers. Same for my legs, feet, and toes. As I sat up, pain overwhelmed the subsiding adrenaline. My right arm was burning, and I could see blood.

A chubby woman in a sea-foam green jogging suit appeared in front of me. "Are you all right?" she called out. The woman dug through the smashed trash cans and smelly garbage to reach me. She knelt down to take a better look. At the top of her lungs she bellowed, "I saw the whole thing! All of it, do you hear me?"

She was already getting on my nerves.

Unabated, she roared, "The person in that truck tried to kill you! Smash you flat. Do you understand? Intentionally! Are you OK?"

I found my voice. "I'll survive. What truck?"

"There was a man, or at least I think it was a man. He wore a ski mask; you know, the knit kind with the eyes and mouth cut out. He was driving a big black pickup truck, and he tried to mow you down! I was doing my daily power walk. Oh, it was freaky, I tell you, freaky! He accelerated right at you. It was a shock! I'm so sorry I didn't warn you. Are you really OK?"

I tried to get up and get away from this chattering monster. But my legs failed me.

"Hold on there, you better take it easy. Sit down. You might be seriously injured. I couldn't believe how you flew through the trash cans. The truck must've been going 40 or 50 miles an hour when it smashed into the houses. I thought you were dead for sure! You should bless your lucky stars there was this little cutout between the homes for the gates. If you had been ten feet in either direction, he would have crushed you!"

Sitting there in increasing pain, I realized that a crowd had formed and others were starting to push in to see if they could help. One man stood calmly talking on a cell phone, reporting the incident to 911. Then I started to feel sick, probably the aftermath of the massive infusion of adrenaline. All I could do was throw up. So I did. My vomiting accomplished at least one positive thing—it made the chubby woman back off. Unfortunately, I don't think that sea foam green outfit will ever be the same.

A few minutes later, I heard sirens in the distance. I knew that the threat was gone, but it still felt reassuring to know emergency personnel were rushing to help. Two other witnesses confirmed the intentional nature of the attack. The truck was a late-model Dodge Ram.

The paramedics wanted me to go to the hospital. I stubbornly refused. Cuts and bruises tattooed my body, but nothing was deep enough to require stitches. There was no concussion either, since I could remember every moment of the drama. Once when I was in a half-pipe, one of my skis fell off in mid-air, and I slammed my head on the icy bottom. Gone forever are the thirty seconds it took my brain to re-boot.

No missing moments here.

Eventually I stood up and tried to respond to the questions a policeman was asking. "No, officer, I have no idea why anyone would want to hurt me. No, sir, I don't know anybody with a black truck. No, there are no recent romances gone bad or discovered by someone jealous. Yes, I often run at about the same time when I'm in town and not surfing." Privately, bookie Reily was the number-one suspect. At that moment, however, it was beyond me to include the Newport cops in my complicated situation.

The damage to the homes was significant. The truck crushed the garage door and edge of the first house. Then, after smashing some of the trash cans near me, it had careened off the corner of the second house. "The lack of skid marks indicates it was a deliberate attempt," one cop pointed out. "The driver never slowed down, even after he made contact with the houses." When I expressed a desire to go home, the police insisted on driving me. Gratefully, I accepted the ride.

Within an hour of my brush with death, I started to recuperate in a hot bath laced with Epsom salts, the healer of all things sore. The miracle substance is absorbed into the skin, reducing inflammation.

Had someone really tried to kill me? If that was also the intent of the thugs on the way home from Las Vegas, that made two attempts in a week and a half. How scary. My mind replayed Milton Reily's threats. Trying not to overlook others who might have a motive, I considered Lenny Hayes. Did he follow me to California or hire someone locally from his home in Texas? How much does that sort of thing cost? Perhaps Slate was behind it, but why? Someone else?

My mind flitted to Linda. Could she be out to get me? Why would she ask for help and then try to dust me? Although, the insurance money was probably in limbo until the police cleared her of criminal suspicion. Maybe I had crossed a line and uncovered something that would hurt her instead of throwing suspicion elsewhere. If so, what had I found?

CHAPTER 24

After soaking in the tub, I toweled off gently and assessed the damage. There was a serious gash on my right elbow and skin missing from my right shin and left hand. A small but deep cut ran across the bridge of my nose, but it was the swollen lower lip that really gave me the prizefighter look. My back was sore, and other areas would need to heal. Fortunately, my well-toned muscles were primed for quick recovery. My next loop for Cary was several weeks away, so there was time enough to mend.

I dabbed Neosporin on the open wounds and employed a variety of bandages to cover them. Four Advil flowed down my gullet with a glass of water, the same 800-milligram dose a doctor would prescribe. I put on a pair of comfortable blue sweat pants, an In-N-Out shirt, and Topsiders without socks.

The next step was clear. Detective Baker hears it all, no more games. Things were out of hand. Time for professionals! I called to confirm that the big man was there and told the receptionist to relay that Shank MacDuff would be down in about an hour to see him. I needed to complete the mission before getting stiff later in the day.

After an uneventful drive to the station, I was admittedly disappointed when a frumpy middle-aged assistant showed me to the conference room. Officer Claire Valentine either had the day off or was engaged in *real* work.

As Baker entered, slightly rumpled as usual, he examined me with interest and asked, "What happened to you?"

"Someone tried to kill me, no doubt this time."

His jovial smile quickly faded. "You're serious?"

"Unfortunately, yes. A maniac in a black truck came within inches of splattering me on some houses." I filled him in on the details of the attack. The detective scribbled on a yellow pad. I then relayed the details about the funeral-day phone call to Linda's house and my sleuthing with Lenny in Dallas. "Hayes might be telling the truth, or he might be making some of it up. His geographic details on Kentucky check out, but there was nothing on the Internet about the shooting itself. If he did give me the straight scoop, it basically fills in Buddy's life before Las Vegas."

Baker looked at me and smiled. "Quite resourceful, MacDuff, although confronting Hayes was risky. We'll start digging and try to verify the remainder of his story. I'm also going to contact the Newport Beach Police and fill them in."

"Sorry about stiff-arming them, but I wanted to keep everything going through you."

"No problem. I'm definitely the point man. Sure looks like you've made *someone* nervous. Let's try and figure out who by having you list everyone you've talked to since agreeing to help the widow Franks. Don't make any judgment calls. Merely list them all. Even if someone isn't a suspect, that person might have innocently told others. Go ahead."

"Chronologically?

"Fine."

"First would be Linda Franks, then Nick Slate, followed by the bartender and the female manager at the Lodge. And let's not forget you," I said, managing a sore smirk. The detective did not seem amused. I continued. "Linda's brother, then the Ocean Verandas clerk. Milton Reily, my FBI Academy friend Tim Fisher—" Realizing the slip, I conceded, "You figured out I talked with him, right?"

"Yeah. By the way, he was cool about everything. Papering his file with the information he already found worked perfectly. Please keep going."

Finding it increasingly hard to focus, I proceeded slowly. "There was the prehistoric manager at the Greystone Park Apartments, but I never got his name. Sloppy, sorry. My pal Cristanos, the English-accent manager at the Lodge, and I guess my brief conversation with your Officer Valentine might count."

"I'll give her the third degree. Go ahead."

"My pro Cary Cline, Buddy's pro Tinny, and then finally Lenny Hayes and maybe the woman at his house, but that's stretching it."

"Anyone else?"

"Not that I can think of."

Baker then asked, "Are you going to tell Mrs. Franks about her husband's hidden past?"

"It looks that way. I'm the logical one."

"Those assignments are always tough." His tone then became more authoritative. "Until we wrap this up, you need to be extra careful. They may get it right the third time. We don't want that."

"Agreed."

"First, don't take runs on public streets."

"Yeah, duh," I said sarcastically.

The detective chuckled and proceeded. "Second, try to be a little less predictable in your patterns. Third, lock everything, including your car when you drive and each building or room you're in."

"You're kidding about locking rooms, aren't you?"

"There is no such thing as being too paranoid when you're a target. If another attack comes, a locked door might be the difference." He then glared at me. "You should seriously consider leaving the investigation to us. The work you've done so far has been a big help, but it's not worth getting killed over."

"Maybe. But it's hard for me abandon ship."

"I'll even give you my personal cell phone number so you can always get hold of me, day or night." He jotted it down on the back of one of his cards. "Keep in touch, even if you think it's trivial. I need to know everything."

During the drive home, I felt increasingly groggy. Once back at my apartment, the phone rang.

"Long time no talk," Baker opened. "They found the smashed black truck abandoned in Santa Ana, ten miles from the scene. The lab is combing the vehicle for evidence, but don't hold your breath. Someone stole it last night at a restaurant in Anaheim. The thief posed as a valet. He apparently gave the owner a fake tear-off ticket and then drove off."

"Clever assassin. I hate that."

"Thought you'd want to know," he said before hanging up.

I spent the balance of the day resting behind a dead-bolted front door. Of course, no sleep came, but lying down was the only thing my body could manage. Daytime TV is brutal, but back-to-back episodes of *Bonanza* eased the boredom. When it was finally dinnertime, I painfully found the freezer and microwaved a package of Hot Pockets, pizza variety. I went for a beer and decided on my last Heineken, leaving a new six-pack of Sam Adams for another day. After eating and changing bandages, I took more Advil before bed. A few hours of fitful sleep followed.

Waking, I sat up, and the room started spinning. I held onto the bed until the unpleasant sensation stopped. The clock showed 2:12 a.m. I had hoped that with the injuries and extreme duress, slumber might have lasted longer— maybe even the rare miracle of REM sleep and a dream. No such luck. I gritted my teeth and stood up.

At times like these, my sleep pattern is savage. I usually eat breakfast after it's light, leaving me four to five hours of nocturnal "dark hours" to fill. At times, this has been a huge advantage. Caltech academics are famously hard, with student life described by the aphorism, "Study, sleep, or socialize: pick two." I didn't have to choose. But now, there is often too much free time in my 21- to 22-hour days. While I manage to read a fair number of novels yearly, sometimes I'm lazy and watch TV, surf the Internet, or thumb through magazines. Occasional projects help, like typing up my notes about Buddy's murder. But there are only so many projects and chores to keep me occupied.

Even during my most productive periods, I'm ruthlessly lonely. Imagine the truant who skips class but has nobody to play with because everyone else is in school. That's me, multiplied by a thousand. I have thought about getting a nocturnal pet like a hamster, but since I am gone for weeks at a time, it does not seem fair to leave an animal alone for that long.

When it's unbearable, pacing seems to help. Occasionally someone will ask why the carpet in my apartment has a path worn in it. My response is vague, since the real reason puts me in line for the loony bin—I walk in one direction, turn, walk back, turn, and do it again. One night when it was really bad, the scientist in me charted my absurd wanderings. In exactly four hours, with each repetition taking an average of 11.4 seconds, I completed 1,263 mini-laps. Nobody can truly understand my dark hours.

When I don't feel well, like I felt after the truck attack, late-night TV is the only option. Luckily, that Tuesday night, American Movie Classics was airing a Humphrey Bogart marathon. I saw the end of my personal favorite, *High Sierra*, enjoyed *The Caine Mutiny*, and finished with the actor's Oscar-winning performance in *The African Queen*. How deep is Bogart's resume? Any of the films I watched that night would have been a career-maker, but the movie icon also starred in what I consider to be the best film ever made—*Casablanca*. Bogie has always been a loyal companion for the truly lonely.

CHAPTER 25

B y the time the sun finally rose Wednesday morning, I was as stiff as one of my surfboards. Getting ready was slow going, even after four more Advil. Nothing healthy for breakfast this time, just a bowl of Lucky Charms. The phone rang, startling me. I answered in a hoarse voice, "Hello?"

"Shank, this is Linda. Are you all right? I was reading the paper this morning, and there was an article about an attack on you yesterday, something about a guy in a truck trying to run you down. Is it true?"

"Afraid so. Somebody in a black pickup tried to scramble me. I dove into some trash cans and escaped an almost certain death."

"How awful! The paper said it was intentional, but that's hard to believe."

"The truck accelerated *after* hitting the houses without ever braking. The facts match the impression of witnesses that there was intent."

"But why?"

"It has to tie to my work on Buddy's death. There's nothing else."

"Is that possible? Oh, Shank, I feel horrible. You ought to stop right now!"

Her voice was not right. Was she angry? Frightened? Something else? If Linda was behind this failed attack, she might hope I was now scared enough to drop the investigation. Linda kills Buddy and asks me to help free up the insurance money? Then when I hit a nerve, she hires a killer to waste me? Were she and Reily linked? I wonder if she used the special betting phone to contact the bookie after Buddy's death.

She continued, "Why didn't you call? Though I wouldn't have been around to help. We spent the night at my neighbor's house. It was good for the kids to have some fun. After we dropped the kids off at school, the other mom and I went out for breakfast and then went shopping."

A prompt and complete alibi. Another coincidence? I listened hard, trying to imagine what Linda looked like while she was talking. Unfortunately, my wandering mind moved from her face to other parts of her nice body. While a person's appearance should not influence believability, I was all man, and it did. This cutie had to be innocent. Right? If she looked like a Russian weightlifter, would she appear guiltier? I needed to change the subject, and now was as good a time as any to fulfill the duty I'd been putting off.

"Linda, I found out something serious about Buddy's past. It's not pretty." The line was silent. "Linda?"

"Yes, Shank, I'm here bracing myself. Go ahead."

I told her everything Lenny Hayes said, word for word, with all the original heat. Editorializing could have put Buddy in a better light, but I resisted the temptation. Linda had the right to know it all, just as Hayes growled it. "I'd always feared something like this. Why else would he have buried his past so deep?" Then she exclaimed, "The kids, how can I tell them? I can't. I can't!" She was barely able to talk.

"Linda, Linda," I tried to calm her. I should have given the news in person. "Don't worry about that yet. The police haven't even confirmed Hayes's story."

She recovered slightly. "I'm so sorry. It's tough enough losing him, but then to find out—"

Her voice waned. My heart went out to her. I tried to comfort her. "Early on, Buddy may have made some mistakes. But after he started over in Las Vegas, he was what you saw—a good husband, father, and breadwinner."

The line was lifeless. Then she said coolly, "Maybe."

What was that in her voice again? I could not tell over the phone. Was this a shocked woman adjusting to her new dead husband—Ben—and her new last name—Fulner? Or was it part of some broader scheme beyond my grasp? I had to assume the former while keeping on guard for the latter.

"Linda, I know it's hard. But Buddy loved you and the kids. Don't let this news destroy the man you knew."

After taking a deep breath, she changed the subject. "Are you sure you're all right? Would you like us to bring you dinner tonight?"

"That's very kind, but I'm still planning on going to Cary's for an appetizer party. It's his daughter's birthday, and Crystal is putting on the party for their friends and family."

"Sounds nice. If you do need anything, please call."

After hanging up, I felt sleepy. Not wanting to look a gift horse in the mouth, I went back to the bedroom and lay down. Next thing I knew, a rarely used alarm clock rang. I struggled to turn the blasted thing off, but it kept ringing. Plowing through the haze, I realized it was not the alarm at all but the doorbell. As I groggily emerged from the bedroom, my senses returned. I had slept like an anesthetized corpse. In the peephole, all I saw was a huge chest that could only belong to one man.

"Detective Baker?" I greeted him.

"In the flesh and alone," a deep voice rumbled.

"What's the secret password?"

"Funny. Properly paranoid, but funny."

As the door swung open, the smiling mammoth walked in. Although he still had armpit rings working their way along the fabric of his dark blue shirt, to my surprise his clothes seemed freshly pressed. Even his tasteful dark red tie looked like it belonged in the current generation.

"What are you doing here?"

"Met with the Newport Police on several items and thought I'd check up on the crash dummy. You sore?"

"Like a pro running back on Monday morning."

"Understood. When I get into a ruckus, the adrenaline often keeps me percolating for a while. But later, look out! It gets worse with age." We talked about my various ailments, and then he looked out the front window. A couple of real honeys walked on the beach. "This is an excellent location, especially for a single guy. The scenery is delightful, *including* the ocean," he joked.

"Yeah, it's got a real pumping vibe," I agreed.

He turned back toward me. "Want to grab lunch? I'm buying."

"Sure."

"Can we walk somewhere? That is, if you can manage."

It was a pleasant, sunny day, so I suggested Charlie's Chili by the pier. The slow trek to Charlie's felt good. My once-a-year nap had helped the stiffness, and I was feeling better. The detective's size 17 shoes pounded the pavement. Half a block from my place, we crossed 22nd Street and entered two blocks of commercial buildings—restaurants, bars, and beach shops renting chairs, umbrellas, and body boards. Small apartments perch above many of these establishments. The area's got tons of character.

After passing the upscale Doryman's Oceanside Inn, Detective Baker wandered over to the plaza monument near the Newport Pier entrance. He read about how the original wharf was built in 1888 and later served as the nucleus for the City of Newport Beach's development.

"Cool, huh?"

"Very," he agreed.

Today, the long wood pier has a recreational focus. From dawn to dusk and beyond, tourists and locals cruise its length. The pier is a favorite of fishermen, fisherwomen, fishercouples, fisherfamilies, and fisherwidows, the last being women who sit on upside-down buckets staring into the sky as their husbands wait for nibbles.

We then shuffled over to Charlie's Chili on the south side of the plaza. It was a weekday in March, so there were several empty tables outside. The big man took my advice, and we both ordered a chili platter, which included a bowl of their headliner dish smothered with cheese and onions. He had a Coke, and I stayed true to form with a Mountain Dew.

When the waitress left, Baker informed me, "On the stolen black truck, the Newport Police found only the owner's fingerprints and a few strays. The driver apparently wore gloves as reported."

Pain shot down my right side as a strong hand grabbed my shoulder from behind. "Shankster! What's goin' on?"

"Pork Rind," I groaned, recognizing his walrus-like roar. Exhibiting unusual sensitivity, the fat slob let go of me as I began to crumple slightly under his heavy grip. He stood there in worn-out sandals, stained shorts, and a faded Hawaiian shirt begging to burst and reveal his basketball-sized beer belly. He calls his straggly meatloaf-colored hair and scruffy beard "classic beachcomber." In reality, however, they look more like a result of lousy personal hygiene.

"Kind of girly today?" he joked.

"Kind of injured. You know, i-n-j-u-r-e-d," I spelled out slowly.

"I get it, bro. Who's the Fezzik?" he asked, turning to my companion. I could only hope that Baker had never seen *The Princess Bride,* because comparing him to André the Giant's character in that movie was nothing short of an insult.

"I'm Gerald Baker," he said while extending a hand and rising.

Looking up at the stone wall that was Detective Baker, the intruder fell silent for once in his life. Finally, he re-engaged with us. "People call me Pork Rind."

Baker might have been expected to ask about his nickname, one that referred to the cooked fat of pigs, but instead he sat back down and quipped, "Better than R.O.U.S."

Pork Rind laughed and slapped the detective on the arm. "This home boy is OK," he said, looking at me. "Not many people can pull out a reference to Rodents Of Unusual Size so quickly."

Obviously, Baker had seen *The Princess Bride.*

Trying not to be too offensive, I said, "P.R., we're kind of talking business here. You mind?"

"Lighten up. I was cruising the boardwalk, and there was the Shank man. Only being a friendly neighbor. What kind of business you two scheming at?"

"The kind that's private," Baker added with a steely glare.

"Whoa, daddy! Both of you are wound too tight. Rum, lots of rum. That's my advice. Later," he said, walking off in hopeless pursuit of a long-legged brunette.

"Close friend?" the detective asked with a smirk.

"What a pig. The nickname fits perfectly."

Baker sat back in the smallish-looking chair and became serious. "Mind if I ask you something personal?"

"Depends on what it is," I answered truthfully.

"What happened to you at the FBI Academy?" He paused, looking at me intently. "It was a point of curiosity before this latest attack, but now we need to know the details. I'd like *you* to tell me, Shank. We can try to get the official version, but it would be so much easier to get it from you instead of the feds." The waitress came by with our salads and drinks, my glorious yellow Dew fizzing freely. "How can you drink that stuff?" Baker asked.

"It's the same as your Coke, only yellow and *styling*."

"If you say so."

Returning to his request, I could see his point about needing to know. Baker had to exclude, at least in his own mind, any connection between the attacks and my FBI stint. In addition, he was correct about the hassle involved in getting information from the bureau.

This was *not* going to be easy. As I started to relive the turning point of my life, every nuance came back with diamond clarity.

CHAPTER 26

The FBI Academy is located on the U.S. Marine Corps
Base at Quantico, Virginia, about an hour south of
Washington, D.C. A thick forest near the Potomac River
surrounds the academy, providing privacy and security as
new agent trainees endure the 18-week course. The main
training complex features three dormitories, a dining hall,
gym, running track, library, and classrooms.

The range of FBI job applicants has broadened over
the years. It used to be that mostly former military and law
enforcement types applied. Now, hopeful agents include
those with technology, language, and international skills.
While my background was valued and unique, it was not off
the charts as it would have been in the past.

Seating was arranged alphabetically in the academy's
stadium-style main classroom. Several levels down from the

entrance, I found my place. As I flipped through the written materials we'd been given, a female voice said with authority, "Excuse me." I looked up, rose, and nearly fell over as the striking woman in khaki pants, pink shirt, and light blue sweater squeezed between me and the seat in front. She put her things down on the seat next to mine. "Jill Mallory," she announced in a friendly tone and stuck out her hand. With short blonde hair, blue eyes, and an effervescent manner, she could have been a young Meg Ryan's twin.

A frog hopped in my throat, and I croaked, "S-h-a-n-k."

"Excuse me?"

Regaining my composure, I tried again. "My name is Henry David MacDuff, but everyone calls me 'Shank.' It's a long story involving golfing buddies and a dead cat." I could not keep my eyes off this woman, and she knew it.

"Are you OK?"

"Mostly, yeah. I'm sure guys fumble through their initial encounters with you all the time."

I could not believe that corny line came out of my mouth. Jill looked me straight in the eyes and said, "Actually, it does happen. I've just never had anyone admit so honestly that I knocked the ball loose."

What a great response! My heart raced. We enjoyed a little more small talk until the instructor began the session. At the first break, Jill got a cup of coffee, and I found a Mountain Dew in the wood-paneled cafeteria. Trainees milled about with laminated ID tags around their necks. I asked, "What did you do before?"

"I was a cop in Phoenix. And you?"

"I worked at a high-tech metals company in Orange County, California. It was a calculated next step toward the FBI."

"Where did you go to school?"

"Caltech."

"I want to be in *your* study group!" she exclaimed enthusiastically. "You don't look like a nerd. What are you really?"

What a funny, yet burrowing question. Smiling mischievously, I responded, "A surfer who ponders thermodynamic principles between sets."

That got her. Realizing I was only half joking, she touched my arm with exaggerated affection. "Just the man I've been looking for!" We both laughed and returned to the classroom, knowing there was already a great connection between us.

At the academy, all training and housing is co-ed, although there is no cross-gender sharing of rooms. Due to the nature of the program, males and females are in close proximity to each other throughout the training period. Even so, opportunities for romance are slim, since there is very little free time during the week. Nights are crammed with study sessions, research, test preparation, and exercise.

Weekends, on the other hand, are open. Onsite entertainment is understandably limited, so on the first Saturday night a bunch of us drove into Quantico proper. With 500 residents, the town has the distinction of being the only city in America surrounded by a military installation.

Quantico has a couple of restaurants, with a favorite being Sam's Inn. Located in a newer brick faced building, Sam's is predictably patriotic. The entry has photos of the owner with high-profile military officers and a glass case displaying historic American and Marine flags. The restaurant and bar are in one big open room, with locals typically hanging out together near the front.

We settled into a couple of large tables and ordered appetizers and beers all around. While we had talked in short bursts during that first week, this was the first time Jill and I really talked in depth. She looked delightful in a sleeveless V-neck purple dress, black leggings, and low black pumps. We were passably social within the group. But we increasingly found ourselves slipping into private conversation.

"Why did you become a cop?" I asked.

"Because a malignant boyfriend beat me up. I swore it would never happen again. Also, cuffing jerks like him might spare other potential victims."

We had already reached a very personal level. I wanted to know more. "What happened?"

Jill looked intrigued. "You don't mince words, do you? That's good; I like people who are direct. Well, up to that point, I had always been a trusting person and believed the best about people. My boyfriend had a mean streak, but it rarely surfaced. I made excuses for him, like he was tired or the argument was my fault. Should have seen it coming.

"One weekend when he was away partying with friends, I ended up going out with one of my former college professors. We had a nice evening and were kicking back listening to music at my apartment when the bully boyfriend came back early from his road trip. Ugly scene. As he was slugging the poor professor, I jumped on his back to stop the attack. His rage turned on me. He gave me a black eye and a bruised sternum, among other things, before he stormed out. We pressed charges, and a jury convicted him for the double assault. It turned my sheltered world upside down. Only by becoming a cop did I finally regain confidence."

How could anyone have hit this beautiful creature? I wanted to hold and protect her, even though the events she had just described occurred years ago. Was I falling for Jill after six days? This could get as messy as a car's glove box.

During the second week, all trainees were expected to complete a five-mile cross-country run. On this occasion, the instructors encouraged us to run diligently but not to max out, since we had a long day ahead. With those parameters, I simply decided to match Jill's pace the whole way. With some effort, she finished in the top third of the women. I cruised the distance, pressing only a little when she sprinted to the finish. We tied, but we both knew I had plenty of energy left.

Huffing significantly, Jill asked, "How many points *did* you score on the PFTs?" Jill was referring to the Physical Fitness Test, or PFT, which each applicant has to pass. It includes doing sit-ups for one minute, a 300-meter sprint, as many push-ups as you can, and a 1.5-mile run. There are male and female tables awarding points for each discipline.

"Does it matter?"

"It matters to *me*, Mr. Hardly Breathing!"

"OK, OK," I said good-naturedly. "In California, 36 of 40 points, and then 37 of 40 during week one here."

"You stud! Which area did you *choke on*?" Jill asked sarcastically as she started to recover from the exertion.

"The sprint," I answered. "Only made 7 points in California, and then improved to 8 here. Never developed those fast-twitch sprinter's muscles. Got all 10s on the sit-ups and push-ups, and 9s both times on the 1.5 run."

Jill was now stretching in cool-down and shaking her head. "Brains *and* brawn—that's a unique combo, MacDuff," she said, looking at me so flirtatiously that I had to turn away for fear of publicly melting.

A few times during training, instructors who were also musicians played a country music session in the common area. The distraction was welcome. On one such occasion, Jill and I were sitting close to each other, listening to the music, when she put her hand on mine. My heart skipped a beat. Jill was wearing a casual dress with stylish sandals. A delightful gold anklet added to the look.

Turning toward me, she asked, "If you could live anywhere in the world, where would it be?"

I thought for a minute and then said, "Near the ocean—otherwise I'd shrivel up like a raisin. Florida is too humid. Tahiti too far from reality. Hawaii would be fun, but isolated. The Pacific Northwest, East Coast, and most of Europe are too cold. France might have a chance, but too French. Australia maybe, but too down under. So that pretty much leaves California. Clearly, a boring choice since that's where I grew up and now live. But it has everything. High intensity, offset by beautiful sunsets over the ocean. You can literally disappear in places like Joshua Tree, a really cool rock-climbing mecca the size of Rhode Island. There's world-class skiing in Mammoth and Lake Tahoe, only a few hours drive from blast furnaces like Palm Springs and Death Valley. The Golden Gate Bridge, the Redwood Forest. Anywhere? California, without a doubt."

Jill was watching me closely now. She looked into my eyes and said, "I adore listening to you, Shank. I knew your answer to that simple question would be a sonnet." She kissed me softly. Our relationship was continuing to blossom, refined in the crucible of the academy.

The FBI spread out the extensive firearm training among eight outdoor firing ranges, an indoor range, and four skeet-shooting areas. Each student spends more than 100 hours firing 3,000 to 5,000 rounds of ammunition with pistols, shotguns, and even the bureau's submachine gun.

Before I graduated from Caltech, the only shooting experience I'd had was one summer at Indian Guide camp when Dad and I shot .22 rifles. They're only a step above BB guns, but to me they were cannons. I can recall the man who ran the rifle range advising me, "Don't *pull* the trigger; gently *squeeze* so the moment of firing is almost a surprise." Wanting to leave nothing to chance in my preparation for the FBI, I took a civilian pistol course, which provided me valuable initial exposure to handguns.

The first day on the pistol range, Jill's experience as a Phoenix cop showed. She adapted quickly to using the .40 caliber 22 Glock handgun, standard issue for an FBI special agent. When it was my turn, I thought back to the advice I'd gotten at camp and squeezed softly. Bulls-eye after bulls-eye was the result. Later, back near the dorms, Jill brushed me off with a chilly, "Not now, Shank." Her warmth returned later in the day, so I never did ask what was wrong.

More than halfway through the academy, we practiced for pistol qualifying. To succeed, a trainee must shoot 80 percent or better on two of three courses, as well as earn a cumulative score of 80 percent on all three qualifications. Jill showed her skill with scores of 90, 97, and 95, for a cumulative 94 percent. That day my rhythm was silky, and I scored 95, 100, and 99, for a cumulative 98 percent.

When the training session was over, I approached Jill to chat while we were walking back from the range. Since she was icy again, I asked, "Is something wrong?" She kept walking. I gently pulled her arm, and she spun around with fury.

"What?" she snapped.

I had never seen her mad before. *Careful, Shank, careful.* As her eyes blazed, I gently tried, "Whatever I've done, I'm sorry."

She railed, "What aren't you good at? I mean, really, name one thing."

I finally clued in. With a fraction of her firearms experience, I had beaten this professional cop on her turf. *Careful.* I said, "Loving without competing?"

Her eyes teared up, and she said softly, "It's tough, Shank. I've risen to the top, but it took a lot of effort. When I'm around you, I'll always be second best. Your hands were as steady as a surgeon's. One instructor commented that in a few more weeks, he'd have a tough time matching you. Shooting doesn't take strength where you have the advantage. Anyone can simply pull the trigger."

It flashed through my mind to offer the suggestion that she gently squeeze instead of pull the trigger. That thought quickly—and wisely—vanished.

She continued. "I do this for a living and have way more hours in training. It should favor me. I know you're not intentionally rubbing my face in it, but your superiority is simply a fact. Some of your buddies and classmates must have hated you for showing them up time and time again." She sighed. Her anger was dissipating, and she managed a little smile before turning from me. Jill walked away muttering, "It's frustrating."

I stood there stunned. The pain at having hurt her, even unintentionally, produced the most gut-wrenching guilt I had ever felt. Then like a ton of bricks it hit me—we were going to spend the rest of our lives together. Emotions that deep don't come without marriage love. Not puppy, sexual, or fleeting love, but *marriage* love. I'd work on Jill and smooth things over. In the meantime, I had to call my folks and craft a game plan.

A few weeks later, I asked her for a Saturday night date. We were going to take out a canoe and have a picnic on the academy's lake. I knocked at her dorm room, and Jill answered. She wore a flowered sundress cut low in the front and devastatingly low in the back. She spun and asked coyly, "Do you approve?"

"Absolutely. Jill, you look incredible!" I approached her with playful lust written all over my face.

"Slow down, Shank," she purred, half-heartedly fending off my kisses on her soft, exposed neck. "Let's at least have dinner before starting on dessert."

We walked down to the lake and found the canoe I had prepared tied to the dock. It was a lovely summer evening, and a breeze was now cooling the air. I helped her in and then launched the boat. As we made our way out onto the lake, she started to look into the picnic basket.

"Say, what do you think you're doing?"

"Come on, Shank, I'm starving."

"All right, but let me do it." I stopped paddling and unpacked Swedish red caviar, with small slices of toast and crème fraiche, serving the treat on real china plates that I found at a local antique store. Next, I opened a bottle of

Dom Pérignon champagne and poured it into two crystal goblets another trainee borrowed for us.

"What's the occasion?" Jill asked cautiously. Before I could answer, the faint sound of music came from around a point on the lake. As we turned toward the sound, a canoe came into sight with a guitarist, flutist, and oarsman. The two musicians played the theme song from *Phantom of the Opera*, Jill's favorite play. As they approached and it became clear that the show was for us, Jill simply looked at me adoringly and waited.

"The other day when you got so mad at me after pistol training, I knew. The guilt I felt at causing you pain was so agonizing, I knew. The first time you put your hand on my arm, right there," I said, pointing to the exact spot, "I now realize I knew. But the emotion was so new that I couldn't put it in context. Now I can."

I reached into the picnic basket and pulled out a small blue velvet box. Jill gasped quietly and began to cry as I opened it, revealing a sparkling diamond engagement ring. While it wasn't the smoothest of maneuvers in a canoe, I dropped onto my right knee and took her hand in mine.

"My heart is lost to all but you. I'm wonderfully, passionately, completely in love. I have to spend the rest of my life with you." Now with me in tears, I asked, "Jill Lynn Mallory, will you do me the highest honor of becoming my wife? Will you marry me?"

Jill didn't keep me in suspense long. She took the box as rivers of joyous tears flooded down her face. "Yes, Henry David Shank MacDuff, yes, yes, yes." She embraced me. The musicians in the boat, whom I hired from nearby Alexandria, finished the song and applauded. It was truly a magical moment.

By Monday, everybody knew our news, and just about everyone offered congratulations. Of course, the staff and many of the other trainees got into the spirit with a litany of wisecracks during classes and training exercises. Later that afternoon, they really set us up during a defensive tactics session focusing on grappling and control holds.

"Today," the instructor started with all seriousness, "we need to explore how a smaller woman would subdue a larger male subject. The importance of positional dominance cannot be underestimated. She will only achieve the goal of submission if she has superior physical positioning during the encounter. MacDuff, step forward." I could see what was coming as a few trainees chuckled. "Mallory, would you like to take a crack at him?" Many more trainees laughed.

Jill replied with a smile, "It would be my pleasure to make him submit to my positional dominance."

Peals of laughter followed. Given the unusual excitement, others had wandered over. Thus, the crowd was substantial as the instructor showed Jill how to twist, grab, and leverage my body. Finally, he declared, "Now for real. MacDuff, you cannot retreat but must stand your ground. Don't let her capture you. Mallory, you have no weapon and face a mortal threat. Subdue him."

It got quiet, and Jill moved toward me. This was clearly no game to her. My fiancée's eyes were steely. The frustration of feeling "second best" to me through much of the academy had come to a boil. She was going to subdue me or lose a few pretty teeth trying. I had three options. First, let her win. This was not palatable for several reasons, including the instructor's directions to resist her and Jill's outrage if she sensed I had let her win. Second, apply 80 percent effort, and then let her win. This had the advantage of outwardly satisfying the training directives and allowing Jill to feel as if she won. But it still felt uncomfortable. Third, I could do my absolute best. This had the obvious downside of minimizing Jill's chance of success. However, it had the advantage of playing it straight with a driven woman who would want nothing less. I chose to give it maximum effort and let the chips fall where they may. After all, someday with a real felon, this training might save her life.

We sparred back and forth for several minutes. She kept moving, but was clever enough not to make a false first attack. She was good. While I outweighed her and was stronger, she was quicker. In a real street fight with a smaller opponent, at some point I would try to seize the initiative. I did so here. When she moved backward after a probe, I pounced. We made contact. I turned Jill slightly then covered her back like a blanket. As my momentum and weight carried us forward, she collapsed under me and appeared to be finished.

Unbeknownst to me, Jill had an ace up her sleeve. After the jerk of a boyfriend had attacked her, she had taken classes in the martial art of kung fu, which of course had been popularized on TV by David Carradine way back in the 1970s. Carradine played a Chinese master who expressed the kung fu approach in this way: "A young tree bends in the wind, then snaps back with force." In other words, go with the aggressor's initial move and then react when he is vulnerable.

Jill used this strategy to perfection. As we started to topple and I relaxed at the prospect of certain victory, she jabbed me in the ribs with one of her sharp elbows and flipped me over. I was so surprised, and Jill so quick, that I couldn't recover. As we hit the ground, Jill used our collective momentum to roll me over. She grabbed my arm, and in a split second, I was face down. Jill had my arm halfway up in the middle of my back, and I was helpless. The crowd shouted for the winner, who perched on me like a hawk over its wounded prey.

While gently pressing my arm further into my shoulder blades, Jill bent low and whispered close into my ear, "I won fair and square, MacDuff, didn't I?"

"Yes, ma'am," I said, confirming what she already knew.

Before letting me go, Jill whispered in a sultry tone, "I'm *so* in love with you."

With that watershed behind us, and our FBI careers and life together ahead, the next few days we were on top of the world.

At the end of that memorable week, our second to last at the academy, we undertook our final situational training at Hogan's Alley, a mock small city with building facades reading Dogwood Inn Restaurant, Bank of Hogan, and All-Med Drugstore. Behind the facades are classrooms, storage, audiovisual facilities, and administrative offices. At Hogan's Alley, trainees are confronted with realistic tasks, like surveillance, and equally realistic crimes, like bank robberies.

Without any apparent ulterior motive, the instructors paired us together alphabetically for a simulated kidnapping. The criminals were paid actors, and the scenario included an "at-speed" ransom drop by our vehicle.

I was behind the wheel, with Jill riding shotgun. The kidnappers told us to drive quickly into town and throw the duffle bag containing the ransom at the entrance to the drugstore and then leave without slowing down. While this was only an exercise, the academy applied all its skill to make it as real as possible. For us, it was. As Jill double-checked the ransom bag, I asked, "You ready?"

"Just get me close enough to the store to throw this bundle, and I'll take care of the rest."

"My pleasure, soon-to-be Agent Mallory."

When the kidnapper ordered us by cell phone to drop the money, I accelerated. As we entered the town, everything looked peaceful; there were just a few bystanders here and there. At 30 mph, I smoothly drove past the store, and Jill tossed the bag to within a few feet of the front door.

"Great shot," I complimented her.

Continuing out of town, I ran over some real debris in the mock road. In what they later determined was a freak accident, the loose metal punctured the gas tank, and it started to leak. The fuel made the back right tire slip, and

I hit a corner of the Dogwood Inn, causing the tire to go flat. The result was a spin to the left and a disabled car. Adrenaline started pumping when we stopped sliding. Terror then struck as I saw fire following the spilled gasoline, heading straight toward us. As I unbuckled my seatbelt and opened the door, the car burst into flames. "Out!" I yelled. After running about thirty feet, I instinctively looked back to the left to make sure Jill was clear. She wasn't.

To this day, nobody knows what happened. The flames may have made her freeze, the seatbelt could have been stuck, or the door lock could have jammed. My legs buckled from stopping so suddenly. As I spun to the left, the car exploded. The gas in the tank had turned it into a lethal bomb. I watched in slow motion as my Jill literally blew up with the car. Our future life was over before it started. The Grim Reaper should have taken me too.

Several days later in the hospital, I heard voices. It was Mom saying, "He's coming out of it!" With terrible cottonmouth, I couldn't find a way to talk. As I tried to move, unrelenting pain raced through my body. *What the heck?* Then I remembered. All the horror flashed through my mind. I screamed, "JILL! NO!" Even though the explosion had ravaged my body, I thrashed in the bed in emotional agony. Several people had to hold me down as a doctor's tranquilizing needle plunged me back into darkness. They continued to sedate me, and the next week was a blur of drugs and nightmares.

At the time of the blast, I had been very low to the ground; the explosion had slammed me down and into a coma. Fortunately, most of the shrapnel, including broken glass, missed me. There were only a few pieces embedded in my shoulders and back. The more serious injuries were fractured ribs, a broken wrist, and a destroyed left eardrum. I was far enough away that the heat only singed my hair. Had I been standing upright or a few feet closer, the explosion would have slammed into my face.

The broken bones and most of the other physical injuries ultimately healed, but the medical team couldn't repair my shattered eardrum. I remain deaf on the left side. Was it my fault? After all, I was the one behind the wheel. I've tried a million times to see the debris we drove over, but I can't. Nobody blamed me. Even Jill's parents seemed to believe it was a divine tragedy. Living became difficult. With my already minimal sleep, the long, dark hours meant unbearable torture. I couldn't make it right, no matter how hard I tried. Nothing could bring Jill, and our wonderful life, back again.

I blinked, rubbing my useless left ear out of habit, and found myself back at Charlie's Chili. Even though Detective Baker was a veteran cop, you could tell the account had moved him. "I'm *so* sorry," was all he could muster.

Wow, I hadn't talked about this in a long time. During my recovery, the FBI had provided counseling. The professionals had all encouraged me to let it out. Realizing they were probably right, I gave it my best. Yet the psychological digging failed to uncover the root of whatever weed was choking my soul.

I could feel myself tearing up. The waitress came back with our check, though I don't consciously recall eating my meal. Embarrassed, I wiped my eyes and tried to maintain control. She looked at me sympathetically, wanting to say something, but decided to leave it alone.

Baker cleared his throat. "Well, that was really tasty food; fine choice," he said kindly.

I appreciated the effort to bring me back from the gruesome images that still haunt me. When it gets bad, I pull out a picture Jill gave me during our time at the academy. It's a headshot of her in a Phoenix police uniform. The photo is now dog-eared, but it helps me remember how she was before the explosion. Still, Jill's death so traumatized me that my deepest emotions went dormant. I wondered if they would ever reawaken.

CHAPTER 27

L ater that evening, it was time to get ready for the Clines' party. Above my black slacks and loafers, I donned a beige turtleneck with long sleeves to help hide my wounds. My swollen lip was looking better, but putting on a fresh bandage was all I could do about the cut on my nose.

Since the route from my place cuts diagonally across much of Orange County, the drive to Cary's place is a cumbersome tangle of streets, freeways, and tollways. The M3 cheerfully played jazz as we drove.

I was looking forward to the evening. Since I first started going to parties as a teenager, I've always experienced a sense of anticipation and excitement. Unlike many people, I was energized by multiple brief encounters with the other guests. Without really thinking about it, I would simply "work the room" the way politicians must.

I'd talk with this redhead for a few minutes, move to that blonde for a while, and tell a few stories to this brunette. I would try to dazzle each girl then move on. Most realized that I wasn't out for anything more than a good talk. This sequential blitz of conversations fired me up. Even though I was now going to a child's birthday party, the old anticipation was still there.

The Clines lived in Dove Canyon, a guard-gated enclave in the foothills of Saddleback Mountain, the county's highest peak at over 5,600 feet. The master-planned community is very nice and not too pretentious. After I spent time waiting behind a few cars at the entrance, the guard checked my identity against the authorized list, gave me a dashboard pass, and waved the M3 through. I glanced over at the Jack Nicklaus-designed golf course at the bottom of the first hill. The superb stonework on the clubhouse, one of my favorites locally, reflects a slate-master gone wild.

The Clines' two-storied Mediterranean-style home looked warm and inviting, especially with all the lights on for the party. Crystal, Cary's wife of a decade, greeted me at the door. In her early 30s with stylish light brown curls, her plump figure matched her embracing manner. She reminds me of the butter lady, TV cook Paula Deen. "Shank, it's good to see you," she greeted me with one of her warm hugs. Unfortunately, the move made me wince in pain. I tried to hide my reaction, but she stepped back and glanced quizzically at the bandage on my nose.

"An accident," I explained.

"Sorry to hear that. Cary is in the kitchen, and your biggest fan is running around somewhere. Enjoy yourself." Turning, she once again became a greeter for new guests.

The Mediterranean motif inside the Cline home matches the exterior, with dark taupe walls and purple accents. There are fresh flowers everywhere. Knowing the house well, I quickly found Cary. My favorite part of the well-equipped kitchen is a seaside mural painted onto a long row of white cabinets. Half a dozen people buzzed about in various stages of food preparation.

My boss was diligently pouring sodas for a couple of his daughter's friends. He looked tailored in black shoes, tan slacks, and a dark green sweater. "Shank, what happened to you?" he questioned, glancing at my face. As the kids scooted away, I motioned Cary into the adjacent formal dining room.

When we were alone, I said, "Somebody tried to run me over with a pickup truck. They nearly succeeded. Several police departments are now involved. Reily, the bookie, is the main suspect, and everyone, including me, thinks it ties in to the investigation of Buddy's death."

He looked at me soberly. "Thankfully, they missed. How badly are you injured?" I knew he was asking not only out of friendly concern but also professionally. He depended on me to lug his heavy bag around the course.

"A gash on my elbow is probably the worst. The rest is mostly bumps and bruises. I'll heal. Go ahead and tell Crystal, but wait until after the party. I don't want anybody to make a fuss." He agreed, and we discussed the details of the incident for a minute or two more.

Cary needed to play host again, so we went back to the kitchen where he poured me a Mountain Dew without even asking. He then helped Crystal's gray-haired mom with frozen pastry appetizers. Thankfully, only one of Cary's friends who knew me had read the newspaper article about the attack. He mentioned it, and I briefly described the incident, leaving things vague.

Later, I saw the same guy talking with a most intriguing woman about my age. As she spoke energetically, her silky black hair happily bounced about her shoulders. She evoked images of Audrey Hepburn. Her smooth skin provided the backdrop for striking eyes that danced with animation. Their vibrant color was unique, projecting the green of new spring leaves. They had a hypnotic way of inviting you into her world. Tasty lips framed a cute mouth. She wore a maroon halter dress, which highlighted her perky body in a suggestive yet classy way.

From what she was saying, bits and pieces of which I could catch without overtly eavesdropping, they both went to the Clines' church. As her dynamic dimples erupted during frequent smiles and laughter, I waited for the familiar tightness in my stomach. Since Jill's death, whenever I was confronted with a serious female contender, I felt uncomfortable. But this time there was no torment in my gut. Interesting, since clearly she was a woman of substance and natural beauty.

Observing my sorrow first-hand, Buddy had encouraged me to date. At one tournament, a golf groupie followed our foursome. She was pretty but ditzy. After Saturday's round, the girl asked me out. I gave her a polite brush-off, but she insisted on giving me her number. Buddy thought I needed female companionship.

"You don't get opportunities like that every day. Kind of like the coal jumping into the furnace—no work but all the fire."

"Got it," I responded without much enthusiasm.

"I'm tired of dancing around Jill's death with you," he said in a seldom-used tone that indicated he meant business. "She's gone. It was horrible, unimaginable. You took a brutal fall off the horse. But you got to dust off and get back in the saddle. Shank, you're the catch of a lifetime for some lucky woman. Smart, handsome, fun. Not every date leads to weddin' bells. Just go have a good time."

Taking Buddy's advice, I called her. We went out and had some fun. But it was so different from going out with women of consequence.

Returning to the present, I continued to drink in the intriguing woman. As I toyed with the idea of joining their conversation, a "Shank!" rang out. Cary's daughter, Rebecca, threw her arms around me. Normally, a greeting like that was a treat, because I really liked their daughter. However, this time I almost passed out. The pain eased as she let go. I bent down to get to her level. Rebecca looked as if she stepped out of a catalog. She wore shiny black Mary Jane shoes and a dress the color of newly baked lemon cookies.

"How does it feel to be eight, kiddo?"

"Great! Did you see Molly, the American Girl doll that Mommy and Daddy gave me? She lived during a world's second war, or something like that—you know, the Germanades?" While providing more scrambled details, Rebecca dutifully straightened Molly's braids and adjusted her wire-rim glasses. Admittedly, this was a cool 18-inch miniature person.

"Very nice, Rebecca. I'm sure she's happy now."

"You betcha," Rebecca squealed. She squeezed Molly and scampered off with a friend who was trying to keep up.

Before we ate, Crystal summoned us all into the kitchen so Cary could bless the food. Without fail, whenever Cary ate anything resembling a meal he would say a blessing. Sometimes he would pause before eating and say it silently. On other occasions, typically with other Christians present, he would pray aloud, even in public settings like a restaurant.

When the guests had gathered, with people peeking around corners from the dining and family rooms, Cary bowed his head and started. "Dear Lord, we thank you for bringing all of our friends and family here tonight to celebrate Rebecca's birthday. We praise you for our precious daughter and for how wonderfully she's growing up. Please bless this food and the hands that prepared it. Guide everyone safely home tonight. Amen."

I opened my eyes a bit right before the "Amen" and peeked at the others in the room. No one seemed put off by the prayer—I guess they were used to it, as I was—but still, there had to be a few guests who weren't prepared for this. Even though I've gotten accustomed to it, it still seemed a little weird to pray at a kid's birthday party.

After a scrumptious meal consisting entirely of appetizers, Rebecca attacked a pile of presents. Included in the stash was my gift—a Barbie detective computer game. It was more than mere coincidence that I bought a detective-themed gift.

Later, Cary and I talked for a few more minutes. "So how goes the overall investigation?"

"There's progress, but the pieces are all jumbled. For instance, there's this whole thing with Lenny Hayes and Buddy's mysterious past." After briefly relaying the discoveries I'd made in Dallas, I kept going. "It must tie in, but I'm uncertain how. And there appears to be a gambling undercurrent. Detective Baker thinks the attacks are happening because I've pushed someone's button hard enough that they felt compelled to act. The question is, which button?"

"Try it from a different perspective," Cary offered. "Forget about logic or proof. If you had to pick one person as the most likely culprit, based on gut feelings alone, who would it be?"

I thought about this for a moment, running through the names of people uncovered so far. "It would be Milton Reily the bookie, with Nick Slate a close second. Of course, Reily is the only one who has threatened me."

"I understand how Reily was connected to Buddy, but what about Slate?"

"Good question. I have no idea. Slate can't remember Buddy's name. I wonder if—"

Just then, Crystal appeared. "I'm sorry to interrupt, gentlemen, but Cary, several people are leaving, and you really ought to say goodbye."

It was also time for me to bail, so I followed them to the door. Seeing Rebecca on the way, I wished her happy birthday one more time. She sped away, chasing some little boy who was laughing hysterically. I waited for Crystal to say goodbye to a couple in front of me and then gave her a gentle hug.

"Thanks. This was a lot of fun, and I really enjoyed the appetizer meal. Neat idea."

"Why of course, Shank. You don't come over often enough. I know your parents are in the desert now, so whenever you feel like a good home-cooked meal, let us know, and we'll put something together."

As Crystal turned to the remaining guests, I found Cary and shook his hand. "Thanks, man, this was a good time."

"You heal quickly now, and watch out. I cherish the friendship and need you on my bag. We'll be praying that God provides you with the wisdom of Solomon." Sensing that I did not really know the story, he elaborated. "Solomon was a Jewish king who prayed for wisdom. There's a story in the Bible about two women who each claimed to be the mother of a particular baby, and Solomon was called on to settle their dispute. Well, he figured the *real* mother would protect her child, so his guard brought a sword to divide the baby, to absurdly provide each woman half. One of the women cried out and gave up her claim in order to save the child's life. Solomon wisely determined that she was the real mother and awarded the baby to her."

"Fair enough," I said leaving. Walking to the M3, I thought about reading the whole story of Solomon. But, I didn't even own a Bible.

CHAPTER 28

On the following morning, I stood stretching at the front window after annotating the "Find My Killer, Shank" file during my dark hours. It was amazing how much better my body felt. My overall fitness had helped the recovery process. A glorious morning drenched the coastline with sun. Nature's grandeur lifted my spirits. Although a northwest swell looked promising, my frame needed several more days to recuperate before absorbing the pounding of waves.

I walked to Mutt Lynch's for breakfast in hopes of running into Cristanos. Sure enough, he was finishing a breakfast burrito—a flour tortilla wrapped around three scrambled eggs, cream cheese, and bacon, topped with Mexican red sauce. As usual, Cristanos had ordered a custom dose of jalapeño peppers on top.

"How can you eat those things?" I asked, gesturing at the little green infernos.

"Helps clean me out," he said, pointing toward his stomach.

Sitting down in the booth, I ordered the Surf Benedict—a toasted English muffin with fresh salmon, poached eggs, and cilantro lime hollandaise sauce. After briefly discussing the encouraging swell, I asked, "Were you serious the other day about helping with the investigation into Buddy's death?"

"I your man," he said, grinning broadly. "Who should I punch on?" he added while flexing his small but tight muscles.

"No, it's nothing like that. I need information that you are simply better suited to uncover. You speak Spanish, right?" He had talked with many Latinos when we were together, but I wasn't sure if he was truly speaking Spanish or a butchered version of his native Portuguese.

"Si," he said. "Uncle Juan from Mexico."

"Good. I need you to go down to Torrey Pines and talk with the Spanish-speaking maids, janitors, and maintenance crews."

He looked confused. "Maids in golf?"

"Sorry, I'm not being clear. Your effort would be at both the golf course and the Lodge, the nice hotel next-door. You may be able to get facts that those workers simply will not give me. I don't speak their language, and even if I could fake it, they might clam up to a gringo." My friend looked confused. I emphasized the "clam up" point by closing two hands together tightly. He nodded. "We need anything they know from the tournament weekend that might shed light on Buddy's murder."

Cristanos shrugged in acceptance. "OK, you drive?" He did not have a car.

Do I dare lend this rogue sidekick my ride? Tagging along might cramp his style. Cristanos needed room to work the witnesses his own way. "Can you drive a stick shift?"

"No worries."

He *was* doing me a favor. The least I could do was trust him for a day. "As long as you park away from other cars, you can take the M3."

He jolted in jest, pretending he was having a heart attack. "No joke? You trust Cristanos?" he exclaimed, pointing both thumbs at himself in disbelief.

"At least this time. Especially because of *why* you're going down there. We're both part of Linda's team. It's work, not a joy ride."

Over coffee, I updated him on my progress and outlined the type of questions he might pose. He appeared to understand.

"What excuse me give for snoop-dogging?"

"Be honest. Tell them you're helping the widow of the murdered caddy. Be sad when you say it. Besides, you are *so* charming I'm sure they will tell you everything—especially the señoritas." Cristanos nodded in naughty agreement. "You also might want to look a little less—surfer," I added gently.

"Why?" He looked confused and a bit offended.

"This place is *really* nice, and you'll want to blend in to the greatest extent possible. We won't get much information if security instantly harasses you. I suggest a shower, jeans, and the nicest shirt you have."

"Can I still wear sandals?" he pleaded in desperation.

Instead of asking if he even owned another type of shoes, I let him keep that last vestige of his clothing-related identity. "No problem. Sandals are *always* looking good."

As he drove off an hour later looking surprisingly good, I suddenly wondered if he had a driver's license. Going back inside, I called him. After two or three rings, he finally picked up.

"Cristanos, it's Shank. I forgot to ask—do you have a driver's license?"

"No. Why?"

"Because you need one to legally drive in this country!" I almost asked him to return, but I slowly chilled. *Take a deep breath.* "You'd better watch yourself. The cops will send you back to South America if they catch you driving without a license. Understand?"

"Stay under 100. I understands." I could just see his childlike smile as he yanked my chain.

"That'll do fine, Cristanos," I said sarcastically. He was laughing as I hung up. Did my insurance cover the car if someone else was driving? *Stop worrying—trust him, trust him.*

I now consider Cristanos a genuine and loyal friend, but our relationship was born from betrayal. One summer evening a couple of years ago, I hosted a "sushi and suds" party. The gathering was starting to rock when in walked Sage with the newly arrived Cristanos. "Shank, I'd like you to meet the cutest little Brazilian," she said, showing him off like a puppy. "His English is spotty, but not all international relations need perfect translations," Sage added with a wink.

"Welcome. Have a beer and try the fish." A blank look greeted my offer. I pretended to eat a piece of food and chug a mug. He then understood and smiled infectiously.

The next day while I was cleaning up, I noticed that my Waterford paperweight was missing. Shortly before her death, my grandmother gave me the cut crystal as a college graduation present. Figuring someone had knocked it off during the previous night's festivities, I looked for it everywhere. No dice. The painful conclusion was inescapable—one of my guests had ripped me off. There was no way to determine who, especially since my memory of the later hours was fuzzy.

Over the next few days and weeks, I vented my frustration. One afternoon over pizza with Sage and Cristanos, I told them what happened and griped, "Can you believe some scum eats my sushi, drinks my beer, and then robs me?"

"Outrageous!" Sage protested. "She ought to have her little hands cut off."

"What makes you think it's a woman?"

"Be serious. Only a chick wants Waterford crystal."

"Maybe. But what gets me is the lost link to my grandmother. Nobody can replace that. Even if she can shop up there"—I looked up—"UPS can't pick it up for delivery." Sage giggled at my attempt at humor. A silent Cristanos nodded in agreement.

Time passed, and the incident was mostly forgotten. Cristanos and I became surfing buddies and beachside friends. Months later, he came knocking at my door. "We talk?" he asked sheepishly.

"Sure, man. Come on in."

Cristanos appeared uncharacteristically nervous as he started. "In Brazil, people take. Little here, little there. So, I'm the scums who stole your glass weight," he admitted, nearly in tears. "No excuse. Call me thief."

The admission shocked me. "I thought we were friends."

"Now, yes. On first night, you just richer than Cristanos. Someone to steal from. After became friends, I feel bad. Real bad. So, I tries get glass back. Remember cut below ear?" he asked, pointing to a spot on his neck.

"Yeah," I affirmed, recalling the nasty gash. "But you said it was a surfing injury."

"I lie. From fight with tattoo guy who buy fancy glass from Cristanos." With the first flicker of pride, he quipped, "I won—he told where glass was. I went. Big house Laguna Beach. Many nights, I take bus down coast and watch house. Finally, guy's old girlfriend leaves with friends. I picked door and go in. Many rich things. But Cristanos not take anything!" he exclaimed, pounding a fist against his leg for emphasis. "I only look for Shank's glass. Nowhere. So I sit in dark and wait."

My pulse quickened as I could imagine all sorts of bad endings to this story.

"Very late, friends drop off rich girl. She drunk. Opens door, turns on light, see me. Screams loud! I stay still and say, 'Cristanos not hurt you, only want heavy glass guy give you.' I held out money. 'Please. Want to buy back. Stole from man now my friend. I sell to guy he give to you.' I looked with sad doggie eyes. Girl believe me and stop shaking. Too crazy for lie. She say, 'I don't have any more. Guy bad news. I gave to army.'"

"To army?" I interrupted.

"Army charity," he replied.

"Salvation Army?"

"That the one. Nothing else can do. Tell girl 'OK' and thumb ride home."

With an angry edge to my voice I asked, "Is this bizarre story true?"

He put his one hand over his heart and the other one up in the air as if giving an oath. He teared up and said, "I sorry, so sorry."

I believed him. His honest show of emotion drained my remaining anger. "Fine," I almost whispered. "At least you tried to get it back."

The elf-like Cristanos then quickly returned. With a huge grin, he handed me something heavy in a souvenir bag from a local shop. I opened the peace offering with a genuine smile. After all, although he had made a mistake, he had worked hard to fix it. To my surprise, a nude surfer girl shooting the curl greeted me.

"Better fancy glass!" Cristanos beamed.

Trying to act impressed, all I could do was laugh inside. The thing reminded me of the tacky leg lamp from the movie *A Christmas Story*. I regret losing Granny's gift, but Cristanos's absurd surfing vamp has been the pride of my apartment ever since.

CHAPTER 29

After sending Cristanos to Torrey Pines, I did some chores and added a few items to the "Desert Properties" grocery list mounted on the fridge. The last time I was out at my parents' place near Palm Springs, I complimented Mom on the grocery list that hung by magnets on their refrigerator. Finding out that her only son did not have one, she went into action. Mom started with a Realtor's giveaway notepad and slapped magnetic tape on the back. She then took some string, and in one of the messiest operations I have ever seen, glued it to the top of the pad. While it looked like a joke, it dried clear and worked fine. The string hung down on one side, and I tied a pencil to it. Mom had made me a refrigerator notepad that cost virtually nothing.

My parents lived in San Clemente for three decades. When Dad semi-retired, they sold the family home and bought a place two hours inland in the desert. Phone calls were thus more frequent than visits. We have always been close, and I call them at least once a week, even when I'm on the road. I dialed and waited to hear a familiar voice on the other end.

"Hello?"

"Mom, it's me."

"Henry David, how are you, darling?" She is the only person who uses my full given name. My sisters and Dad embraced "Shank" before I made it out of high school.

"Where's Dad?"

"What am I, chopped liver?" she replied.

"Of course not. I wanted to pick his brain." When I called them the week before from Florida, Linda's project was merely a footnote to the conversation. Now that everything was more serious, I wanted Dad's input.

"He's down at a dealership on Highway 111 looking at those fancy golf carts. The silly things look like safari Jeeps or fire engines, and gosh only knows what else."

"He isn't really going to buy one of those?"

"Sure looks like it. A friend out here got one that looks like a mini military vehicle. Your father wants one now." Sounded like Dad, the king of gadgets.

"How are *you* doing?" I asked directly to avoid a further chopped liver comment.

"Very well. I'm taking tennis lessons. Can you believe that?" It was actually hard to imagine. Although she was thin, my mother was a non-athlete. She seemed to enjoy watching the kids do sports. But her? Forget it.

"Wow, Mom, that's pretty risky."

"Risky?" she said, with perfect timing.

"Yeah, you might actually break a sweat!"

"You're terrible. All kidding aside, I'm full steam ahead. My instructor, the Baron, says he's never seen such progress in a mature woman before."

"The Baron?"

"Why, yes, he's from a prestigious German family that still owns a castle and vineyards."

"Does Dad know you're taking lessons from *the Baron*?"

"Of course, silly. You aren't suggesting he would be jealous. What a funny thought." I could hear commotion on her end. "Well, speak of the devil. It's your son." I could feel her point to the phone. "Lovely speaking with you, sweetheart. Maybe we can talk longer next time. Hugs and kisses. Here's your father."

"Shank?"

"Yeah, Dad, it's me. Did you buy a custom golf cart?"

"Oh, so Mom spilled the beans, huh? Well, not yet, but I'm close. It's between a safari Jeep and a Lakers basketball. What do you think?"

"You mean a golf cart with all sorts of Lakers stickers and stuff?"

"No, it actually looks like the top half of a basketball. It has 'Lakers' printed on it several times for sure. However, it's definitely a big ball."

At that point trying to tell him that it sounded ridiculous was a waste of breath. "I'd go for the basketball and really wow your friends."

"That's kind of what I'm thinking. So what's up with you?" He redirected the conversation.

"It's a long story. Linda's project has turned ugly, and I could use your advice. There are some twists. We'll need a good hour. Mom won't be happy with all of it. So how about a one-on-one, and then you can fill her in as you see fit?"

"When and where?" No questions asked, just action. I love my father.

"How about halfway between us? Lunch tomorrow, say noon, at the Mission Inn in Riverside?"

"You got it."

I was about to change topics when Mom's agitated voice filled the background. Dad said something back with his hand over the phone then returned to me. "Sorry, son, I've got to go. Mom caught her dress in the dishwasher. I can't imagine how, but it looks like the Jaws of Life might be required," he said, referring to the huge tool that's used to rescue people from crushed vehicles. He hung up, saying calmly, "Yes, yes, I'll get the tool box..."

How long would either of them last once the other one died? They were such partners, even in the little things. As I sat for a minute meditating on this, I realized what a contrast their relationship was to the Franks'. On the gambling issue, Buddy's separate account ensured that he completely cut Linda out of that aspect of his life. Wondering if Linda ever gained access to the secret account, I called her.

"Good morning," she answered cheerfully on the third ring.

"Linda, it's Shank. How are you doing?"

When she recognized my voice, her tone changed. "Not good. The district attorney is going to officially charge me with Buddy's murder." Her tears started flowing as if on cue. "Shank, what am I going to do? The kids! What will happen to them? How will—"

"Linda, slow down. We're a long way from anything permanent. There is a little thing called a trial and the concept of innocent-until-proven-guilty. Let's take a step back. Who told you?"

"My lawyer. He has a friend in the D.A.'s office who told him."

What is the deal with her lawyer? I'm dodging potentially lethal attacks, and where is he? Is his absence because he charges several hundred dollars an hour? That is actually a good reason. Linda is no fool. I regrouped. "Has something changed? I mean, things were quiet for the last few weeks."

"Apparently, the district attorney is feeling pressure to charge someone. And once he files, it's a fight to the death."

"Who said that?"

"I asked the same thing, but my lawyer doesn't know. That's all his friend would say. What should I do?"

"Nothing, absolutely nothing. Remember, you've got me. It's possible the D.A. is running on empty and getting desperate. He could have fed misinformation to your lawyer's friend, knowing the attorney would pass it on. He may be hoping you'll get nervous, do something stupid, and incriminate yourself."

After a long pause, Linda responded, "Shank, I never thought of it that way. Oh, wouldn't that be wonderful?"

"Yeah, but it's pure speculation on my part. Please don't do anything rash or unusual. We're making progress, but there's nothing clear-cut yet. By the way, the reason I called was to see if you ever got access to Buddy's gambling account."

"They finally gave me clearance. The account didn't have much in it."

"How much had Buddy deposited over the last few months?"

"I looked at that. Going back half a year, it wasn't *that* much." She sounded disgusted.

"So, while it was real money, the amounts weren't earth-shaking?"

"That's fair." After a pause, she added, "Shank, please figure this out. I'm starting to suffocate."

"I'm trying. Please be patient." If the latest news was simply a ruse by the D.A., then Linda was home free. If not, the noose was tightening.

She waited a moment and then said, "Can you take me to dinner and a movie this weekend? I need a change of routine. My life has been a real grind since that horrible Sunday."

Did she just solicit me for a date? Trying to be objective, I acknowledged to myself that all the family responsibilities were now on Linda's shoulders. There had to be major hassles that come with wrapping up the affairs of a deceased husband. In addition, hundreds of little daily things must remind her of Buddy. A temporary escape, even for a few hours, would probably do wonders. Yet taking out this new widow was *very* awkward. Predicting her behavior was becoming as random as trying to figure out which kernel of popcorn will pop first.

"Sure," I replied tentatively.

"Wonderful. You're so sweet, Shank. How can I *ever* thank you?"

After we finished the call, I continued to hear the unmistakable emphasis in Linda's last sentence. Where was this all heading?

CHAPTER 30

The gambling aspect of this whole situation was really never on the surface, but was certainly an undercurrent near the murky bottom. Having an entire day free waiting for Cristanos, I decided to explore this angle further. But in what direction? Clearly, I was not going near Milton Reily again. What about Slate? For him, the only avenue that came to mind was Del Mar Race Track. Slate told me he worked there before becoming involved with the Torrey Pines Classic. While it might end up being nothing more than a pleasant field trip, I decided to poke around the track.

I was not a horse person. Thus it was only through Internet research that I discovered Del Mar's racing season is limited to a seven-week summer "meeting" that ends on Labor Day weekend in September. While I was disappointed that I could not go to a race, there had to be someone minding the store during the off-season who might answer a few questions. Small logistical problem—Cristanos had the M3! Imitating Winnie the Pooh, I tapped my temple—*think, think, think.* The silly gesture seemed to work. Researching "Amtrak" yielded a game plan. I would start with a fifteen-minute taxi ride to the Irvine station, followed by a one-hour train trip to Solana Beach, and finish with another taxi to Del Mar. Sounded kind of fun.

Amtrak's Pacific Surfliner, painted in distinctive blue and silver, runs from San Luis Obispo, several hours north of Los Angeles, to San Diego near the Mexican border. Sitting in an upper deck seat comparable to that on an airplane, I gazed out the window as the ocean whizzed by on my right. In Orange County, the train's route stays inland until San Juan Capistrano, where it then hugs the coast for fifty miles in San Diego County until past Del Mar. This portion of the trip gives the Surfliner its name and glory. Getting off at Solana Beach, I approached a waiting taxi. Had it been racing season, there would have been free double-decker buses waiting.

"Where to?" the friendly Asian driver inquired.

"The race track."

"You know the horses don't run until mid-July?"

"Yeah, thanks. I've got other business." Many times during the day's journey, I checked for someone tailing me. Without the M3, I felt vulnerable. There was nobody I could see. Approaching our destination, I asked, "Could you come back and pick me up? I'll make it worth your while." We arranged a time. I figured it was less likely that this driver, who had picked me up at random, would be under Reily or anyone else's influence. Of course, if the price was right, he might sell his sister.

Del Mar Race Track is a thoroughbred horse racing complex that overlooks the Pacific. Designed in a Spanish Mission style, the facility epitomizes the laid-back California attitude.

Famous singer Bing Crosby and a few of his Hollywood cronies built the track as a summer escape. Entertainment icons, including W.C. Fields, Betty Grable, and later TV stars Lucille Ball and Desi Arnaz, were among those who frequented the adult playground. Tapping into its Hollywood connection, Del Mar employed the world's first photo-finish camera during its inaugural season in 1937.

Two publicity moves during the track's second season further made Del Mar famous. First, Crosby created a brilliant marketing ditty that he sang with class and style: "*Where the turf meets the surf down at old Del Mar, take a plane, take a train, take a car. There is a smile on every face, and a winner in each race, where the turf meets the surf at Del Mar.*" The tune instantly became the track's theme song and has been played several times each racing day for seven decades. Second, Del Mar hosted the historic winner-take-all match race between domestic and international heavyweights Seabiscuit and Ligaroti. At least 20,000 fans flocked to the track for the event. Crosby, who owned a piece of Ligaroti, broadcast the race coast-to-coast on radio. After a thrilling battle, where the lead changed multiple times, America's hero, "The Biscuit," won by a nose.

The taxi driver turned off Jimmy Durante Boulevard and let me off at the racing office. At the impressive entrance, there is a collage of paintings depicting winners of Del Mar's signature race adjacent to a large antique scale for weighing the jockeys. As I stood taking it all in, a woman walked past. She stopped and politely asked, "May I help you?"

"Actually you can. A research project leads me here, and—"

Before I could continue, she jumped in. "Oh, wonderful, you'll want to talk to the director of operations. Right in there," she said pointing to the office as she went the other way.

Thinking the encounter strange, I nevertheless followed her directions. Through the office doors, a middle-aged receptionist was bent over, fiddling with her computer. When she sat up and saw me patiently standing there, the woman yelped in surprise. She was dressed to impress in a flirtatious way, but it did not work; everything about her was overdone as she tried too hard to retain her fading youth. The receptionist put a hand over her chest. "You gave me a heart attack; I didn't hear you come in."

"I'm sorry. My sisters used to complain about the same thing."

"Are you looking for someone?" she asked, irritated.

"I'm doing research and came here today to talk with—"

"I'll buzz Jerry right away," she abruptly warded off any further discussion.

What is the deal with these people? Soon a pleasant-looking Latino man who appeared to be in his 50s entered the room. He wore a tailored suit and nice wing-tipped shoes. With a broad smile, he bounded toward, me extending his hand.

"Jerry Diaz, so pleased you came. We were unsure if SI was really going to come through."

Shaking his hand, I said in confusion, "SI?"

He pulled back. "You are from *Sports Illustrated*, right?"

"Sorry, no. My name is Shank MacDuff. A research project brought me here but I'm not with any magazine."

"What type of research?"

Finally able to tell these people my mission, I said, "I'm looking into the death of Buddy Franks at Torrey Pines—he was a professional golf caddy—and I need background information on Nick Slate."

Diaz's expression changed dramatically as the curious receptionist listened with interest. Without another word, he turned and motioned me to follow. Once inside his office, Diaz closed the door and offered me a seat. He walked behind the desk and fell back into a well-worn brown chair. "Now, please explain what this is all about."

Wanting to gain his trust but feeling some discretion was in order, I took a middle-of-the-road approach. "I'm a professional golf caddy myself, and Buddy's widow asked me to help. Do you know about the murder at Torrey Pines?"

He affirmed by a stoic nod.

"I've interviewed Slate, and he mentioned working here before moving into golf and the exotic adventure business. What I'm after is any background on Slate that might help. While it's unlikely he was involved, there are loose threads that seem to weave back toward him."

Diaz considered the request carefully. "Will Slate know we've talked?"

Sensing that he was leaning in my direction, I tried to be encouraging. "Not from me, that's for sure."

Diaz looked at me with a solemn face. Deciding to play ball, he opened up. "Slate worked in promotions but always wanted to be transferred to the paymaster's office, which handles the betting. When track management denied his requests, he took it personally and quit. Never liked the man. He was too slick and even a bit scary. Putting him in with the money would have been letting the coyote watch the herd. You know, like that cartoon with Wile E. Coyote in the zippered sheep outfit?"

At least we now had common ground. I said, "Technically, Wile E. Coyote was in the Road Runner cartoons. He was later renamed Ralph Wolf in the cartoon you're referencing. Sam Sheepdog guarded the flock, and Ralph's job was to try and steal lambs. They both punched time clocks. Absurd, right?"

He smiled a real lip cracker and threw his head back roaring. "You know your Looney Tunes! I watched those with my kids many a Saturday morning."

"Bugs Bunny and his pals are the best," I heartily agreed. Realizing this likable man was an ally, my questions bore deeper. "When Slate was here, did he bet a lot on the horses himself?"

"Not on the ponies. He wasn't here long enough. Quit right before the season."

The answer led to a natural follow-up. "Did he bet on something else?"

"Name it. He was like a one-man advertisement for Gamblers Anonymous. The guy could barely work during March Madness since the NCAA basketball tournament made him crazy."

"How did Slate make his bets?"

"Some bookie."

"From Las Vegas?"

"No idea."

"Do you recall the bookie's name?"

"Nope."

"Have you seen Slate since he left?"

"Oh yeah, he's a regular. Flashy high roller now. Belongs to the private Turf Club up on the fourth floor. Hangs out and acts superior. He takes every opportunity to look down his nose at us track staff."

"Any special women?"

Diaz nodded. "Slate thinks of himself as a real Casanova. During his working stint at the track, he dated several of the girls. Now, he's always got some new bimbo hanging on his arm."

"Ever heard of a guy by the name of Milton Reily?"

"I knew a Horton Reily once. Owned a few Del Mar winners. But a Milton—no, sorry."

"You described Slate as 'scary.' Why?"

"Nothing firm. Simply don't trust the slickster. Wouldn't turn my back on him, especially if there was money around."

"I'll remember that."

The phone rang, and Diaz answered. "Si, si. Are you kidding? Didn't your people fix that last week? Uno momento," he said with obvious frustration, holding his hand over the receiver. "Unfortunately, my friend, I've got to handle this."

"Can someone give me a brief tour?"

"Sure, have our receptionist call marketing. Tell her I said so."

As he went back to the phone, I mouthed "thanks" and left him starting to argue in Spanish.

Back out front, the abrasive receptionist called marketing. Soon an older gentleman arrived.

"You'd like a tour?"

"Yes, sir. That would be great. It's my first time here." We left with the receptionist giving me the evil eye. "What's with her?" I asked when we were outside.

"Oh, she's been here a while and thinks she owns the place." The gentleman showed me areas of interest starting with the paddock, where the horses are assembled, saddled, and paraded before each race. Next, we saw the stables at the north end of the track, where the horses are fed and groomed. Eventually we made our way up to the Seabiscuit Skyroom Patio, on the west side of the main grandstands. This must be the highlight of every tour. On one side, we had a splendid view of the track, with its lakes in the center. In the other direction, the Pacific relentlessly rolled in.

The man was all marketing in describing Del Mar's history, including a few modern highlights: "In 1970, we lucked out to have famed jockey Bill Shoemaker ride to his 6,033rd career victory here, surpassing John Longden as the winningest rider of all time."

My mind wandered. Slate was a true gambler—interesting. With a little more work, that undercurrent might turn into a riptide.

My guide continued: "In 1989, Del Mar started an impressive run of years as the nation's number-one horse racing venue, both in terms of daily attendance and bets handled. In 1995, a suicidal man shocked everyone when he ran into the field of oncoming horses. Amazingly, no people or horses were hurt. In—"

Interrupting him, I asked, "Are there records of who attends races?"

"Sort of. There's no sign-in sheet or anything like that. However, for advanced sales of reserved seats, there would be detailed records. Obviously, for regular admission tickets, which never sell out and can be purchased at the gate, there are only total sales data."

"How about guests to the private Turf Club?"

"Members' attendance? Probably."

"Their guests?"

"I don't believe so, since the member simply pays for the guests and they're in."

Linda said Reily was in California every summer for the horse racing at Del Mar. He confirmed that fact by stating he had not been to California since the ponies at Del Mar last summer. Did Slate and Reily hook up annually at the races? Could Reily be Slate's bookie also? Apparently, there was no way to reverse engineer the answer from the track's records, even if the police or I could somehow get hold of them.

As my guide finished the track history, I soaked in the scene from a majestic vantage point. While there were no thundering thoroughbreds or deafening crowds, I could almost hear crooner Bing Crosby's melodic voice singing, "Where the turf meets the surf down at old Del Mar…"

CHAPTER 31

After a peaceful trip back to Orange County, I was home by late afternoon. There had been no word from Cristanos. Hopefully he was diligently hunting information. But "diligent" and "Cristanos" created an oxymoron. Call him lovable, playful, crazy—but diligent?

His Latino targets were an important yet often invisible part of Southern California's work force. Many people higher on the socio-economic ladder tended to ignore them because of their lowly jobs and limited English. A majority are illegals. Police or other authoritative gringos pose the threat of a quick trip back to Mexico or other parts of Latin America. They often simply hide behind the language barrier and say nothing. That's why I hoped Cristanos could find a few nuggets as a Spanish-speaking peer.

For dinner, I made "skillet surprise," a flexible feast that uses creativity and handy ingredients. On this night, the meat was leftover rib-eye steak that I cut into cubes. The sauce was whipping cream and sherry, with a touch of honey for sweetness. Lacking anything fresh, I used a can of diced Ortega chilies and a sprinkling of French's fried onions as the vegetable component. After adding spices and salt, I set it on the stove to cook over a slow heat. When it was ready, I poured the concoction on top of a bed of Fritos. Maybe not a recipe chefs would teach at *Le Cordon Bleu*, but tasty nonetheless.

After the satisfying meal, I again opened the "Find My Killer, Shank" file. I thought about adding a "Now" to the end of the file name but passed on the motivational gimmick. However, the pressure was increasing. The possible action against Linda had turned up the heat. Once I added to the sections for gambling and Slate, the document was now significant in length. Wanting an overview, I read the entire mountain of information and insights. The summit was near. "Buddy, we're close, really close," I said aloud.

Unable to reach Cristanos all day, I changed into my volleyball shorts and a "Got Milk?" T-shirt. As I crawled into bed, the lack of communication with my pal made me uneasy. Let me clarify—I was afraid something had happened to the M3, not to the ever-resourceful Brazilian.

When the phone rang the next morning, I quickly picked up. "Shanks, it's Cristanos. You buy me big breakfast at Mutt Lynch's?"

"Sure, sure," I responded. "My car?"

"You nervous?" he questioned with an elf-like tone. "Not really trust Cristanos?"

"I do, I mean did, you know but—"

"The beauty beast fine. We eat, and I tell all. Fifteen minutes?"

After agreeing, I showered, dressed in jeans, and headed over to Mutt Lynch's. Cristanos sat with a coffee in front of him and my keys on the table. "I order, you pay?" he confirmed our deal.

"That's fine. Where's the M3?"

"In Shank's garage, safe and happy. I get home late. Your lights out, so I use garage remote and park."

I had slept right through it. Not surprising, however. I have grown immune to noisy people late at night in the pier district. A pierced young waitress arrived, and I pointed at Cristanos. "Whatever he wants, it's on me."

My companion took great pleasure in ordering a large glass of orange juice and the No Faces specialty omelet—three eggs filled with mushrooms and other goodies, including a custom dose of jalapeños, and topped with melted Sonoma Jack cheese and avocado. Enjoying himself, he also ordered a side of Mad Mike's Sausage.

"So tell me, what did you find?" I asked.

He shook his head from side to side wearily. "Long day. Señorita maid tell Cristanos how Buddy no sleep in bed Saturday night. She cleaned room Sunday like normal, but bed no sleep."

I had to absorb this tidbit. The police would not necessarily have caught it, because by the time they saw the murder scene on Sunday evening, it was well after the maid's normal service. Was Buddy so nervous about the potential big paycheck that he could not sleep? Nah. He was a seasoned veteran. Buddy would not have stayed up all night because of nerves. So what did he do, or where did he go, the night before he died?

"Very interesting," I said to Cristanos. "Good job. Anything else?"

"Buddy's golfer, Tinnly?"

"Tinny Wilcox?"

"Yeah him. The guy pass out on floor of manager's office after Buddy found dead."

"OK. A lot of sources confirmed that Tinny took the news hard. Anything more?"

"Cemetery janitor saw—"

"Wait," I stopped him. Cemetery? This was kind of like talking to Sage. "Oh, do you mean a janitor that works the graveyard shift—all night?"

Cristanos nodded yes, as if he could not understand why I had stopped him. "The janitor saw tournament big man Slage or Slight in golf shop late Friday, maybe three in the morning, alone with a bucket from janitor room. Very strange."

"Could that be Slate, Nick Slate?"

He shrugged his shoulders. "Tournament big man?"

"Yeah, he's the man in charge."

"That him I guess."

Did that mean anything? At first, I doubted it. The tournament director was probably always around during the event weekend. Although being around in the dead of night did seem extreme. Moreover, what was the reference to a bucket?

"Did you ask what he was doing with the bucket?"

"Playing balls."

"What?"

"Janitor said, 'Playing balls.' He know no more. Said ask tournament big man himself." Breakfast arrived, and Cristanos dug in with abandon.

What did "playing balls" mean? Surely, something was getting lost in the translation. The more I thought about it, the more curious I became. After working the Classic all Friday and knowing Saturday was huge, Slate would have been a fool, or a low-sleep specimen like me, to spend precious hours playing with anything in the middle of the night.

When Cristanos finished breakfast, the South American groaned in delight to exaggerate how full he was. Then he spent a half hour more over coffee telling me gossip and other little things. He told several risqué tales he'd heard at the Lodge, with a lecherous glee. It was entertaining, but nothing was even remotely relevant. When he had exhausted his memory, I said, "Thanks, amigo, you did great. I really appreciate your effort, and I'm sure Linda does too. We owe you."

He frowned seriously. "Breakfast you pay?"

"Yeah, sure."

He smiled once again. "We cool." The simplicity of my friend was awesome.

Returning to my apartment, the next step became clear—confront Slate. When in doubt, charge! If I did it at his busy office, what could possibly happen? I found his number and called. After I had been on hold for several minutes, he finally answered, "Slate."

"This is Shank MacDuff."

"And?" he replied impatiently.

"We've got a few more things to discuss."

"Such as?"

"I'd rather talk in person. Are you free near the end of the day?"

He paused and then asked, "Three o'clock?"

Not wanting to cut short my lunch with Dad, I asked, "Can we meet a little later?"

"Look, MacDuff, you called me. I'm a busy guy and—" then someone interrupted him. I could hear him bark back, irritated. Next he said, "If he's got lots of dead presidents, maybe we'll consider it. Otherwise, he has to stick with the dive spots from the brochure." He returned to me. "Where were we?"

"I'm sorry to eavesdrop, but what are 'dead presidents?'"

He sighed audibly and indulged me. "Dollars, dead presidents, greenbacks, they're all the same. Anyway, three o'clock is the best I can do. Take it or leave it."

"I'll be there."

Without another word, he slammed me into cyber-nothingness.

CHAPTER 32

Around noon, I arrived in Riverside for lunch with my father. Located an hour from Newport, the city is in the heart of an area now referred to as the "Inland Empire." While Riverside bustled in the early 1900s as wealthy Easterners desired warm winters and citrus riches, when the major agricultural players moved away, the city's fortunes dwindled. The restored Mission Inn in downtown proudly reflects Riverside's earlier splendor. Opening in 1876, the resort has hosted ten Presidents; Richard Nixon was married in one of the wedding chapels, while Ronald Regan honeymooned there. The Mission Inn's flying buttresses, spiraling staircases, and towers bring Old California to life in a powerful way.

"Shank," Dad greeted me as I peeled off my sunglasses and tried to adjust to the subdued light of the museum-like lobby. We shook hands, and then he grabbed my arm affectionately. I winced. "Are you hurt?" he asked, letting go and surveying my bandaged nose.

"I'll survive. Let's talk about it at lunch."

A friendly hostess seated us on the Spanish Patio. This far from the coast, it was sunny and toasty outside. Dad ordered soup and salad, and I opted for the "Mahi Mahi Tacos"—grilled dolphin wrapped in corn tortillas with tomatillo sauce. A cold Mountain Dew rounded out the basic food groups.

When the waiter left, Dad asked me, "How can you eat Flipper like that?"

The reference to the star of the old TV show I've watched in reruns made me smile. "This is restaurant mahi-mahi," I explained. "They call it dolphin, but it's not related to the mammal of the same name. These are brilliantly colored fish that can reach 60 or 70 pounds and prefer tropical waters."

He shook his head and said, "When I'm not around you all the time, I forget the staggering breadth of your knowledge. Thanks for the marine biology lesson."

Our drinks arrived, and I studied my Dad. He looked good and acted spry. Even as some of his skills were now fading, Dad was still sharp. Before retiring, he worked as a security analyst in the banking industry. He advised people on everything from armored car procedures to ATM surveillance, but uncovering embezzlement was his highest calling. After establishing himself as one of the best in the field, he often worked as an independent contractor for a contingency fee. I got sidetracked with the memory.

"Dad, remember the time that Texas bank didn't pay your percentage of the recovery fee and you went after them in court?"

"Sure. It was my first job for them. The initial discrepancies were only the tip of the proverbial iceberg. By the time the rest of the iceberg surfaced, it was huge. When we crunched the numbers, the bank owed me a small fortune. They called it extortion and refused to pay. So I sued. The judge ruled that the bank was a big boy, knew what it was doing, and had sought out my expertise. It was irrelevant that the crime was bigger than anyone anticipated. I got every dime!"

"Remember how you indulged the family with the windfall?" I asked, smiling.

"Sure. That ski trip to the Alps was spectacular, wasn't it?"

"Absolutely. Salzburg in the snow was very cool."

"Well, enough about the old days. What's up, son?"

I gave him a condensed version of my latest work for Linda. He stopped me several times to ask questions. After I described the two attacks, he leaned forward with intensity and understandable parental concern. The veins at the sides of his gray temples pumped with the effort.

"So how can I help?"

"Whatever wisdom you could share."

My father thought for a moment and then offered, "Pretty Fair Maiden. PFM."

"Excuse me?" I replied. I had no idea what he meant.

He repeated with emphasis: "Pretty Fair Maiden. First explore the passion, the *P*—emotions like love, hate, honor, and revenge. Whatever people get passionate about, they will act upon, sometimes to destructive extremes. Second, look for fear, the *F*. Remember—a cornered animal is the most dangerous. Third, follow the money, the *M*. Where does it start, where does it flow, and most importantly, where does it end up? Pretty Fair Maiden." As was usually the case, Dad had something significant to contribute. "Let's work through it," he said.

"Pretty Fair Maiden," I repeated as I was thinking. "OK. In this case, there must be passion, Pretty or *P*, because of the method the killer employed. Shoving a golf ball down someone's throat was *not* a detached action. It was an enraged, vicious act. But which passion? Love seems unlikely, unless Buddy was unfaithful to Linda. However, there is no evidence of that type of betrayal. Honor is a bit vague, and there are no facts showing that anyone had to kill Buddy to defend their dignity. Hate and revenge are the most likely. Lenny Hayes admitted he despised Buddy. Are there others who hated Buddy? Possibly."

"Good thoughts; keep going."

"Fear," I listed next. "That would be the Fair or *F* in your mnemonic technique. Was someone scared of Buddy and acting like a cornered animal? I'm drawing a blank. Buddy was not intimidating or threatening."

"That's fine. It simply may not apply."

"Finally, there is money, your Maiden or *M*. The police sure attacked this angle hard. The multimillion dollar insurance proceeds for Linda are a huge *M*. What other money is there? I keep coming back to the gambling undercurrent. Betting linked Buddy, Milton Reily, and probably Slate."

"Do any of those people have alibis?"

While I had kept track in a casual way, I had not done this exercise formally. My spreadsheet needed another column. "Good point. Let's see. As tournament director, Slate was undoubtedly busy and visible immediately after the Classic ended. Someone would have noticed his absence. But that same bustling might have allowed him to scamper over to the Lodge for mischief."

"Wouldn't that have been incredibly risky, since someone might have recognized him?"

"Yes, if he *intended* on murdering someone. Perhaps Slate, or whoever the killer was, merely wanted to talk to Buddy. In that case, they wouldn't have been concerned about someone spotting them on the way to his room. Once the person gets there, the two get into an argument and things get out of hand. Buddy ends up dead. A stealthy escape is then the only tricky part."

"So he's still a possibility. What about the others?"

"The bookie Reily—who knows? Even if that reptile had an ironclad alibi, he could have hired someone to do the dirty work. No use speculating further, too dark a hole. Lenny Hayes's story is like Swiss cheese. He was alone, staying at a cheap motel in Inglewood. There's nobody to corroborate his account. He could have made the two-hour trip to San Diego. The cops will undoubtedly check the mileage. But for now, Lenny remains a suspect."

Dad nodded and then asked with hesitation, "Has Linda's alibi improved?"

"No. She still has a 'window of opportunity' at Torrey Pines, given her excuses about traffic, being turned around, and parking problems. Nobody can vouch for her either."

"Tinny's got one, right?"

"For sure. Lots of people saw him on the practice green pathetically trying to figure out what went wrong. I personally verified it with the bartender and Slate. The cops apparently have other witnesses too. Tinny was still there when the Lodge manager sent someone to fetch him after security found Buddy dead."

"Crash and burn on the alibi approach," Dad commented.

"Guess so," I reluctantly agreed.

We continued to exchange ideas and then finished lunch. After a minor verbal scuffle over who was going to pay, which I won, we finally strolled outside.

"Thanks, Dad, it was helpful to hash this out. Also, nice to see you."

"My pleasure. Don't know how much I've helped, but it felt good to try."

When asked who their heroes are, most American males first list athletes and movie stars. Not me. Dad has always been my hero. We hugged gingerly, and he said quietly, "Watch out, Shank. We love you and want our only son in one piece."

I should have listened to Dad's warning more carefully.

CHAPTER 33

Driving south the hundred miles from Riverside to Del Mar Heights, my mind revisited that morning's call with Slate. He had explained that "dead presidents" meant money. In the first cryptic call Slate took in my presence, he mentioned "Madison." James Madison was the fourth U.S. President. Was he on a bill? The faces adorning most U.S. currency are presidents. But Benjamin Franklin is on the $100, and he never held the highest office.

I knew that the U.S. Mint used to issue a variety of large denomination bills but stopped because the government wanted to force major criminals to lug around more bulky money. Needing assistance to confirm a hunch, I called Cristanos.

"Yo," my pal answered.

"Cristanos, it's Shank. I need your help."

"Names it."

I told him to go to my place and then call me back. I had trusted him completely for some time now, so he knew my hidden key location. In about ten minutes, the phone rang.

"I in. What to do?"

"Go to the computer and return it from sleep mode."

I heard him whistle with enthusiasm as a swimsuit model greeted him from the screen. "Find the Internet and type in U.S. currency, c-u-r-r-e-n-c-y," I instructed.

He did so and said, "OK. Big list. What now?"

"Read them starting at the top."

He struggled through a few hits that didn't sound promising. With some effort, he finally found a viable one that included a pictorial trip through the history of U.S. paper money. Cristanos labored through the site but finally found the 1928 and 1934 series Federal Reserve Notes that had James Madison's picture on the front.

"That's it. What's the value? How much money does it say?"

My heart began to race when he carefully read, "5-0-0-0."

Score! Madison was on a long-forgotten $5,000 bill. As I had a significant drive ahead and Cristanos appeared to be enjoying himself, I had him get more information on Madison. We laughed at part of his biography that read: "At his inauguration, James Madison, a small, wizened man, appeared old and worn. But whatever his deficiencies in charm, Madison's buxom wife Dolley compensated for them with her warmth and gaiety. She was the toast of Washington."

While he clicked away distractedly, I asked, "Cristanos, you know what this information on Madison means?"

"Nopes."

"Slate was placing a bet that first time we met at his office. That's why he had *two* cell phones on his desk. Over the betting phone, the bookie probably said, 'I'm giving so-and-so odds on this-or-that event.' Slate then considered the offer and replied, 'Madison,' meaning he wanted to place a $5,000 bet." I wondered if the wizened Madison, or at least his buxom wife Dolley, would have approved of being integral to such a clever, yet simple, gambling shorthand.

"Me lost, but that's bueno," the Brazilian-in-bliss said before whistling at something else he found online.

Dad's Maiden, *M*, or "follow the money" resurfaced like an attack submarine. Buddy and Slate each had gambling connections. Milton Reily had to be the common bookie for both of them! Other bookies may use a special phone to handle the transactions of their good clients, but Slate and Reily's parallel, and personal, appearances at Del Mar made the conclusion inescapable that they were connected face-to-face. I felt like Agatha Christie's fictional detective, Hercule Poirot—my little gray cells were working! Several groups of puzzle pieces fit into place. Was I about to put the entire picture together?

"Thanks, Cristanos."

"No worries, Shanks. This a good time!"

"Go ahead and play around all you want. Please make sure to lock the door on your way out."

"Yeah, OK," he muttered.

After hanging up, I immediately called Baker. Excitedly, I blurted, "Detective, it's Shank. I'm pretty sure Slate is connected to Reily, like Buddy was."

"Slow down, cowboy. Lay it out slowly."

I proceeded to outline my earlier conversation with Slate and the "dead presidents" revelation.

"Interesting. It's not surprising, though, since my prior encounter with Slate involved gambling. When I first came on the force, we arrested him but had to drop the charges for lack of evidence. He rubbed my face in it."

I said, "There are still gaps. I had Cristanos go do some snooping at Torrey Pines and he—"

"Wait a minute! You had who do what?"

"My surfing buddy Cristanos. Remember? I mentioned him to you."

"Vaguely, but what was he doing?"

"Since he speaks Spanish and offered to help, I figured he had a much better chance of getting information from the Latino workers than a Sweedoregian."

"A what?"

"Sorry, a made-up word. My ancestors were mostly Swedish and Norwegian, thus I'm a self-proclaimed 'Sweedoregian.'"

"Got it. Let's stick to the subject. Obviously you trust this Cris guy?"

"It's Cristanos, and yes, I do now. He found at least one nugget. The maid that cleaned on Sunday reported that Buddy didn't sleep in his bed Saturday night."

It took a moment for this information to register. "Is that possible?" I could hear Baker muttering to himself.

I tried to ease the embarrassment. "You guys wouldn't have known, since by the time of the murder, it was well after maid service. You would have assumed she made the bed up in the normal course."

"Thanks for trying to bail us out, but there's no excuse. We simply missed it. Do you know where he was?"

"Not yet."

"Anything else?" Baker inquired.

"I think something got lost in the translation, but the graveyard-shift janitor saw Slate alone in the pro shop late Friday night with a bucket 'playing balls.' I tried to clarify the story, but Cristanos swears that's what the man said."

"Real late?"

"Yeah, like middle of the night."

"And?"

"Not sure. If the description is accurate, Slate's either a total tripper or up to something mighty mysterious.

Maybe we'll find out shortly. I'm meeting with him at three o'clock."

"Where?"

"His office, Del Mar Heights."

"How big an operation is it? Are there a lot of people around?"

"Upscale digs. Perhaps twenty employees. Plenty of witnesses."

"Fine. But be cautious and keep in touch."

"That's what my Dad said at lunch."

"Nobody wants a dead Shank."

"Agreed."

After ending the call, I once again debated the detective's motives and methods. He expressed concern about my meeting with Slate, but as long as the situation was relatively safe, Baker would risk it. Should I be mad? Nah, he was not hiding the fact. Besides, I got the feeling that if calamity struck, the colossal cop would lead the cavalry charge.

CHAPTER 34

Arriving at Slate's building, I should have realized something was wrong. The parking lot was mostly empty, and the M3 easily found an end spot. But it could have merely been a slow afternoon; after all, I didn't know the parking pattern of the small office building.

The door to Slate's second-floor office was locked. I banged and waited. Nothing. I started back to my car to retrieve my cell phone. He was probably deep inside and could not hear the banging. Halfway down the stairs, I heard the door open. I looked back. There was Slate.

"MacDuff, where are you going?"

I walked back up. "What gives? The door was locked."

"I let some of the staff go early to start the weekend. Enhance employee morale and all that." Looking at my wounded nose, he popped off, "Whoa, pal, did her boyfriend finally catch you?" I frowned. "Lighten up. This way," he said, ushering me through the door and locking it. The office was dim and quiet. Apparently, he had given *all* the staff the afternoon off. I sensed danger, but it was too embarrassing to turn back. Pesky male ego. As we passed the reception desk, the phone rang. He kept walking. There was probably a night recording that guided the disappointed caller into a voicemail maze. When we reached his office, the torture chair was still my only option. As his desk phone rang, he let the door close on its own. Slate ignored the ringing and nestled down into his comfortable swivel chair.

"Are you still poking around the caddy's murder?"

"His name was Buddy Franks. And yes." Something was different about Slate, but I could not put my finger on it. After all, I had only talked with him once face-to-face. Was he more cocky or less? Either way, I did not like it.

"So what did you want to discuss in person?"

Being a conditioned athlete, I can sense even small changes in my body. At that point, my heart rate was elevated and a measured flow of adrenaline was starting to work its magic. Time for business. "I have two topics, which may lead to more depending upon your answers. First, what were you doing on the Friday night of the Classic in the Torrey Pines pro shop, around three o'clock in the morning?"

Direct hit! The question visibly stunned him. He sat still for a long moment. Finally, he punted. "Why?"

This guy was skilled and not to be underestimated. "Because I have an eyewitness placing you there."

"While it's none of your business, I was checking tournament figures."

His lie forced me to play my ace, although I could not tell whether it was worth one or eleven. "Why were you playing balls with the bucket?" I chose to use the precise phraseology from Cristanos. I did not know what the janitor had meant, but Slate would. He showed no emotion.

"What bucket? What golf balls?"

Straight denial. Either Cristanos had mixed up the story, or he was going to lie about everything. Then something dawned on me—his denial contained an admission! "Why did you mention *golf* balls when I asked about 'playing balls'?"

Slate tensed and said, "You said golf balls. What are you trying to pull?"

Shank scores!

He then asked, "What kind of eyewitnesses do you have who saw anything at three in the morning?" The blood vessels on his temples were pulsing. While trying to remain unruffled, he was really working hard at it. I was ever so close.

"No dice. Ask the cops." Follow-up questions were pointless. Therefore, I switched gears. "Second topic. Did you win the $5,000 bet you made the last time I was here?" While eyeing me suspiciously, he genuinely did not understand. "Remember? The 'Madison' you placed with your bookie, probably Milton Reily, on the private betting phone." All my cards were now on the table. Would he pass, fold, call, or raise? Had I put the pieces together correctly?

His eyes narrowed a fraction. "What do you want from me?"

So I was right! Excellent. But now where to go? Was he hinting at a payoff or hush money? "The truth," I said, glaring at him.

His eyes became slits as his pupils dilated. Like clockwork, that wonderful but horrible warning system once again triggered within me. I had hit some sort of sinister jackpot and was now in mortal danger. Slate reached beneath the desk and hit a button. The lock on the door behind me snapped into place remotely.

As I started to rise, he growled, "You're not going anywhere, caddy." He opened his top desk drawer and pulled out a gun. Experience told me the pistol was a .45 caliber. Slate undoubtedly knew how to use it. I was in serious trouble. "Put your hands behind your head and sit back down."

I complied. Slate laid the gun on the desk within easy reach. He had gone all in and called my hand with winning cards. The man could grab the gun and fire before I could get out of the chair. I might have to try a death leap over the desk, but it did not seem that we were there yet. The gun had enhanced his dark power, and he was scary calm.

"You couldn't leave it alone, could you? Some people would call you brave or tenacious. I think you're a fool! Now you'll get what a fool deserves."

That did not sound good. My mouth had gone dry. I swallowed and spoke, with considerable effort.

"You were connected to Buddy through Milton Reily, right?"

"Bright boy. I knew you'd figure it out once you showed up at Del Mar yesterday and started talking to that loud mouth Diaz."

I flinched with surprise, confident nobody had followed me.

Noticing my reaction, he said, "No, you didn't screw up. I got lucky. The receptionist and I started dating when I worked there. We've been on and off for years. She followed you back to Diaz's office and eavesdropped, catching enough to know that my private affairs were the topic of conversation. Like a good little girl, she immediately called. That's why I made sure we'd be all alone this afternoon."

I started to hyperventilate. If he was confessing secrets, there was no way he was going to let me live to tell about it. Then I heard what sounded like a train. It started as a low rumble and had to be the Pacific Surfliner I rode the day before. I had gotten off at Solana Beach, before the route headed inland near here on the way to downtown San Diego. Buddy and I used to go to a Mexican restaurant in Irvine that shook something awful when an Amtrak thundered over the adjacent track. But I had not noticed any trains or nearby tracks during my first session with Slate.

As the noise grew louder, I turned so my good ear could pinpoint the source. Slate was trying to figure it out too. Sitting frozen, his eyes grew wide. The thunderous sound was coming from the hallway. Before either of us could react, the place virtually exploded!

CHAPTER 35

With a deafening crash, a rumbling refrigerator, or so it seemed, creamed me from behind. The impact sent me flying. Pieces of splintering door flew past. Slate was in shock, eyes bulging. My already bruised body crumpled in a heap on the floor. The roaring appliance buried me.

As the explosion began to subside, there were shouts in two distinct choruses. The first was a single booming voice commanding, "Shank, down, down!" Detective Baker, the human "refrigerator," was using his massive body to protect me. The second set of voices belonged to a multitude that kept yelling at Slate, "Freeze! Freeze!" When the other officers had subdued Slate, my 300-pound rescuer finally rolled off me.

"Are you OK?" he bellowed.

For the second time that week, I checked my body for functioning parts. "Apparently so," I said, dazed.

Baker got up and gave me his huge hand. He about pulled my arm off. I got to my feet as the other officers took a handcuffed Slate through what remained of the doorframe. He was already asking for his lawyer.

"Nice timing, detective."

"Don't even go there. You should be glad we're here at all! After we talked, I second-guessed letting you meet Slate alone. On the one hand, you had done a great job to date, the place would be full of people, and I admit I wanted more information. But the guy's a scumbag. I tried your cell but no luck. Then I called the office here to see if everything was still kosher. No receptionist, just a general mailbox. I then used the auto-attendant and tried Slate's extension directly. Again nothing."

"Both office calls rang, but Slate ignored them," I confirmed.

While dusting debris off his permanently wrinkled clothes, Baker continued. "Now I was officially worried, so I requested backup and hit the road. We were here in less than five minutes, turning off the siren the last mile. One patrol car was waiting and another arrived soon after."

"How did you get inside?"

"I saw that your distinctive wheels were still here, and my gut felt you were in real danger. So we 'opened' the front door lock. Not hard with the right tools and a little practice. It was too quiet, and I had a bad feeling. We found Slate's nameplate outside this office. When we heard voices, we tried to open the door, but it was locked."

"Man, you guys were quiet. I didn't hear a thing until you started imitating a train. That must have hurt when you demolished the door."

The giant smiled proudly. "I'll probably feel it later. Old football philosophy—you have to hit the other object harder than it hits you. Try a breakdown at half speed, and the door might win. But when my mass gets going full throttle, physics controls the outcome."

Baker looked around the office, noted the gun still on Slate's desk, and escorted me outside. A crowd was gathering beyond a growing police armada.

"Was your car involved?"

"Not except for bringing me here."

"Good, leave it for now. We'll bring you back after taking a statement."

He showed me to a patrol car and instructed the uniformed officer to go directly to the station. The young cop obeyed. A few minutes later, I was in the now familiar conference room a final time. Different faces greeted me. Because of Baker's involvement, they took our statements independently "to keep everything above board."

The gray-haired examining officer had a friendly demeanor. An assistant took notes. A stenographer, or court reporter, phonetically "typed" every word on one of those funky black machines. The cop took nothing for granted. He started *before* the beginning. I had to detail my background, including my education and work experience. Then he turned the subject to how I knew the various players. Next, he wanted details about Linda's request for help. Here, my caution interrupted the flow. By now, I was accustomed to protecting her privacy. We had cracked the case, but the confidentiality persisted. It was slow going as I chose my words carefully. He questioned me extensively about the actions I had taken during the investigation, exploring everything that Baker said or asked me to do. The only thing I omitted was Tim Fisher. There would be no transcription of my exploiting an FBI special agent's friendship.

At first the drill was fun, especially the part where I was treated like a hero. They joked about my new career in crime fighting. The banter was ego stroking—I liked it. But after several hours, fatigue set in, and we took a break. Someone brought me a vending-machine sandwich, chips, and a Mountain Dew. Then we kept going, finally finishing at about eight o'clock.

As we broke, a tired-looking Detective Baker came in.

"Exhausting, huh?" he asked sympathetically.

"Stick a fork in me; I'm done! Did your session take four hours also?"

"Maybe three. I've been doing paperwork since the questioning ended. Have you eaten?"

"Kind of. They treated me to food from your vending machine."

"The department spares no expense."

"What's happening to Slate?" I asked.

"He'll only say four words: 'I want my lawyer.' He's too slick a customer to be intimidated or confess without his attorney's input. But I'm sure the evidence will come pouring in, now that we know where to look."

We walked back toward the lobby and then outside.

"I've made arrangements to get you back to Slate's office to pick up the M3. There's your ride," he said, pointing at a waiting Honda.

Officer Claire Valentine emerged from the driver's side. She was now off duty and wore a pair of snug jeans and a tight purple sweater. The look was casual but dangerous in a very female way. The noise of the traffic faded into the background. Was that her heart beating? I could hear mine. Imagining how the soft material must feel over her full figure, I tingled. But I was beat. A dull male cop would have made a fine chauffeur. Instead, I had to gear it up again.

Baker shrugged and smiled. Raising his eyebrows and leaning in closely he whispered, "Shank, she *volunteered* and hung around. Enjoy." As he walked off, the detective's massive frame seemed to leave imprints in the pavement.

I moved toward the car, and she opened the passenger's door. The edge of her perfume's tentacles teased me. After closing my door with a pop, everything went silent. She knew I was watching her walk around the front. My seat was cold, my body hot. The sounds outside returned as she opened the driver's door and slid in.

"I heard all about the excitement today. Glad you're OK."

She snapped the seatbelt in the buckle and let the diagonal belt settle softly in her breasts' valley. Energized by the innocently seductive maneuver, my fingers fidgeted. Trying to focus on something else, I joked, "Creeps with guns are always locking me in rooms that ogres demolish."

She laughed delightfully and started the car. Pulling away from the station, we were soon on the I-5 freeway heading north.

"Have you told Mrs. Franks?"

"Not yet."

"She will be so relieved it's over."

"No doubt. I'll call her on my drive back to Newport."

With a playful tone, she asked, "I know you had a snack, but would you like a real meal? There's this great Italian place in Del Mar, a local hangout, and—"

I interrupted, "Please don't take this personally, especially since you're being so sweet. But this week has been brutal. I'm dust."

"Of course. That was thoughtless of me. I just thought since your involvement with the department was over, well—" What this cutie left unsaid spoke volumes.

An exit went by in silence. But she did not wait long and dove back in. "Detective Baker told me what happened to your FBI Academy partner, your—fiancée. I'm so sorry. It must have been horrible."

That got me. Since the year of Jill's death, the only women I had opened up to were my mother and sisters.

Even with them, though, we seldom discussed the topic; it was too painful. Was I ready to unload all the baggage I'd been carrying around? My molten emotions started to churn. Not wanting an eruption, I nodded and stayed silent. Soon we were at Slate's parking lot. The M3 sat alone. There was yellow police caution tape across the entrance to Slate Sports. She shut off the engine and faced me. I turned toward her so my good right ear could hear. Even in the dim light, she was delicious. A soft hand touched mine. With smoldering intensity, she whispered, "Whenever you're ready to talk, eat Italian, or *whatever*, just call."

She leaned forward and kissed me gently on the cheek. My heart raced and body shivered. Her delightful perfume, now in full attack mode, delivered the knockout blow. I was one big bundle of raw emotions. Saying anything would cause me to lose it. I merely nodded in acknowledgement and got out. She waited until I revved the engine before she drove off.

After a short stretch on the freeway, the M3 exited, found a residential neighborhood, and somberly parked. The dam finally broke. I started crying. Softly at first, then louder and harder. I could not help it. The need to sob overwhelmed me. I felt so alone and miserable, sitting there bawling on that dark street. I imagined happy people in cozy homes. How wonderful it would be to make dinner together, watch a movie, or hold hands while strolling the beach. I wanted to love someone again so badly it physically hurt. Why Jill? Why me?

I must have sat there in misery for thirty minutes. My shirt was soaked from using it as a towel to wipe the torrent of tears. Pulling myself back together, I felt relieved. Allowing the intense pressure to build up over several years had been unhealthy. The release was wonderful.

On the way back to the freeway, I stopped at a gas station for something to drink. Losing fluids from crying had parched me. Inside the mini-mart, I put my hand on a Mountain Dew and then stopped. Instead, I picked Gatorade. Liquid nutrients were called for. I opened it and took a long gulp. It tasted good. The cashier looked at me quizzically, but I figured he was used to seeing strange people during the night shift. On the road again, we drove north in silence. While I had planned to call Linda with the good news, I did not have it in me. She would be just as happy tomorrow.

The M3 parked itself in the garage. After opening the locked door to my apartment, I tried the light. Nothing. So much for the reliability of light switches. As I wondered if there were any replacement bulbs in the cupboard, I slowly worked my way across the dark room toward the kitchen.

I never heard it coming. After all the excitement and drama of the day, the emotional tension and tears, the *coup de grâce* was a white-hot flash punctuating the crushing blow to my skull.

CHAPTER 36

I had been unconscious only once before, after the car explosion at the academy. The timeless void is strange. It is not like sleep, where you are often aware of surrounding conditions and background noises. Most people who nap on the beach can later recall sand kicked on their legs, kids yelling, or the breeze stiffening. Unconsciousness is different. It is binary—either on or off.

Starting to come to life again, my throbbing head dominated the emerging reality. The blow had nearly killed me. My brain struggled to reboot. A wave of nausea threatened to cause a tsunami in my stomach—a clear indication I had a concussion. My eyelids were inoperable. *Am I sitting?* A few synapses fired. *Yeah, I am sitting. Are my arms paralyzed?* No, my fingers wiggled. But my hands were bound behind me. That realization sent a surge of adrenaline that primed the pump. My eyes finally rolled opened.

There was my kitchen. I tried to rise, but my feet were bound too. Suppressing a threatening release of bile, I looked left but merely saw an empty room. To the right, however, Tinny Wilcox sat relaxing at the table. The pro was dressed in cheap brown slacks and a bottom-drawer argyle sweater. He was reading and had on rubber gloves. I tried to speak but merely gurgled. On the second attempt, I sputtered, "Tinny?"

"Well, there you are," he squeaked like a constipated squirrel.

The clock on the microwave read 2:24 a.m. I had been out for four hours. Under normal circumstances, that would have been quite a luxurious sleep.

"What are you doing?"

"Looking at your *Surfer* magazine. Quite impressive. Does Newport ever get towering surf? This article's entitled 'Neptune's Revenge,' and it lists Jaws, Maui, Hawaii; Mavericks, Half Moon Bay, California; and Todos Santos, Baja, Mexico, as the largest rideable mega-waves in the world. I would have thought—"

"Forget that! Why am I tied up?"

"Actually, you're ducted. Since I used duct tape, you're not tied but 'ducted' up. Get it?"

I looked at my feet and confirmed that duct tape was holding my ankles to the chair.

"I have a duct tape joke. Let's see how clever you really are. Why is duct tape like 'The Force' in the *Star Wars* movies?"

He stared at me, expecting an answer. I resisted the impulse to play along.

"Stubborn, or is that bump on your head draining your brain power? Either way, I guess that means you give up. The answer is they both have a dark side and a light side and hold the universe together!" With the grin of the Grinch, he chuckled.

"What are you babbling about?"

As he took a deep sigh, the smile left his face. "I was hoping that my blow would kill you. Too bad. You're a tough one all right. Once you were down, I should have kept beating you. But I couldn't. Just not man enough. Now we have to wait for Plan B." He hesitated and then continued, "Where did that saying come from anyway? Why not Plan 2? Perhaps it started with the Greek gods." He attempted to deepen his voice and then said with manufactured drama, "What do you think Hades, should we implement Plan Beta? Or maybe—"

This guy had lost it! I interrupted and asked, "How did you get in here to ambush me?"

"Found your spare key inside the circuit panel. I was all set to break a window, but you provided me painless access." Shaking his sheathed index finger at me, he said, "You should have been more careful. A *criminal* could have gotten in here."

Admittedly, that was lame. Baker hadn't mentioned spare keys during his post truck-attack security briefing, but still, there was nobody to blame but myself.

Tinny kept going, boasting now. "I removed the bulb from the corner lamp and then sat in the dark, waiting. I've replaced it now—see?" he said, gesturing with a fluttering latex-gloved hand.

Turning, I confirmed the light was working fine. *Note to self*: Never blindly walk into a dark room when you did not see the bulb blow. "What did you hit me with?"

"A marble rolling pin from on top of the fridge."

"And the gloves?"

"Got these at Pep Boys. You know—'Manny, Moe, and Jack,'" he sang the familiar automotive store jingle. "Can't leave any fingerprints. That would never do." He was staring past me with a distant look in his eyes.

I cut to the chase. "Did you kill Buddy?"

"Yes, that would be me."

Even though I knew that answer was coming, it was still hard to absorb. Earlier in the day, didn't we find the murderer—Slate? Obviously not.

A burning anger replaced the distant look in Tinny's eyes. "He deserved to die after what he did to me."

"Which was what?"

"Switched the balls!"

"I don't fully understand. Can you explain?"

Tinny took a deep breath and looked at the clock. Shrugging, he said, "Why not? You've got a little time left."

CHAPTER 37

Being a hostage is frustrating and scary, especially when you're bound tightly to a chair. There is no way to improvise an escape. My extremities were as useless as a scarecrow's. I could yell, but it would be a long shot that anyone would hear me this late. Neighbors might catch a word or two, but most people do not immediately figure out if they are dreaming or not. Besides, a shout would be short lived since Tinny would clobber me, tape my mouth, or both. Inciting him to club me again was not very appealing. Better to engage him verbally and look out for an opening. Stay the course.

Tinny rose and said mockingly, "Don't bother getting up; I'll get another beer myself."

He opened the refrigerator and grabbed one of the two remaining Samuel Adams. There were four empty bottles sitting on the sink next to a plastic garbage bag. Was it good or bad that he was getting drunk? Only time would tell. Watching him, I realized how thirsty I was again. That beer looked *really* good. I thought about asking for one or at least a glass of water but decided not to let him know I was suffering. "Make yourself comfortable," I popped off with an attitude.

"Sassy to the end." He shook his head in disapproval and sat back down. "Where to start? Let's go way back, since you're the curious type. I grew up in Chicago during the 1970s. The local sports teams were lousy. Not like later with Walter Payton's Bears and Michael Jordan's Bulls."

Sweat started to dampen my shirt.

Tinny kept rambling. "That left my old man to watch golf on TV. He was a demoted shipping clerk, a lifetime underachieving alcoholic. What a loser. He took out his misery on me. But athletes like Jack Nicklaus inspired me, and I begged Mom for golf lessons. She finally agreed, running interference with the drunken dictator. The game came easily to me, and by high school, I could really play. I won often, but the two times Dad actually showed up, I tanked. He would complain that I wasted his time. Dad started calling me a choker. During one whiskey binge, he wrote it on my bedroom door with a permanent marker. Mom painted over it the next day.

"I tried to ignore the criticism and ultimately received a partial scholarship to Northwestern, about fifteen minutes from Chicago. I played all four years for the Wildcats, finishing as an All-American. Of course, Dad drank himself to death the year before I graduated.

"You probably know much of the story after that. I had both success and failure at Q-School, resulting in stints on and off the big Tour. The best I could muster in all those years were several second places. Every bloody time I was in contention late on Sunday, something would happen.

Usually my fault. But I didn't deserve the 'choker' label from the press. I could hear *him* laughing from the grave."

As Tinny continued unburdening himself, my thoughts returned to escaping the mad man. Plan B sounded bad. The tape held my helpless legs to the chair; my bound wrists were anchored behind me. I could tip the chair over, but where would that get me? My only option was to sit and listen.

"Then came Torrey Pines," Wilcox slurred on. "I'd never played better. All week I hit the ball long and straight, my short game was sharp, putting was unbelievable. It felt different from every other pro tournament. Going into Sunday, I knew victory was mine. Finally, I was going to shed that choker label and chalk up a Tour win. Forget the money; this was going to be my redemption day!

"We cruised the front nine. A couple of big boys were chasing, but my four-stroke lead was bulletproof. I had a snack and soda at the turn. Felt great. However, Buddy looked sick. I asked him if he was OK. He said he had some bug, hadn't slept the night before, but could manage the bag and finish the round.

"On the 10th hole, the 405-yard par four, tee to green I was fine. Then the putting debacle began. I three-putted for bogey from ten feet! While I tried to shake it off, the torture continued. On the 11th hole, the nasty 220-yard par three, I purred my tee shot to eight feet. One of my best of the week. I three-putted again! The crowd moaned.

"Typically, Buddy gave me a new ball every third hole unless there was a reason to reload more often. On the tee at the 12th, I asked him for a new ball early and tossed the old one into the crowd. That hole is brutal, a 504-yard par four into the wind. I spanked my tee shot and hit a beautiful four iron onto the front of the green. While the pin was in the back, I still thought I could lag it close and tap in for par. Instead, I four-putted! Goodbye lead. The wheels flew off. On the back, I had five three-putts and that grotesque four-putt. Every stinking hole. I would set up perfectly square, stroke it smoothly, and the ball would miss the mark. There was no pattern, sometimes left, then right, then straight. Made no sense!"

Listening to Tinny's tale, my mind spun like a roulette wheel. Finally, the bouncing silver sphere fell into place. "Buddy gave you unbalanced balls. That would explain your proficiency tee to green, but random errors putting."

"Exactly!" he snarled. "Afterwards, I did a little research." He grabbed his wallet and pulled out several small dog-eared papers. "I quote from a *Golf Magazine* article by Dave Pelz, 'Does Balance Matter? A Tiny Offset in a Golf Ball's Weighting Can Cause You to Miss Putts': 'I've been saying for 20 years that many balls are out of balance, sometimes enough to affect the roll and results of your putts. I'm not talking about a particular brand or model. Ball manufacturing is so exacting that if a ball's weight is not perfectly distributed or centered, and its balance is off even a tiny bit, it can make a putt move one way or another and do serious damage.'"

Tinny jumped up and started pacing around the kitchen. "Serious damage! Did you hear that? No joke, Pelz baby; I was seriously damaged all right."

His face was flush as the agitation grew like a weed. This was going the wrong direction. I had to calm him down.

"What else does Pelz say?"

The maniac chugged more beer, sat down, and continued. "The following month, Pelz wrote a companion article titled 'Playing in Balance, Don't Let an Out-of-Balance Ball Cost You Strokes.' It says, 'When the ball's weight isn't perfectly centered, it will tend to roll off line. If the ball is positioned with the weight on the right side, the ball will roll off line toward the right (even on perfectly flat surfaces).' Pelz even has a nifty home test for determining if, and to what extent, a ball is out of balance. You float the balls in 'heavy water' made from tap water, Epsom salts, and some drops of Jet Dry dishwashing liquid. I've tried it since, and it works. The heavy side sinks, the light side floats."

Another piece of the puzzle snapped into place. This had to be what Slate was doing late on that Friday night. "Playing balls" was the best way the Latino janitor could describe how Slate was dropping balls in a bucket of heavy water to find the ones with the worst balance. But why Slate? What was his connection to, or leverage on, Buddy?

"When did you suspect the balls?" I asked.

"On the practice putting green afterwards. I was in shock. I signed my scorecard then walked through the crowd toward the locker room in the Lodge. Several people in the crowd dropped the 'choker' bomb on me. I couldn't let it go and wandered out to the practice green. Crews were starting to tear things down, but the practice green was still sectioned-off. Nobody seemed to mind.

"There were two practice balls on the fringe and a demo putter near the remnants of a display. I added the ball from my pocket and stroked a few. Admittedly, it was a pathetic scene—the 'choker' trying to find his stroke after losing. But I was beyond caring.

"Soon a pattern emerged. The practice balls found the center of the hole, while my tournament ball was inconsistent. Putting systematically for a few more minutes confirmed it. I hadn't choked; the problem was the balls!

"I ran up to Buddy's room and gushed my revelation. He looked horrible, white as a hockey player. Then it dawned on me—he *knew* about the unbalanced balls. I was dumbfounded. My 'loyal' caddy? Didn't take long before the weakling confessed. Buddy had this hidden life before Las Vegas that involved a gas station shooting."

"Got that part. Lenny Hayes told me."

"Didn't do you much good, did it?" he chuckled.

"Apparently not," I responded dejectedly.

"Buddy was afraid of being found out; he thought it would destroy everything. He had made friends with a bookie named Milton Reily while he was living in Vegas. One night the two were drinking and Buddy shot his mouth off. Reily tucked away the ugly confession for future use. Buddy swears the snake was the only one who knew."

"That appears to be the case," I confirmed for no good reason.

"The bookie, like everyone else, considered it a long shot for me to win *any* tournament. Yet, for some reason, two gamblers had separately made sizable bets on me to win the Classic. A victory would have cost Reily a small fortune. Slate was heavily in debt to Reily, so the bookie offered his old client a deal. Reily would wipe out Slate's gambling tab, provided Slate sabotaged me if I was still leading on the back nine Sunday."

"So Reily *was* at the center," I said, finally understanding who was the linchpin.

Tinny jumped up again, his blood vessels pounding on his neck and temples. "Yep, Reily to Slate to Buddy. I was the innocent victim, the pawn! Slate got the call after my great second round on Friday. He then found the most unbalanced balls from the stockpile of my brand at the pro shop. Slate met with Buddy on Saturday night and played his blackmail card. He provided Buddy the screwed-up balls to use if I was still in contention.

"Buddy said he was a wreck the rest of that night, never even trying to go to sleep. Instead, he wandered the Lodge grounds and nearby streets. Ultimately, he decided that it was merely a golf tournament for everyone else, but it was *his* family and freedom. So he hung me out to dry to save his own skin!" Tinny was now shaking with rage.

"So you killed him in revenge?"

"Not intentionally—at least, not at first. He was sitting on the chair facing the bed after he confessed, hanging his head down in shame. My blood boiled. I grabbed that old putter he travels with and whacked him hard across the head."

The puzzle was almost complete. The fact that Buddy was looking down explained why there was no struggle.

"He fell against the end table, knocking it into the wall," Tinny continued.

"That was the crash the hotel guests next door heard. By the way, did you still have your playing glove on?"

"Yup," Tinny mumbled. "I had put it back on earlier at the practice green. I've always putted that way."

Tinny is left handed. I learned that tidbit at our Florida lunch when he accidentally stabbed his right hand with the knife. But like some lefties, he plays right-handed on purpose. In theory, it is better to have your dominant side pulling through the swing rather than pushing from behind. Phil Mickelson, known worldwide as "Lefty," is the most high-profile example in reverse. During the attack, Tinny probably picked up the putter and hit Buddy with his dominant left hand. The glove was still on it; thus, there were no prints on the putter.

"What was with the golf ball theatrics?"

"Inspired touch, huh? Just came to me," he said proudly. "My blow had knocked him unconscious, so I propped him upright and then picked up one of his practice balls from the floor. I was so enraged, I shoved it down his throat. Now who was *the choker*?" He smiled and laughed sadistically. "Really, Shank, you and the police overlooked the biggest clue—the 'choker' connection."

He was right. We totally missed it.

"Why did you place the putter across his legs?"

"Habit. After years of competitive golf, I always take care of putters."

What a freak! He bludgeons a guy, leaves a macabre calling card down his gullet, and then worries about golf etiquette?

"Really, I didn't think he'd die. But he had it coming."

"Then you bailed?"

"Immediately. I opened the door with my gloved hand and returned to the practice green."

"Wait a minute. There were witnesses who swore you putted for a long time on the practice green."

"Dumb luck. I was gone for maybe ten minutes. While the witnesses all said they remembered seeing me, I bet if they were questioned *properly*, none of them could swear they saw me the whole time. People came, went, and had other things going on. But their combined sightings gave me a neat little alibi."

Amazing. I remember the partial view from inside the bar near the practice green. The building and Tolleson's Weeping tree obstructed the putting surface. The bartender I interviewed—apparently *poorly* interviewed—recalled that the place was packed after the tournament. He was not obsessively watching Tinny but simply noticed him outside. He unconsciously filled in time gaps, assuming the pro was merely out of sight.

Tinny kept rolling, as he finished the beer.

"In the Lodge, I saw almost nobody in the hallways. They all seemed wrapped up in handling luggage, trying to open doors, that sort of thing. I only had to walk through a few main areas. Nobody knows *me* out of context," he barked bitterly.

"Back at the practice green, I kept stroking putts like before. A few minutes later, I heard all the sirens. After following the Lodge staffer to the office, the manager told me Buddy was dead. The stress of the tournament, the putting meltdown, the confrontation and attack of Buddy, everything combined to suck the blood from my brain. Bam, I'm out. Next thing I knew, smelling salts were making me gag. Everyone was treating me very nicely, telling me how sorry they were for my loss. Nobody suspected. I flew back to Tucson the next day. The cops and press were easy to manipulate. Everything was fine until *you* started poking around.

"I knew Buddy was only the front man, so I called Slate the week after the tournament and confronted him. He's smart. Figured out right away I was the one who killed Buddy. Used it as defensive blackmail, saying we all had something on each other. It was a stalemate until you grilled me in Florida. There was no way two measly caddies in a row were going to take me down."

"Did you drive the black truck yourself or hire someone to try and run me down?"

"Not me; probably Slate or Reily. Too bad they missed."

Tinny looked at the clock, which now read 3:03 a.m.

"It's the witching hour," he said ominously.

The killer stood up and opened several kitchen drawers, finally pulling out one of my long cooking knives. He balanced it in his hand approvingly. I was *not* thrilled about Plan B.

CHAPTER 38
The Final Chapter

While recuperating from the accident at the academy, I watched a lot of TV. A few cooking shows caught my attention. It sounded fun to expand my skills beyond hitting buttons on the microwave. Mom encouraged me, primarily with cooking accessories such as the marble rolling pin that Tinny used to bludgeon me. While some of the utensils merely collect dust, I use Mom's gift of Cutco knives constantly.

The cutlery's razor-sharp blades are legendary. Teeth on each side of square serrations cut forward, backward, or straight down with equal ease. Sage is afraid to use them because she once witnessed a nasty Cutco accident. Her paranoia seemed ridiculous—that is, until I almost sliced off my finger while chopping onions. The emergency room doc recounted stories about several similar Cutco incidents as he stitched my finger back together.

Tinny held the large fourteen-inch carver, its blade gleaming menacingly. Mom's culinary encouragement was going to allow this guy to slice me without ragged edges! A line from Disney's *Pirates of the Caribbean* flooded over me: "Dead men tell no tales." I sweated more and started talking fast.

"Look, man, I'm sure if you don't take this any further, the police and D.A. will take into serious consideration all the stress you were under. Anybody would have snapped. They simply want to close their files. However, if you start butchering me, then you're really in for it. Don't make it any worse because—"

"Shut up!" he growled.

I was running at the mouth but was helpless to do much else. Tinny put the empty beer bottles in the trash bag, along with the magazine. He then moved to the hall closet and started sifting through the hanging clothes. After a few seconds, he pulled out my red and black North Face parka, which typically only saw action during ski season.

"Here's the deal," the pro said ominously. "After I put this parka on you we're going to take a little walk. Don't even think about trying to escape. I really don't want to have to cut you," he said, waving the wicked knife just inches from my face. "But if you cause me any headaches, I'll fillet you. Got it?"

I nodded, since my vocal cords had frozen. I was scared. It was not like the intoxicating raw fear I gulp thirstily when riding big waves. Then you have choices. That freedom produces nervous energy bordering on euphoria. Not here. I had no control over the situation and was going to die. The combination produced panic. What a pathetic way to go. I thought back to a conversation I once had with Buddy over a game of pool in Ohio.

"How do you want to die?" I had asked my friend.

"Sleepin'."

"You're kidding. How boring," I chided.

"Painless and unknowing. Like an old bear that never gits out of hibernation."

"Not me," I protested. "Dying should be an honor. I want to go out in a blaze of glory, like my Scottish ancestors stopping the Romans or in the footsteps of America's bravest at Iwo Jima or Normandy."

"What do you care? You'll be dead!"

"Yeah, but what about a legacy? If you died rescuing a baby from a burning building, your eulogy would be grand: 'Here lies Buddy Franks. He died a hero.'"

"Not for this simple Southern boy. If the Grim Reaper's listening, put me down for a slumbering death."

Tinny pulled me up roughly so my bound hands cleared the chair back. Duct tape still bound my legs tight. He put the jacket on me and zipped it up. For a moment, I felt like a kid again, playing the "armless man" in one of Dad's coats. Tinny tucked the empty sleeves into the parka's pockets. Next, he put the hood over my head and cinched the elastic band tight, as if he was concerned about sub-zero temperatures.

After pulling me to a standing position, he cut my ankles free, unbuttoned my jeans, and pulled them down to my knees. Was it possible this night could get weirder? He then duct taped my upper thighs several times. Funny what goes through your mind in times of extreme peril, like Lenny Hayes mentioning that his mind focused on the cigarettes as he lay there bleeding in the gas station after Buddy ran out on him. All I could think was that if I somehow survived, it was going to be brutal taking the sticky silver tape off my hairy legs. Tinny pulled my pants back up and re-buttoned them clumsily. While I felt like a zombie in training, at least I was mobile again, sort of. I could walk with tiny steps like a geisha girl but could not possibly run.

"Let's go. Remember, any trouble and I'll *Kill Bill* you," he said, wielding the Cutco like a sword from the martial arts revenge movie.

Why was he going through all this? I could have been dead hours ago. Then I remembered his comment about not having enough nerve to keep clobbering me after the ambush. This heat-of-the-moment murderer could not kill in cold blood. It is one thing to hit someone and maybe he dies. Quite another to intentionally kill. I bet he wanted something else to deliver the final blow. The coward!

Tinny put on his jacket, put the remaining bottles in the trash bag, and led me outside. Had it not been such a lethal game, I would have considered the effort expended trying to get ol' duct-taped thighs down the stairs to be comical. We struggled, since I had a limited range of motion, and he was determined to stay above me. Once we were out the front of my duplex and onto the boardwalk, I scanned the area for help. Nobody. At that hour, the landscape was deserted. The valets were long gone from Portofino's restaurant and the Doryman's Inn.

If I got the chance, I could gamble and yell. My booming voice would carry. So why had he skipped duct-taping my mouth? Perhaps he needed me to look as "normal" as possible in case we encountered someone. A taped mouth would advertise malicious intent. But if I yelled, he would thrust the Cutco through me like butter.

We had not taken very many steps when I heard a familiar walrus voice miserably attempting to sing a Kinks classic: "Lola, L-O-L-A, Lola, lo-lo-lo-lo-Lola." The song quickly deteriorated even further. "Lola Loletta, when can we meet 'ya"—not even close. A plump and wobbly figure emerged from between two houses.

Tinny ducked behind me.

"Is that you, Shankster?" Pork Rind slurred in our direction.

His dirty jacket and torn jeans made him look like a Skid Row bum, but at that moment he had never looked so beautiful to me.

"Don't say a word," Tinny whispered to me with Cutco emphasis.

As P.R. staggered slowly toward us, it was clear that the beach oaf was drunk, plastered. This was my rescuer? Oh well, any port in a storm. Pork Rind stopped several houses away. Barely able to stand, he took a bottle from his coat. He then blubbered, half talking, half belching, "Rum'ee dum-dum, time to be done!"

"Don't drink anymore. I need you!" I wanted to shout. P.R. gazed intently at his liquid seducer; its lure proved too powerful. P.R. threw his head back and started guzzling the rum just like Johnny Depp, a.k.a. Captain Jack Sparrow, in the original *Pirates of the Caribbean* movie. The upside-down bottle sloshed as air bubbles rose. *He is toast.* To Pork Rind's sick credit, he finished the bottle. And then, just as Depp's character did in the movie, P.R. passed out. The slob fell backwards over a small fence and disappeared into a neighbor's front yard. The bottle landed quietly in a nearby bush and hung suspended. The last drops of alcohol drained out, along with my hope.

Tinny snickered smugly and said, "Let's go."

Instead of following the boardwalk past the shops, we went across the empty parking lot toward the water. I did a slow shuffle. He held me lightly around the waist. We mounted the sidewalk next to the beach. As we passed one of the many round Dumpsters lining the walk, Tinny stopped. He took off his gloves, shoved them in the trash bag, and pushed the package deep into the receptacle. We continued walking.

Soon we came to the century-old Dory fishing fleet. The colorful boats looked drab in the darkness. Hope rekindled in me as a car entered the one-way loop around the parking lot. Miracle of miracles, it was a Newport Beach cop! Tinny tensed and held me tight.

"Don't even think about it," he whispered cruelly. I could feel the Cutco prod me in the back. We kept moving slowly toward the pier. *Should I yell?* As I drew in a breath to go for it, Tinny pierced the jacket and then my skin with the tip of the weapon. I winced and shut down the verbal blast before it reached critical mass. A small but painful puncture wound started to bleed. The opportunity slipped away, since the cops had already passed us. My only chance was if they circled around the parking lot counter-clockwise. No such luck. My would-be saviors simply turned right at Mutt Lynch's and disappeared. The cops were likely trolling for late-night misfits like Pork Rind. As the patrol car abandoned me, blood dripped down my back. I became dizzy.

"I'm going to black out."

"None of that," Tinny replied suspiciously.

My knees started to buckle. He had to hold me up. When my vision returned, so did some of the strength in my legs.

"Serves you right," he scolded. "I wasn't joking. Try another stunt like that, and I'll have to cut you again."

In a few moments, we were at the pier. On the left side was the city's marine department headquarters. Another possibility for rescue went nowhere. The building was vacant at this hour. What about the web camera? It showed waves north of the pier twenty-four hours a day. This desperate thought was also fruitless, since the camera never showed the pier itself. At night, it barely showed the murky ocean with occasional rows of white foam.

We crept up the concrete entrance ramp and onto the wood planks, looking like a shuffling mummy and its date. Covered with barnacles and driven deep into the ocean floor, large wood pilings support the structure against the ocean. To the north, I could see the Huntington Beach Pier lights against the moonless night. A padlocked gate stopped us in our tracks. The city closes it nightly to keep out vagrants and evildoers.

"What the heck?" Tinny exclaimed.

I started to shake. Fear and loathing were causing tremors. We stood for a moment, and then he moved me toward the edge.

"This ought to be interesting," I chipped in, with attitude.

He worked me over the railing that runs the entire perimeter of the pier. "I'm going to slide you over the edge, OK? The knife will be ready." He held the Cutco close to my neck as he struggled to lift me over the edge of the pier. If I made a desperate lunge over the side, I would crash onto the beach below and become a pile of broken bones. Then what would I do? Roll away like a slow log? Tinny would just jog down and retrieve me. No good.

He manipulated my corpse-like body until it fell hard over the rail and onto the planks past the fence. My body writhed in pain. Just as I had started to recover from the attack of the black truck, Detective Baker had crushed me in Slate's office, and then Tinny clubbed me into unconsciousness. The dive onto the wooden planks was the final insult. I tried in vain to get up, but the tape destroyed my ability to flee or fight. Tinny climbed around the fence and over the rail too.

Plan B was now clear. Tinny was going to take me to the end of the pier and throw me off into deep water. Wrapped up like a Thanksgiving goose, I would quickly drown. Sweat soaked me. While the parka I was wearing amplified the amount of sweat I was producing, the situation was what really caused my pores to erupt. My mind worked overtime looking for options. Zero; I had nothing.

"What a gutless wonder!" I finally barked as Tinny pulled me up. "You're going to let the faceless Pacific do the dirty work, aren't you?" I had nothing to lose now by mouthing off.

"Just zip it," he replied.

"Threats of a knifing won't work anymore," I barked with an outburst born of frustration and indignation. "How could a stand-up guy like Buddy caddy for a worm like you?"

"Oh, that's rich," he shot back as he lifted me and began to inch us forward. "He's the one who betrayed me, remember?"

My cooperation ended right then and there. It was not going to save me anyway. He was going to have to struggle to kill me. The only weapon I had left was my weight. It was not much, but it was something. I dropped to the planks a final time like a sack of cement.

"Get up!" he ordered.

"Make me!" I dared him.

Tinny put the knife in his back pocket and started dragging me. I took great pleasure in hearing him grunt and swear. Near the snoozing restaurant and sushi bar at the end of the pier, he stopped and stood up panting. I began rolling away while he caught his breath. He swore, ran over, and hauled me over the rough planks again, this time all the way to the north side of the pier. Not taking anything for granted, he pulled out the remaining duct tape and bound my ankles. Then he quickly sealed my mouth too.

"Tired of listening to you," he snorted. He tossed the duct tape over the side and stood looking at me, his eyes glazed by the late hour, digested beer, and ugly task. "I'm sorry about this. You don't really deserve it the way Buddy did. However, your relentless snooping makes it necessary. If it's me or you, then bye-bye, Shank."

Did Buddy deserve to die as Tinny had maintained? True, he had acted with treachery in sabotaging his pro's best shot at an elusive first victory. Moreover, Buddy had twice saved himself without regard to the fate of another man. He had sacrificed Lenny Hayes and later Tinny. But the two acts were fundamentally different. After the gas station shooting, there was no reason to run except to save himself. With the Classic, his family was top of mind. Right? Regardless, Tinny's deadly actions were beyond justification. Murder always is.

Considering my options for a last time, only one came to mind. If he got close enough, I could try to knock him out with a vicious head-butt. The plan made me woozy, since such a blow added to my concussion might be terminal in any case. But it was all I had. Failing that, my only chance was to make it out of the water alive. Unfortunately, there was no rational basis to believe such a result was possible.

I never got the chance to try the head-butt since Tinny merely sat down and used his legs to roll me under the bottom rail.

The long fall in blackness was terrifying. More as a reaction than a conscious effort, I took a huge breath through my nose on the way down. It was similar to a wipeout while surfing—you want maximum oxygen before submersion. I twisted slightly in mid-air and pointed my Nikes in the direction I thought was down. Fortunately, I entered the water feet first. Still, the impact was significant from that height, and I went deep.

The stinging cold Pacific slapped my face. The friction of the water ripped my jacket upward. While the wet parka covered my head, the duct tape binding my wrists was now totally exposed. If only I could find something sharp. Anything. Bobbing up like a cork, I tried desperately to break the surface and take a breath. No way. Fully clothed and without free arms or legs to fight gravity, I remained underwater. As the ocean current pushed me under the pier, I banged into one of the crusty pilings. My shirt ripped and something dug into my left shoulder. Barnacles! The wonderfully sharp little creatures covered every piling holding up the pier. I had recently read of a man who dove off the Huntington Beach Pier to save his prized parrot. The bird died, and the barnacles cut the man badly.

I tried to find another pier piling and lunge backward with the next tidal push. Apart from gashing my hand, I accomplished little else. Panic made me start thrashing. Of course, this was the worst thing to do since it used up precious oxygen. Early in my surfing life, a mentor counseled me that the cornerstone to survival in the ocean is to relax, relax, relax. In large waves, the trick is to act like a rag doll until the sea relents and you can legitimately fight for the surface. Years of practice swept over me, and I relaxed a fraction. Anything more than that, however, was becoming increasingly difficult.

Things started to dim, and the drowning began. Buddy's similar experience up on the tower came to mind as my life began to flash before me in vivid color. In a split second, I saw my favorite grandmother quoting a poem about Indians that she learned as a child. Then there was our childhood dog Nutmeg, a brown terrier I had dearly loved. He was lying in our family room, his long red tongue getting every real or imaginary drop out of a beer can Dad had recently finished. Mom appeared, baking an apple pie. Next was Jill. She started intense, like the first day I met her at the academy. Then she was soft and sultry, soaking in a bubble bath. Ultimately, however, she exploded in a firestorm.

This last image transitioned into a strange dream-like sequence. There were my sisters opening presents on Christmas, Sage surfing, Claire Valentine in uniform, and the beautiful woman of substance from the Clines' party. Then, the ladies all stood together and tossed me a giant life preserver with the word "Titanic" emblazoned on it. Next, an unsolvable calculus equation appeared with living numbers leaping off the chalkboard. Things slowed down, and one final image overtook the others. A cross of biblical proportions stood ominously on an inky hill surrounded by lightning. A crucified Cary hung on it, bleeding, suffocating, and about dead. Yet he smiled peacefully.

Death tugged hard when the sea surged and tossed me backward against another piling. My hands once more scraped against the barnacles. However, this time, the sharp edges slashed the duct tape before digging into more flesh. I rotated my wrists outward and the binding broke. I was energized by a near-fatal dose of adrenaline. Every ounce of survival instinct fired! My lungs were about to burst as I made one prodigious push down through the water with my newly liberated arms. Breaking the surface, I had to exhale before breathing. The resulting carbon dioxide bomb out my nose pushed the jacket far enough away from my face that I got a small dose of precious oxygen.

Mauling the jacket with both hands, I pulled it down and tried again. More air came in but not enough. I reached up and searched for the duct tape on my mouth. Finding an end, I yanked. Gulping for air, I got ocean instead as my body sank. Gagging and choking, I pushed up violently. Reaching the top, I tried to clear my lungs of salt water. More out of anger than anything else, I pulled the jacket off over my head, just about ripping my ears off. Over the next minute, I began to breathe more rhythmically, and my heart rate stabilized to merely outrageous. I developed an adequate arms-only treading motion that managed to keep me afloat.

While it was irrelevant before, the cold mid-50s water now began to assault me. With no wetsuit, hypothermia—the lowering of the body's temperature to damaging levels—would soon set in. I had to get out. But before attempting to swim, I needed to become more seaworthy. Taking a deep breath, I slipped underwater and shed my burdensome Nikes. Not wearing socks served me well as it saved removing an additional soaking layer. Resurfacing with a sense of progress, I tried to get my ankles free but could not. The wet duct tape was too difficult to remove. I resigned to swimming with arms only. My well-trained upper body stroked aggressively as I escaped the labyrinth of pilings and made it to the open ocean on the side of the pier. With my head up, as was my typical surfing style, I swam toward shore, settling into a surprisingly nice rhythm.

Suddenly, I thought of Tinny. Had he looked over the railing and watched my drama from above? Probably not, since it was dark, the waves were loud, and most of the action took place between the pilings. Also, my mouth had been taped most of the time, so I didn't yell. Was he watching from the shore? Would he stab me when I made the beach in a morbid Plan C? My eyes scanned the horizon. I could not see anyone, but there were plenty of structures to hide behind. While playing cat and mouse might have been feasible in other circumstances, I had an immediate need to get out of the frigid water. The exercise was helping keep up my core temperature. However, if I messed around too long, the icy Pacific would finish me off. *Biggest threat, first response.* I decided to worry about a Cutco-wielding Tinny later.

In about five minutes, my hand hit the sand. I rolled over several times in the shallow water, dragging myself onto the shore and crumpling into shivering heap. Land never felt so good! After a moment, someone materialized from the shadows under the pier. I was cold and tired, had duct-taped legs, and was bleeding from multiple wounds. This time the coward was going to have to do his own butchery. Even if he slashed me brutally, he was *not* going to finish me on *my* beach, in view of *my* home. No way! Calling on yet untapped reserves, I rose to my knees and steeled for the grand finale.

The figure then spoke in a tottery voice. "What the dickens are you doing, son?" An old man with fishing gear stepped toward me. "Is this a fraternity prank or something?"

Relief washed over me. While a quip was in order, my body was battered, and I could not muster one. As the sound of the ocean soothed my senses, I collapsed onto the glorious California sand.

EPILOGUE

The ancient fisherman helped me back to my apartment, earning the best fish tale he would ever tell. Still soaking wet, I called the giant detective.

"Baker," he answered groggily on the fifth ring.

"It's Shank. Sorry about the hour, but Tinny attacked me when I got home. He's the killer, not Slate! Confessed the whole thing before throwing me off the pier. Quite the escape. A fisherman found me bleeding on the beach."

The drama of the previous afternoon had built a bridge of trust between us. He did not even question my wild story. "Where are you?"

"My apartment."

"Where's Tinny?"

"No idea."

"Lock your door, grab a weapon, and barricade yourself in the bathroom. Stay on the line while I call for help on my other phone."

I obeyed. With sirens blaring, Newport's finest arrived within two minutes. They promptly cleared me to emerge from hiding. The paramedics showed up next. They had me put on a pair of swim trunks and get into a hot shower. After emptying the water heater, the professionals took me via ambulance to Hoag Hospital. The emergency room doc stitched up the Cutco puncture wound and several deep barnacle gashes on my shoulder, arms, and hand. He diagnosed me with a Grade III concussion and gave me meds to reduce the swelling and ease the pounding headache. Thankfully, I had no broken bones.

Once back home, I answered an extensive set of questions from the police. As it was now morning, one of the cops went out for fresh donuts and delightfully hot coffee. There had been no sign of the villain. By noon, however, the Tucson police had arrested Tinny Wilcox at his house without incident. He had apparently left Orange County shortly after 3:30 a.m. and headed back to Arizona. His evil mission to California took less than twenty hours.

Mid-afternoon, Linda Franks arrived. She looked better than I had seen her in weeks. Color was returning to her cheeks. She wore white slacks and a cheerful pink blouse. Linda brought me a large bouquet of sunflowers and a case of Mountain Dew.

"How are you?" she asked.

"Pretty beat up, if you want to know the truth."

"I feel so bad. If I hadn't asked you to help—"

"Buddy's murderer would still be on the loose," I finished. "The bad guys did the damage, not you."

For at least an hour, I downloaded the details, to a barrage of comments like, "No way!" "Really?" and "Oh,

Shank!" Over my mild protests, Linda later went shopping and cooked me a tasty dinner.

After the dust settled, the insurance company finally paid her Buddy's death benefits. I was glad the suspicions about Linda were wrong. She graciously thanked me and rewarded my efforts with a surprise trip to Hawaii. I eventually made good on my promise to take her out for a friendly dinner and movie.

Beyond the obvious loss of Buddy, one of the hardest fallouts for Linda was telling the kids about their father's checkered past. She wisely decided to do it herself so they would not hear bits and pieces from potentially cruel classmates. Did they grasp it all? Unclear. But they appeared to understand that Buddy had a prior life where he made a big mistake, leading to another error in judgment that got him killed. To her credit, Linda often repeated that their dad loved them very much.

The authorities ultimately convicted Tinny for Buddy's murder and separately for assault, kidnapping, and attempted murder on me. Smug throughout, he admitted nothing. Reportedly, he went broke paying lawyers.

As for Nick Slate, because he locked his office door and refused to let me leave, the authorities also charged him with kidnapping. True to form, he chucked and jived into a plea-bargain. In exchange for helping nail Milton Reily, he received a reduced sentence. Only time will tell if Slate made a good bet this time; nowhere is safe after handing over a well-connected snake like Reily. Of course, the industry will never allow Slate near another golf tournament.

As it turned out, Reily *did* hire the desert gas station thugs to "persuade" me to abandon the investigation. He met me at The Venetian in Las Vegas to determine how dedicated I was to uncovering the tournament sabotage he had put in motion. Seeing I was fully committed, he authorized the attack. When his goons failed so miserably, he blew a fuse. The bookie then decided on a more permanent solution and issued orders for my demise. Thankfully, the truck attack also failed.

The police closed the file on Lenny Hayes. There was no evidence that Hayes committed any crimes against Buddy, and I did not press charges for the front-yard assault in Texas. No harm, no foul. His life was tough enough.

My parents were understandably horrified to hear about the most recent events. While leaving out certain facts for Mom's sake, I told Dad everything. We spent additional time reviewing the mystery, especially placing actual facts within his Pretty Fair Maiden framework. Passion, or P, was clear. When Tinny figured out that Buddy was involved in his putting debacle, revenge, frustration, and hatred erupted with violent consequences. Fear, or F, was also present. Buddy was so afraid of his past misdeeds coming to light that he sabotaged Tinny. Slate, Reily, and Tinny were all fearful that I would implicate them, prompting each of them to attack me. Money, or M, was *not* central in Buddy's actual death. Yet it was an important factor in motivating the upstream players. Large gambling payouts threatened Reily, so he offered to wipe out Slate's sizable debt to entice action. Pretty Fair Maiden—very cool, Dad.

Even though I was injured, I never missed a loop for Cary Cline. While he had encouraged me to take time off, I worked through the pain and recovery period. Had the barnacles slashed my dominant right shoulder instead of my left, it would have been tougher. The Clines were relieved to hear it was over. Cary told me, "We thought you might be in danger after Rebecca's party. So Crystal and I provided prayer coverage. We know the Lord protected you." While I appreciated the gesture, I was clueless about what "prayer coverage" was and how, or if, it worked.

A modest level of notoriety flowed from my efforts. Even though I refused to grant interviews, news and human-interest stories appeared on TV, in newspapers, and on the Internet. True to form, Pork Rind tried to capitalize on his chance meeting with Tinny and me on the boardwalk. Although he was so drunk that he did not even remember it, the clown later claimed to be my partner. I refused to make joint "personal appearances." He swears my refusal dimmed his rising star.

Cristanos continues to be my closest beach friend. Our time together increased as that summer blossomed in all its Orange County glory. "Hey, Shanks," the Brazilian greeted me one morning at Mutt Lynch's. "Miss Linda gave me a 'thanks' present." Beaming, he produced a small box containing a shiny new surf watch. It was a Tidemaster, built for tracking tide height and direction.

Inspecting the watch closely, I said, "This is top-drawer, pal. Why aren't you wearing it?"

"No expecting gift. I just help you and Miss Linda."

"Cristanos, she *wants* to thank you. Admittedly, it cost serious cash, but she now has piles of insurance money. No biggie, right? Go for it."

He hesitated a little longer and then shrugged in humble acceptance while putting the timepiece around his dark bronze wrist. He hasn't had it off since.

The women in my life? Sage continues to be a great friend who keeps me entertained. Officer Valentine, who insisted I call her Claire, provided me a much needed outlet for long-bottled emotions. We dated for a while; I showed her Newport and she found us good Italian restaurants in San Diego. It was fun while it lasted, but she moved to Vermont after securing a law enforcement job with more responsibility. The intriguing woman from the Clines' party? That's a long story for another day. For now, suffice it to say that we challenge each other and don't yet know what the future holds.

Apart from the brutality, I enjoyed the adrenaline rushes while investigating the treachery at Torrey Pines. It felt good to help Linda and exact justice for Buddy's murder. I may have made several blunders during my rookie sleuthing campaign, but I certainly predicted one thing right—pulling the duct tape off my hairy thighs was absolute torture!

Acknowledgements

The author wishes to thank and acknowledge the assistance and support of the following individuals (alphabetically):

Denny Bellisi (co-author of *The Kingdom Assignment*); Kim Davis; Marsha Ford (Editor-in-Chief); Chuck Higgins (PGA Professional, Keeton Park, Dallas, Texas); Daniel Kippen, Esq.; Jim Long (Special Agent, F.B.I.); Denise Moon, Ernie E. Owen ("the dean of Christian publishing" who influenced the writing careers of Billy Graham, James Dobson, Max Lucado, and now John Van Vlear); Minor and Guy Owen; Gary & Toni Smith; Ken and Val Smith; Robin Smith; Chuck Stain; Kim Van Vlear; Megan Van Vlear; Victoria Van Vlear (Publishing Manager/ Polishing Editor); John Webb; and Denyse Yolken.

About the Author

John Edward Van Vlear is an award-winning writer, Christian, sports enthusiast, and prominent environmental lawyer.

A third-generation Californian, Mr. Van Vlear was raised in South Pasadena. Attending the University of California Irvine and Pepperdine University School of Law, he earned extensive academic honors including the distinguished *Sorenson Memorial Award for Literary Excellence* and West Publishing's *Most Significant Contribution to Overall Legal Scholarship* for a ground-breaking published piece on land use aesthetics. In addition to writing numerous articles in local, regional, and national publications, Mr. Van Vlear authored a legal treatise–*The Environmental Handbook*, 1996 (ISBN 0-9652553-0-1). He has been interviewed on television several times, served as an adjunct law professor, and has presented more than 60 professional speeches and seminars. [Cont.]

Among various athletic pursuits, Mr. Van Vlear is a passionate road cyclist who continues to summit some of world's most challenging and famous *hors catégorie* "beyond categorization" mountain climbs. He is actively involved in church and supports ministries worldwide. Mr. Van Vlear has traveled extensively, lived in London, and played many of the top golf courses in America and Scotland. He resides with his family in Southern California.

Learn more at: *JohnVanVlear.com*

47063671R00160

Made in the USA
Lexington, KY
03 August 2019